GLIMMER TRAIN
STORIES

EDITORS
Susan Burmeister-Brown   Linda B. Swanson-Davies
CONSULTING EDITOR
Roz Wais
COPY EDITOR
Scott Stuart Allie
TYPESETTING & LAYOUT
Paul Morris
COVER ART
Moving On, by Jane Zwinger
PUBLISHED QUARTERLY
in spring, summer, fall, and winter by Glimmer Train Press, Inc.
1211 NW Glisan Street, Suite 207, Portland, Oregon 97209-3054
Telephone: 503/221-0836   Facsimile: 503/221-0837
www.glimmertrain.org

PRINTED IN U.S.A.
Indexed in *The American Humanities Index*.
Member of the Council of Literary Magazines and Presses

STATEMENT OF OWNERSHIP, MANAGEMENT, AND CIRCULATION. Required by 39 USC 3685, file date: 7/20/07.
Publication name: Glimmer Train, publication #10557520. Published quarterly (4x/yr). Publisher and owner: Glimmer Train Press,
Inc. Complete mailing address of known office of publication and headquarters is 1211 NW Glisan, Suite 207, Portland, OR 97209-
3054. One-year subscription price: $36. Editors and co-presidents: Susan Burmeister-Brown and Linda Burmeister Swanson-Davies,
1211 NW Glisan, Suite 207, Portland, OR 97209-3054. Known bondholders: none. Extent and nature of circulation: a) average
number of copies each issue during preceding 12 months, b) actual number of copies of single issue published nearest to filing date.
Net press run: a) eight thousand, six hundred twenty-five; b) seven thousand. Paid or requested mailed outside-county mail subscriptions: a) four thousand, one hundred four; b) three thousand, nine hundred ninety-four. Paid or requested mailed inside-county
mail subscriptions: a) none; b) none; Sales through distributors: a) two thousand, three hundred twenty-five; b) one thousand, seven
hundred fifty. Other Classes: a) one hundred; b) one hundred. Total paid/requested circulation: a) six thousand, four hundred seventy-
nine; b) six thousand, seven hundred ninety-four. Free distribution outside-county by mail: a) one hundred; b) one hundred. Free
distribution inside-county by mail: a) none; b) none. Free distribution, other classes: a) none; b) none. Free distribution outside of
mail: a) two hundred forty; b) two hundred forty. Total free distribution: a) three hundred forty; b) three hundred forty. Total distribution: a) six thousand, eight hundred nineteen; b) seven thousand, one hundred thirty-four. Copies not distributed: a) one thousand, eight
hundred six; b) eight hundred sixty-six. Total sum of distributed and not distributed copies: a) eight thousand, six hundred twenty-
five; b) seven thousand. Percent Paid and or requested Circulation: a) ninety-five; b) ninety-four. I certify that the statements made by
me above are correct and complete—Linda Swanson-Davies, Co-editor.

Glimmer Train (ISSN #1055-7520), registered in U.S. Patent and Trademark Office, is published quarterly, $36 per
year in the U.S., by Glimmer Train Press, Inc., Suite 207, 1211 NW Glisan, Portland, OR 97209. Periodicals postage
paid at Portland, OR, and additional mailing offices. POSTMASTER: Send address changes to Glimmer Train Press,
P.O. Box 3000, Denville, NJ 07834-9929.

ISSN # 1055-7520, **ISBN # 1-59553-014-2**, CPDA BIPAD # 79021

DISTRIBUTION: Bookstores can purchase *Glimmer Train Stories* through these distributors:
DEMCO, Inc., 4810 Forest Run Road, Madison, WI 53707 ph: 800/356-1200
Peribo PTY Ltd., 58 Beaumont Rd., Mt. Kuring-Gai, NSW 2080, AUSTRALIA
Source Interlink, 27500 Riverview Center Blvd., Suite 400, Bonita Sprints, FL 36134
Ubiquity, 607 Degraw St., Brooklyn, NY 11217
SUBSCRIPTION SVCS: EBSCO, Divine, Subscription Services of America, Blackwell's UK.

Subscription rates: Order online at www.glimmertrain.org.
or by mail—one year, $36 within the U.S. (Visa/MC/check).
Airmail to Canada, $46; outside North America, $59.
Payable by Visa/MC or check for U.S. dollars drawn on a U.S. bank.

Attention established and emerging short-story writers: We pay $700 for first publication
and onetime anthology rights. We welcome your work via our **online submission procedure:**
www.glimmertrain.org.

Glimmer Train Press also offers **Writers Ask**—*nuts, bolts, and informed perspectives*—*a*
quarterly non-newsletter for the committed writer. One year, four issues, $20 within the U.S.
($26 beyond the U.S.), Visa, MC, or check to Glimmer Train Press, Inc., or order online at
www.glimmertrain.org.

Dorothy Ann, 1947.

We dedicate this 65th issue to our sister, born Dorothy
Ann Burmeister and immediately nicknamed Dabby
by our grandfather—a name which has held now for
65 years, this month. Our lives would not be the same
without her easy laugh and her constant love.

Susan & Linda

PAST CONTRIBUTING AUTHORS AND ARTISTS

Many of issues 1 through 64 are available for thirteen dollars each.

Robert A. Abel • David Abrams • Linsey Abrams • Steve Adams • Diane King Akers • Daniel Alarcón • Susan Alenick • Will Allison • Rosemary Altea • Julia Alvarez • Brian Ames • A. Manette Ansay • Margaret Atwood • Dalia Azim • Kevin Bacon • Michael Bahler • Doreen Baingana • Aida Baker • Kerry Neville Bakken • Russell Banks • Brad Barkley • Andrea Barrett • Kyle Ann Bates • Richard Bausch • Robert Bausch • Charles Baxter • Ann Beattie • Sean Beaudoin • Barbara Bechtold • Cathie Beck • Jeff Becker • Janet Belding • Sallie Bingham • Kristen Birchett • Melanie Bishop • James Carlos Blake • Corinne Demas Bliss • Valerie Block • Belle Boggs • Joan Bohorfoush • Matt Bondurant • David Borofka • Robin Bradford • Harold Brodkey • Oliver Broudy • Danit Brown • Kurt McGinnis Brown • Nic Brown • Paul Brownfield • Ayse Papatya Bucak • Judy Budnitz • Susanna Bullock • Christopher Busa • Jenny A. Burkholder • Evan Burton • Robert Olen Butler • Michael Byers • Christine Byl • Gerard Byrne • Jack Cady • Annie Callan • Kevin Canty • Peter Carey • Ioanna Carlsen • Ron Carlson • H. G. Carroll • David Cates • Brian Champeau • Vikram Chandra • Diane Chang • Mike Chasar • Xiaofei Chen • Yunny Chen • Robert Chibka • Chieh Chieng • Carolyn Chute • Christi Clancy • George Makana Clark • Dennis Clemmens • Aaron Cohen • Robert Cohen • Evan S. Connell • Joan Connor • Ellen Cooney • Rand Richards Cooper • Lydia E. Copeland • Michelle Coppedge • Rita D. Costello • Wendy Counsil • Doug Crandell • M. Allen Cunningham • Ronald F. Currie Jr. • William J. Cyr • Quinn Dalton • Bilal Dardai • Tristan Davies • C. V. Davis • Annie Dawid • Laurence de Looze • Toi Derricotte • Janet Desaulniers • Tiziana di Marina • Junot Díaz • Stephen Dixon • Matthew Doherty • Leslie Dormen • Michael Dorris • Siobhan Dowd • Greg Downs • Eugenie Doyle • Tiffany Drever • Alan Arthur Drew • Andre Dubus • Andre Dubus III • Stuart Dybek • Wayne Dyer • Melodie S. Edwards • Ron Egatz • Barbara Eiswerth • Mary Relindes Ellis • Sherry Ellis • Susan Engberg • Lin Enger • James English • Tony Eprile • Louise Erdrich • Zoë Evamy • Nomi Eve • George Fahey • Edward Falco • Anthony Farrington • Merrill Feitell • J. M. Ferguson Jr. • Lisa Fetchko • Joseph Flanagan • Charlotte Forbes • Patricia Foster • Susan Fox • Michael Frank • Pete Fromm • Abby Frucht • Daniel Gabriel • Avital Gad-Cykman • Ernest Gaines • Mary Gaitskill • Tess Gallagher • Louis Gallo • Elizabeth Gallu • Kent Gardien • Ellen Gilchrist • Myla Goldberg • Allyson Goldin • Mary Gordon • Peter Gordon • Jean Colgan Gould • Elizabeth Graver • Lisa Graley • Jo-Ann Graziano • Andrew Sean Greer • Gail Greiner • John Griesemer • Zoë Griffith-Jones • Paul Griner • Aaron Gwyn • L. B. Haas • Patricia Hampl • Christian Hansen • Ann Harleman • Elizabeth Logan Harris • Marina Harris • Erin Hart • Kent Haruf • Ethan Hauser • Jake Hawkes • Daniel Hayes • David Haynes • Daniel Hecht • Ursula Hegi • Amy Hempel • Joshua Henkin • Cristina Henríquez • David Hicks • Julie Hirsch • Andee Hochman • Alice Hoffman • Cary Holladay • Jack Holland • Noy Holland • Travis Holland • Lucy Honig • Ann Hood • Linda Hornbuckle • David Huddle • Sandra Hunter • Tim Hurd • Siri Hustvedt • Quang Huynh • Frances Hwang • Leo Hwang • Catherine Ryan Hyde • Stewart David Ikeda • Lawson Fusao Inada • Elizabeth Inness-Brown • Debra Innocenti • Bruce Jacobson • Andrea Jeyaveeran • Ha Jin • Charles Johnson • Cheri Johnson • Leslie Johnson • Sarah Anne Johnson • Wayne Johnson • Allen Morris Jones • Nalini Jones • Thom Jones • Cyril Jones-Kellet • Elizabeth Judd • Tom Miller Juvik • Jiri Kajanë • Anita Shah Kapadia • Hester Kaplan • Wayne Karlin • Amy Karr • Ariana-Sophia Kartsonis • Andrew Kass • Kate Kasten • Tom Kealey • David Kear • Andrea King Kelly • Jenny Kennedy • Thomas E. Kennedy • Tim Keppel • Jamaica Kincaid • Lily King • Maina wa Kinyatti • Carolyn Kizer • Perri Klass • Rachel Klein • Carrie Knowles • Clark E. Knowles • N. S. Köenings • Jonathan Kooker • David Koon • Karen Kovacik • Justin Kramon • Jake Kreilkamp • Nita Krevans • Erika Krouse • Marilyn Krysl • Frances Kuffel • Evan Kuhlman • Mandy Dawn Kuntz • Anatoly Kurchatkin • W. Tsung-yan Kwong • Victoria Lancelotta • Christiana Langenberg • Rattawut Lapcharoensap • Jenni Lapidus • Doug Lawson • Don Lee • Frances Lefkowitz • Peter Lefcourt • Jon Leon • Doris Lessing • Jennifer Levasseur • Debra Levy • Janice Levy • Yiyun Li • Christine Liotta • Rosina Lippi-Green • David Long • Nathan Long • Salvatore Diego Lopez • Melissa Lowver • William Luvaas • Barry Lyga • David H. Lynn • Richard Lyons • Bruce Machart • Jeff MacNelly • R. Kevin Maler • Kelly Malone • Paul Mandelbaum • George Manner • Jana Martin • Lee Martin • Valerie Martin • Juan Martinez • Daniel Mason • Brendan Mathews • Alice Mattison • Bruce McAllister • Jane McCafferty • Sean Padraic McCarthy • Judith McClain • Cammie McGovern • Cate McGowan • Eileen McGuire • Susan McInnis • Gregory McNamee • Jenny Drake McPhee • Amalia Melis • Askold Melnyczuk • Susan Messer • Frank Michel • Paul Michel • Nancy Middleton • Alyce Miller • Greg Miller • Katherine Min • Mary McGarry Morris • Ted Morrissey • Mary Morrissy • Bernard Mulligan • Abdelrahman Munif • Manuel Muñoz • Karen Munro • Paula Nangle • Antonya Nelson • Kent Nelson • Randy F. Nelson • Lucia Nevai • Thisbe Nissen • Katherin Nolte • Miriam Novogrodsky • Sigrid Nunez • N. Nye • Ron Nyren • Joyce Carol Oates • Tim O'Brien • Vana O'Brien • Mary O'Dell • Chris Offutt • Jennifer Oh • Laura Oliver • Felicia Olivera • Jimmy Olsen • Thomas O'Malley • Stewart O'Nan • Elizabeth Oness • Gina Oschner • Karen Outen • Mary Overton • Patricia Page • Ann Pancake • Peter Parsons • Roy Parvin • Karenmary Penn • Susan Perabo • Benjamin Percy • Susan Petrone • Dawn Karima Pettigrew • Constance Pierce • William Pierce • D. B. C. Pierre • Angela Pneuman • Steven Polansky • John Prendergast • Jessica Printz • Melissa Pritchard • Annie Proulx • Eric Puchner • Kevin Rabalais • Jonathan Raban • George Rabasa • Margo Rabb • Mark Rader • Paul Rawlins • Yosefa Raz • Karen Regen-Tuero • Frederick Reiken • Nancy Reisman • Yelizaveta P. Renfro • Linda Reynolds • Kurt Rheinheimer • Anne Rice • Michelle Richmond • Alberto Ríos • Roxana Robinson • Anya Robyak • Susan Jackson Rodgers • Andrew Roe • Paulette Roeske • Stan Rogal • Carol Roh-Spaulding • Frank Ronan • Julie Rose • Elizabeth Rosen • Janice Rosenberg • Jane Rosenzweig • Elissa Minor Rust • Karen Sagstetter • Kiran Kaur Saini • Mark Salzman • Mark Sanders • Carl Schaffer • R. K. Scher • Robert Schirmer • Libby Schmais • Natalie Schoech • Natalie Schoen • Adam Schuitema • Jim Schumock • Lynn Sharon Schwartz • Barbara Scot • Peter Selgin • Amy Selwyn • James Sepsey • Catherine Seto • Bob Shacochis • Evelyn Sharenov • Karen Shepard • Sally Shivnan • Evan Shopper • Daryl Siegel • Ami Silber • Al Sim • Mark Sindecuse • George Singleton • Floyd Skloot • Brian Slattery • Louise Farmer Smith • Janice D. Soderling • Roland Sodowsky • Scott Southwick • R. Clifton Spargo • Gregory Spatz • Brent Spencer • L. M. Spencer • Lara Stapleton • Lori Ann Stephens • Barbara Stevens • John Stinson • George Stolz • William Styron • Virgil Suárez • Karen Swenson • Liz Szabla • Shimon Tanaka • Mika Tanner • Deborah Tarnoff • Lois Taylor • Paul Theroux • Abigail Thomas • Randolph Thomas • Joyce Thompson • Patrick Tierney • Aaron Tillman • Tamara B. Titus • Andrew Toos • Pauls Toutonghi • Vu Tran • Patricia Traxler • Jessica Treadway • Doug Trevor • William Trevor • Rob Trucks • Kathryn Trueblood • Jennifer Tseng • Carol Turner • Christine Turner • Kathleen Tyau • Michael Upchurch • Lee Upton • Gerard Varni • Katherine Vaz • A. J. Verdelle • Daniel Villasenor • Robert Vivian • Sergio Gabriel Waisman • Daniel Wallace • Ren Wanding • Eric Wasserman • Mary Yukari Waters • Jonathan Wei • Eric Weinberger • Jamie Weisman • Lance Weller • Ed Weyhing • J. Patrice Whetsell • Joan Wickersham • Vinnie Wilhelm • Lex Williford • Gary Wilson • Robin Winick • Mark Wisniewski • Terry Wolverton • Monica Wood • Christopher Woods • Leslie A. Wootten • wormser • Celia Wren • Callie Wright • Calvin Wright • Brennen Wysong • June Unjoo Yang • Paul Yoon • Nancy Zafris • Silas Zobal • Jane Zwinger

CONTENTS

Here I am with my father at New Smyrna Beach, Florida in 1981.

Kim Brooks is a graduate of the Iowa Writers' Workshop and a recipient of the Michener-Copernicus fellowship. Her stories have appeared in *One Story*, *Epoch*, the *Missouri Review*, *Meridian*, and *Alaska Quarterly Review*. She is completing a collection of short stories and is at work on a novel. She lives in Chicago with her husband and dogs and is studying to become a nurse practitioner.

THE SHELTER

Kim Brooks (signature)

Kim Brooks

On the tenth and final day of the raid, André woke as the sun was setting. He had a bad taste in his mouth and an uncharacteristically clear head. The bottle beside his bed was empty. He peered in with one eye, a small brown bead of liquid trickled toward him, reflecting a prism of color as it slid along the curved glass and landed on the bridge of his nose. He wiped it away without remorse. The sun had sunk low in the sky and was suspended exactly in the middle of his curtain-less window, a fiery orange sphere as large as the plastic balls he and Yalla used to give to the children on the beach. Between his window and the sun were miles of sand, dust, buildings crushed like bugs, heaps of sweltering rubble, bodies in every stage of decomposition, dry, white bones picked clean by vultures, and all the way on the other side of town, Yalla, his wife, still walled up in the cold, dark basement he had abandoned months ago when the bombing started and the thought of being trapped there with her had filled him with a fear worse than the fear of death. He knew Yalla was still alive because two days ago, three days ago, the only other man left in André's building had mentioned seeing her near a garbage pile, scavenging for food.

When they had met in the hallway, André's only remaining neighbor was carrying a sack over his shoulder and seemed to be in a hurry. He was filthy like André; there hadn't been water in their building for weeks, and his hair clung to the sweaty sides of his neck. Before the war, he'd been a professional polyglot, offering underwater tours of the Tortoise Islands in six different languages. He had bedded women of every nationality, kept samples of sand from shores across the globe. Now, he scavenged like everyone else, and also, André suspected, worked as a translator for the invading army. It was a hunch, only, and André had no desire to confirm or disprove it. He liked his neighbor. The man knew how to drink and how to not drink, how to make do. He had the cold, truthful eyes of a visionary.

"You're leaving?" André had said.

"It's about time, don't you think? They'll flood the city before long to get rid of the vermin, and then all the stray food will mold. In the countryside there's still fruit, seeds, tubers."

"Which way will you go? Not west."

"North," he said. "Or maybe south. I think I'll start walking and see where I end up."

"A sensible plan," André had said as he opened another bottle, the one that now sat empty beside him.

After his neighbor had left, André thought about Yalla scavenging the garbage, and couldn't help but smile. This from the woman who had once thrown a still-warm Cornish hen in his face when he'd come home thirty minutes late from work, shouting, "It's ruined, you cock-sucker. You ruined it." And yet now, he felt the urge to see her once again. He was curious how she would appear now that he wanted or needed nothing from her. Had utter devastation humbled her? For so long, he had believed his dying wish would be to see her vanquished and humiliated, begging him to give her another chance, but this venom, which had once felt imperishable, as much a part of himself as his fear of spiders or his love of the sea, was now missing, eviscerated, dissipating like a thin fog inside his eyes. He wanted to see her one last time. One last time? Was he expecting this to be the end? Planning on it? He couldn't be certain. But he felt he was approaching a finale of one kind or another, and he couldn't think of a more fitting ending than a conversation with the woman who had destroyed him.

Hanover Street was empty, deserted, the storefronts, the once-gleaming buildings—restaurants and clothing stores and night clubs—toppled and rotting, crisscrossed by fallen phone lines and enormous chunks of concrete, floating about the blasted glass and drywall like icebergs in the sea. Where four-story apartment buildings had been, there were now only chimneys protruding at precarious angles from smoldering piles. Stray pieces of furniture, now liberated from their homes, were strewn shamelessly along the darkening sidewalk: a recliner with the stuffing pulled out, a capsized baby grand piano. *What kind of invaders leave a beautiful baby grand to rot on the street?* André wondered. *Pillage and plunder, you cowards. Rape our women and quarter your soldiers in our homes and make us kiss your emperor's feet, you spineless technophiles.* But no, all they had to offer were fireworks, night after night of fireworks, and by the looks of it, this thoroughfare had taken its share.

Everything smelled burnt. The air was hot, but he could not tell if the heat emanated down from the sky or up from the earth. He stepped over a dead man who was wearing a fine wool jacket, holding onto its lapels as if it might do him some good. Where had he gotten a jacket like that? It was something André had noticed of late; no one had anything, but most people got what they really wanted. For this man it had been a fine wool jacket. For André it was whiskey, which most people were willing to trade for food or medicine. André leaned over and checked the man's pockets, then walked on.

The north end of Hanover Street was in slightly better shape—there were still some elm trees in the ground, a few intact houses—before the war, this was where well-to-do intellectuals and university professors lived—the homes were large and old, built of stone instead of cement with wide porches and colorful doors. André was reminded of riding his bike along the sidewalk as a child, usually intent on catching up with his older brother who wanted nothing to do with him. He could still feel the satisfying whoosh of his tires along the fresh, even cement, the warm sea air in his hair and in his nose as he pedaled, pedaled with all his strength. And later, closer to the city's center, he had walked with students from the university, following them to some vaguely known destination or sitting on a hard little chair at an outdoor café, sipping bitter coffee and discussing politics and soccer and watching women. He was sitting at such a café the first time he saw Yalla. A boy on a skateboard had slammed into her backside and she was letting him have it. There had always been something about the state of rage that made her face extremely arousing, beatific, almost.

He continued to walk west and gradually the smell of burnt matter subsided, or his nose adjusted. The sky, which had been a deep blue when he set out, was now gray in places, purple in others, the color of summer storms, though it was nearly winter, and there was not a cloud in sight. It was the sort of evening that made André intensely aware of the smallness of his country, his proximity to the sea. He turned off Hanover onto a cobblestoned side street, and a block or two beyond, a tank with a helmeted soldier poking his head through the middle passed by, slow but determined. He always felt sorry for the fellows. He wondered how it was decided which men were sent to monitor the deserted streets and clean up corpses while the others soared thousands of feet above in their slick, black birds. André smiled and waved. Had this one here started a brawl, been caught stealing, overslept? Was he afraid of heights? The soldier rotated. He had pale, pockmarked skin, a narrow face, and blistered lips. It seemed for a moment that he would shoot. I'm ready for it, thought André. As a child, he'd dreamt of war, real war with swords and muskets and battleships and cannonballs, oceans of soldiers washing over each other like waves—but if this was it, so be it. The soldier squinted at André, then ducked inside his turtle of a tank and, a few moments later, it was gone.

By the time André reached his destination, the day's last light was nearly gone and the city seemed to be settling down into itself, and into darkness. The darkness was of no concern for André; he could have been blind and deaf and armless and still found his way in this city that had been his since birth. As he descended the stairs, the darkness grew thicker, blacker, a moonless blanket that seemed to get inside his skin. He fumbled with the door.

"Who is it?" she called out, her voice just as it had always been.

"Who do you think?"

"André, is that you?"

"It's me, my love, I've come at last."

He waded through the darkness toward the sound of her voice.

"Get out of here," she said. "I didn't invite you."

"I need an invitation?"

"Get out of here or I'll scream."

"Go ahead. There isn't a soul left in the city. A few tanks is all."

"There's plenty of people, hiding. How did you get here?"

"I walked. How else?"

"You're always very brave when bravery is useless."

"But it's not useless. I wanted to see you once more. Where are you?"

Silence again. Then, "I'm right next to you."

He reached forward. His arm grazed a portion of her skin, but she grabbed his wrist. Her eyes were better adjusted to the dark. "Don't touch me," she said.

"I guess it's been quite a while since you spoke those words."

"The last time I saw you. Now let go."

"Have it your way." He sat down on the hard cement. "I hear you were rummaging through the garbage. Find anything good?"

"Nothing I'm willing to share."

He laughed.

"What's funny?"

"Just that nothing changes you. Not war nor death. A fiery meteor the size of Mars could slam into the earth, and you'd still be bitching about the neighbor's nectarine tree sucking up the water from your yard."

"It was our yard. Your yard, too. Where have you been? You don't sound drunk."

"Dry as the desert skies. I woke up this evening and I was cured."

"Then what do you want? I don't have anything for you."

"I only wanted to tell you that I was leaving."

"You left three years ago. But I suppose you never can do anything without a proper audience."

"Yes, Yalla. That's right. Everything I do is in service of your amusement and entertainment. You are my sun, my moon, and my stars."

"Your sarcasm lost its charm two decades ago. Where are you going?"

"North, or maybe south. I'm not sure. I thought I'd start walking and see where I ended up."

"They'll kill you at the border. They'll shoot you in the head."

"Maybe so," he said, and realized then that this, indeed, was his mission. With a good supply of whiskey, he could wait for death. Dry, he'd need to claim it. "Well," he said. "No one could ask for a better end than that."

Neither of them spoke. Below ground, it was so quiet, only a faint scratching in the walls. He moved as if to leave. She spoke his name. "André," she said. "Don't go tonight. You can stay here. Maybe you'll change your mind."

"All right," he said. "Why not? I can see you now, a little." He could see only the dark orange silhouette of her skin, the gentle slope of her nose, her chin.

"Your eyes adjust."

"How long have you been staying here?"

"Weeks. I don't know. The others left and I didn't have the energy or will to follow. Sometimes a woman comes with her son and I play with him while she goes looking for food."

"You were always good with children."

"I wish I could say the same for you."

"I loved our children."

"You loved everyone when you were drunk. You loved the mailman and the gypsy whore down the street."

"I'm going to lie down now." The floor was hard against his head, but it felt good to take weight off his shoulders. She kicked at his feet.

"I'm sorry," she said.

"Don't apologize. I knew it would be this way. You and I are constant, a constellation."

She lay down beside him and they were quiet for a while. Then she reached out and touched his face. "You have a beard."

"The water comes and goes. It's easier."

"I've never seen you with a beard. I would guess it suits you." She withdrew her hand.

"Please," he said. "Leave it there."

She laid her fingers across the side of his face and he held them with his own hand. She had the same fingers as his mother, thick and soft and smelling of the forest, never painted or adorned like those of other women he had known. He slept. In his sleep, he saw what he always saw, a man whose face was peeling off in sodden strips. He walked across a whitewashed landscape holding his face in his hands.

"André?"

He opened his eyes to darkness.

"What is it, my love?"

"I don't think about the children anymore. It's strange; do you know what I think about?"

"What?"

"I think about Sasha. I think about how we left her there, about what she must have gone through in those days after we left."

"Don't, Yalla. Please."

"It's the only thing I haven't forgiven you for, making me leave her. I think about how we closed her in the house, with a couple days of food and water, as if that would have made a difference, how she must have run around to all the windows, watching us go. I hear her whimper. I see her pressing her snout against the sill trying to catch our scent, I see the way she would have wagged her tail against the ground whenever she heard a noise, thinking it was us returning for her."

"We had no choice."

"Yes, that's what you said. Of course it wasn't true. There was a choice. We could have stayed there with her and been killed. All of us together. Do you remember when we used to walk her along the beach, how joyful she was. She'd swim so far out we were certain she'd drown, but then she always came back, triumphant with a clump of seaweed on her head, her fur glistening with salt." She paused. "Listen, do you hear it?"

What he heard was the rising, inhuman wail spreading overhead. When he closed his eyes, he could see the sound, a dark red light, the opposite of stars, a dark tarp cast out over the city like an invisible fisherman's net. "I hear it," he said.

"Who are they warning? There's no one left. They're warning the air, the cockroaches."

"We're left."

"My god, André, what do they want from us?"

"They want us to die. Or disappear, at least. Our existence complicates their plans. They want everything simple."

"André, I'm frightened."

"There's nothing to be afraid of anymore."

"And I'm sorry for what I did to you, leaving to go with him."

"I can hardly blame you."

"I was angry. I wanted to hurt you." The wailing grew louder. "Sometimes I want to go onto the roof. I want to raise my face to the sky and then it will be over and I'll be in Paradise with Sasha."

"There is no Paradise."

"How can you be sure?"

"There's only here."

"Then I want to be wherever is not here. I want to be in nothing."

He closed his eyes and listened to the sounds of the sky. It was strange how this sound could be both familiar and foreign. It was as if an alien machine had fallen from space, and they'd all built their lives around it, learning to live inside its structure and spaces without understanding its essence, what it was or where it came from. It was the opposite of Sasha, who they'd found on the side of the road, caked in mud and crazed with hunger, but who had loved them instantly, grafting her life onto theirs, becoming as familiar to André as his own arms or legs. André had loved her as much as Yalla, maybe more. He'd take her for long walks through the forest, and then later along the beach. She allowed him to be alone with his thoughts, but not too alone with them. Sometimes he'd watch her poking her wet nose into a bed of mushrooms, taking in the peculiar air around dead jellyfish, such simple curiosity and hunger for the world, and he'd think, this was how we were meant to be, innocent, grateful for mushrooms and jellyfish, and he'd feel sad and at peace.

When news came of the invasion and the bombings, they left their home in such a hurry—the neighboring suburb had been completely destroyed on the first night of bombing. They were told about a camp twenty miles east that would take them; they were told not to bring pets or other nonessential belongings. He knew that if he let Sasha out of the house she would follow them; she would follow them into the desert or the sea, across a bed of burning coals, so he closed her in with an open bag of food and a tub full of water and he promised himself he'd go back for her. Three weeks after they left, he set out. He hitchhiked half the distance to town and walked the rest. When he arrived, a neighbor told him one of the soldiers, one of the not-so-bad ones, had heard her howling and broken a window. She had followed him around for a few days. The soldiers took a liking to her, named her something the neighbor couldn't understand. When they rolled out the next week, the soldier who had found her took her with him. André's heart had felt both heavy and light when he heard the news, and he'd gone back to the camp with every intention of telling Yalla. By the time he arrived, she was sleeping beside the engineer, the children off playing on their own and she, sitting between the savage's legs, smoking one of his filthy brown cigarettes. He called her an inconstant whore and she spat in his face, and after that, he hadn't felt so much like telling her about Sasha. But now, why hide it from her now? There came a point when inflicting additional pain became meaningless, like pressing a pen to a sheet of black ink. And besides, there had been a time when he loved her, when he would have gladly given all he owned to feel her skin against his, her eyes on him. Was that moment less real than this one, or than all the ones between?

"Yalla," he said. "Are you awake?"

"Yes. I hardly ever sleep."

"I have something to tell you."

"No more fighting, André. I haven't the energy for it anymore."

"No, it's about Sasha."

"What about her?"

"A few weeks after we left, I went back to see if I could find her. Remember, I told you I was going to try to look into buying papers. I wasn't. I was going to bring her back to the camp. I had seen other pets there. It was practically Noah's ark. I walked all the way back, stopping only once to sleep."

"And when you got there, she was dead. Why do you tell me this?"

"No, she wasn't dead. That's just it. An officer had adopted her. He was taking excellent care of her, feeding and playing with her; I saw with my own two eyes, so I told him he could keep her. I knew she'd be happier with him than in some godforsaken camp. I should have told you then. I know I should have. Can you forgive me?"

She didn't answer at first. The noise from above had momentarily ceased and André's eyes were growing accustomed to the dark. The space between them no longer seemed black, but a rich and twilit purple. He reached for her again and this time she didn't push him away. Her face was hot and wet with tears, and yet she made no noise. He touched his tongue to her cheek. Her tears tasted like the sea—not like any sea but like the one they had lived beside in another life. What were tears? What were they made of and what was their purpose? It seemed that the longer he lived, the less he knew. Things had a way of dissolving, but this was not entirely bad.

His wife, a good woman and a whore, gathered him up in her arms and stroked his head, and thanked him, as the wailing resumed.

SHORT-STORY AWARD
FOR NEW WRITERS

1ST PLACE

Scott Alan Anderson receives $1200 for "Saints Alive."

Anderson's bio is on page 18, preceding his story.

2ND PLACE

Marc Basch receives $500 for "Morth."

He had a Monkees-style haircut parted down the middle that looked not quite sane, and his tennis shirt was unbuttoned all the way down to his sternum.

Marc Basch lives in Brooklyn. He is working on a novel. "Morth" will be his first published story.

3RD PLACE

Laura van den Berg receives $300 for
"Goodbye My Loveds."

"I think that's just a puddle, Denver."
"No, Shelby. It's a hole." And to prove it, he reaches inside, his arm disappearing to the elbow.

Laura van den Berg attends the MFA program at Emerson College, where she is the incoming editor-in-chief of *Redivider* and an editorial assistant for *Ploughshares*. Her stories have or will soon appear in the *Northwest Review*, *Literary Imagination*, *Third Coast*, the *Greensboro Review*, *Indiana Review*, *Literary Review*, and *StoryQuarterly*.

---

*We invite you to visit **www.glimmertrain.org** to see a list of the top twenty-five winners and finalists. We thank all entrants for sending in their work.*

Shortly thereafter the lion devoured me from the
waist down. I'm lucky to be alive.

Scott Alan Anderson grew up in Burleson, Texas, the hometown of Kelly Clarkson. His family swears he used to know her, but he doesn't remember. He recently earned his MFA from Old Dominion University and lives with his wife and son in Norfolk, Virginia. This is his first published story.

SAINTS ALIVE

Scott Alan Anderson

Scott Alan Anderson

Mamma Idelfa came home one Saturday from Haymarket, set her bags of produce next to the refrigerator, and glanced through her bedroom door, only to find the statue of Saint Jude gone. At first, she suspected the saint had ascended into heaven, although she didn't understand why he hadn't taken her along. Her husband and all their good friends had already passed on to heaven, and she prayed every night that Saint Jude would help her die too. She entertained the notion that the saint had walked out into the winding streets of Boston's North End and was at that moment performing miracles. But that made no sense! For the past few months he had devoted himself strictly to her. Maybe the saint was hiding. She searched the house—the closets, the pantry, the bathtub—just to make sure she hadn't misplaced the five-foot statue. Then she panicked. The votive candles at the saint's feet had been carelessly lifted to the dresser, while her prayer cards on the dresser now lay scattered on the floor. Worst of all, the small, enshrined photo of her late husband, passed away some two years, lay facedown upon her bed. She held her breath in disbelief. The statue did not transmogrify and walk out on its own. Someone had taken it.

Mamma Idelfa never liked to visit her neighbors and preferred that they didn't visit her either. But without too much deliberation she went to all the doors of those who shared the building and asked if they had seen the saint.

"*La mia statua,*" she said, "*non la ha vista?*"

"I'm sorry, I don't understand Italian," said the young woman upstairs. Inside the doorway, a child sat on the floor crying and shaking an empty sippy cup. The woman rubbed her neck. "What can I do to help?"

"The statue," Mamma Idelfa mumbled. "Saint Jude. He is missing."

"No, I'm sorry, I haven't seen him." The young woman replied. She scrunched her face pityingly and once more exclaimed before shutting the door: "Sorry!"

Mamma Idelfa hesitated to knock on the door across from hers. She could feel the loud hip-hop music vibrating through her shawl, her polyester dress, and into her chest.

"A saint?" The young man scratched his bare knee and brushed his hair forward. He turned to his friend inside. "No saints here. Right, bro?"

It was the same at every door. No one seemed to know Saint Jude existed, much less in a five-foot plaster form.

The search left her exhausted. She returned to her apartment, unbuttoned the top of her blouse, and poured herself some water from the faucet. How could anyone be so callous as to steal an old woman's comfort in her final hours? A small cloud outside her window blocked the sun, and for a moment, everything turned gray. Mamma Idelfa lumbered past her groceries and lay down upon her bed to sleep.

She'd first found Saint Jude in the damp storage basement of Saint Leonard's church. After her husband's death, she had no desire for anything but the church. Every day she would kneel in front of the Virgin and pray for comfort in her time of great loss. Father Joseph had told her she would find some extra votive candles in the basement, and it was there among the dusty banners, paintings, and a folded ping-pong table that Saint Jude first revealed himself to her. In his shiny plaster mold, aqua-green robe, and dark flowing beard, he welcomed her as a dear child. Leaning on the handle of his tall club, symbol of his martyrdom, he bowed to her, while the tongue of fire danced upon his head. Though covered with soft gray dust, he shone with fluorescent splendor.

Mamma Idelfa stood before him, rapt, and didn't even notice that Father Joseph had followed her down until he complained about the flickering overhead lights. Then Father Joseph stood behind her and put his hand on her shoulder. "Pray to Saint Jude in time of loss," he said. "He is the saint of lost causes."

She knelt on the concrete floor, lit one of the candles at the statue's feet, crossed herself, and prayed. She felt the saint's grace upon her shoulder, which, though she didn't notice, was actually the priest's hand, and she no longer felt alone.

"It's no good for him down here," she said. "Let me take him. He helps me, and I can take care of him."

The priest assented, with one condition: the church could take back the statue when needed. Mamma Idelfa ignored the condition; she just wanted the saint. With her son's help, she carried the statue home and gave him a place of honor, not under the vaulting roof of a church, but beside her headboard.

Every night, she knelt and prayed: "Do not forget the needs and difficulties of Christ's little ones like me, still struggling on the way home to God."

She was eighty-nine years old. But in the saint's painted green eyes, she was a special child of God, soon to cast this ugly world aside to see His face. Her little world had grown so unfamiliar since all her old neighbors had either passed away or moved to the assisted living on Parmenter Street. The saint taught her contentment. He helped her forget her present sorrows and focus on the life to come. In the meantime, he always listened to her complaints. He even played solitaire with her and let her win. They would sit together for hours at a time, the way she imagined she would have sat with Salvatore had he lived longer.

Sleep was a kind of peace, but it only dulled her pain. Her dreams troubled her; they were as empty as the bedside corner where the saint had once perched. She woke intermittently, jumping from the sensation that everything in the world had been stripped from her, including the bed beneath her.

Her son Gaetano found her in bed at about four o'clock later that afternoon. The restaurant he owned, Piccola Venezia on Hanover Street, kept him busy, but every Saturday he came by to check on her. She felt a sour tinge of disappointment when she saw him. Salvatore was more ill tempered, and they had often argued, but at least he didn't grovel for people the way Gaetano did. He was so nervous. How could she respect someone whose greatest ambition was a full house every Friday night? Gaetano bumbled into the room and hovered over her. He was not a tall man, but whenever he talked to her, he hunched over so he looked almost as tiny as she was. "Mamma," he said, "*che successo?*"

"My Saint Jude," she said. "He disappeared."

"Ah, Mamma," Gaetano said. "I'm sorry. I meant to tell you. Father Joseph asked me to pick it up for him. They're having a big festival for Saint Jude this year." He went and leaned against her dresser, bumping a couple more prayer cards to the floor. "I thought you'd be happy about it. It's been twenty years since they had a feast for Saint Jude."

She sat up, pushed herself out of bed, and marched past him into the kitchen, snatching at her hair. She leaned against the counter and stared at the cracks in the black and white floor tiles. Didn't he have better things to do than steal from her, she thought, like fixing the house?

"It'll be fun, Ma," he said, holding out his arms. "We'll go to the festival. You need to get out more anyway. You could…"

"*Idiota!*" she shouted. "You don't think!"

She threw her arms at him, shooing him away, and sat at the kitchen table. She felt her blood rush to her temples. She put her head in her hands, took a deep breath, and peeked through her fingers at the groceries by the fridge. The romaine lettuce poked its head out of its plastic bag, glared back at her, and stuck out its tongue.

She felt a sharp pang of regret. Gaetano stood in the bedroom doorway with his head bowed. She shouldn't have snapped. After all, she had taught him respect for the priesthood. Finally, she motioned him to her, and he came and kissed her on the cheek.

"*Sta bene*," she said. "Tomorrow I talk to Father Joseph. He tells me where I can find the saint."

But that night she couldn't sleep. She kept staring at the big empty spot in the corner where the five-foot-tall statue had once guarded over her. The room, at first, felt enormously empty. But the more she stared, the smaller the room seemed. It shrunk until it was no bigger than a penny, and her where Abe Lincoln sits. When it shrunk to nothing, she opened her eyes—she must have shut them—her throat constricted, and the whole process started over again.

The next morning at mass, Mamma Idelfa sat in her pew by the altar, bowed her head, and folded her hands in her lap, but she could not pray. Neither could she pay much attention to Father Joseph's words. Her one thought was to find her saint of lost causes. She looked around at the fading murals—Jesus and the apostles, the story of His life and death, the feeding of the five thousand. She particularly liked the mural of Joseph and Mary riding the donkey to Bethlehem. She always wondered about the fate of Joseph and how hard it must have been for Mary after he died. She studied the stained-glass saints in case Saint Jude appeared there as a clue. She scrutinized each plaster statue with its coin box and candles, every few paces around the sanctuary—the Virgin Mary, St. Agrippina, St. Lucy, St. Leonard. Still she found no trace of her beloved Saint Jude.

After mass, Mamma Idelfa waited until only a few lingered in the foyer. She caught Father Joseph gathering the collection of books he had brought with him.

"Padre," she said, her hands trembling, "why did you take my saint?"

Father Joseph scratched his neck, puzzled. "The feast," he said. "You must know." He stretched his hand from his neck to his head, which he scratched with lavish attention. "I told your son. We're going to celebrate the saint again this year." With one quick nod the old priest puckered his entire face to a position of complete satisfaction.

Mamma Idelfa suddenly lost all patience with him. She crossed and uncrossed her arms a few times over and demanded to know where he'd hidden the statue.

"For the moment," he said, with a weak smile, "he shares my office. He's wonderful. I've already found several lost items, including my extra set of keys and my favorite pipe."

"Of course," said Mamma Idelfa, her hands shaking violently by her sides. "Why do you think I keep him in my own home?" She had rescued the statue. Father Joseph hadn't cared for him. He'd banished Saint Jude to the basement where he kept company with an old coffee maker and an oversized photo of Father Joseph's sister. She felt betrayed.

Father Joseph only nodded, muttered, "*Si, si, si*," under his breath, and smiled. He waddled away to his office as fast as his stiff legs and heavy wool suit allowed.

She stared at the altar. It was the priest's job, as her spiritual father, to take care of her. Didn't he know how much the saint had helped her? Her footsteps echoed as she walked back down the aisle of the big hollow sanctuary. She bundled herself up tight, cursed the priest, and went home.

Mamma Idelfa shut her blinds and kept the lights so dim that she bumped into furniture. She tried to survive on the groceries that were already in the house. She didn't eat that much, especially since a little into the third day she lost her dentures.

On Saturday her son Gaetano visited her. He found her in bed again, and he went and stood beside her like before.

"I'm worried about you, Ma," he said. "You haven't been this bad off since Pop passed away."

At the mention of her late husband, Mamma Idelfa crossed herself. Gaetano bowed his head and crossed himself, too.

"Why you leave me here all by myself?" Mamma Idelfa said. "I carried you around in my arms. All this time you spend at the restaurant."

She could see his eyes gaze over the room. "I don't know, Ma," he said. "Maybe if you moved in with us, I could help out more. We'd eat dinner together. I'd take you out on the town or something. What you think?"

She shook her head.

"I brought you a present, Mamma," Gaetano said. He handed her a shoebox, which she opened, and inside, wrapped in the Sunday comics, she found a smaller version of the saint.

"It's hand carved," he said, stooping over, some of his slicked-back hair falling over his ear. "Made from olive wood," he said. "A saint for a saint."

The little brown eight-inch saint glared up at her with a stern smile and one eyebrow cocked up full of suspicion.

"I don't like it," Mamma Idelfa said, handing it back.

"What's the matter with it?" Gaetano asked.

"You take it home with you. You pray to it. Ask it to give me back the real one."

"No, Ma," Gaetano said. He stood up straight and loosened his shoulders. "I'll leave it here for you. I'll stop by tomorrow to see how you're doing."

She set the saint on the bed. She wanted Gaetano to stay, but couldn't just ask. "Your father…," she started, and then crossed herself. Gaetano stopped and crossed himself, too. "If your father…" This time Gaetano crossed himself, and she followed.

"Pop's been gone over two years now," he said, leaning his arm against the doorframe. "I hate seeing you like this, Ma."

Mamma Idelfa crossed herself once more, and Gaetano did likewise, halfhearted.

"I'll see you tomorrow," he said.

She motioned him out. She refused to look at him. "You're an ungrateful son," she told him. Once he'd gone, she got up, took the little statue to the dresser, and turned it on its head. Then she flipped off the light.

She lived in darkness and shadows. Long-forgotten memories possessed the shadows around her and flitted along the walls. The smaller shadows along the living-room wall took the form of her two children: Gaetano and little Antonella, the one who died at age two. The children crawled and fought silently as slivers of moonlight filtered through them. In the kitchen, a larger shadow slouched back in a chair and kicked up his heels.

"You?" Mamma Idelfa said aloud. "Why you show up now?"

The shadow only shrugged.

"You want something?" she asked. "I can pour us wine and we can talk a little. You want that?"

The shadow shook his head. He shook his whole body as a group of people walked by outside laughing with each other.

"It's just like you," she said. "You're not worth nothing. Even with you here I raise the kids myself. I have a baby in my arms, and I help at the restaurant. You stay out late. You don't help. Then you leave."

The shadow stood and made as if to leave.

"No," she cried. "Stay here, then. You stay here and help me."

The shadow slunk back in the chair, and for a moment she felt relieved. Then it floated and angled against the wall toward the window. She called out for her husband to stay. She even cursed him. But that only seemed to hasten his departure. And once again she found herself alone with only the dark memory of his death.

The next day was Sunday, and she called Gaetano and asked him to go with her to St. Leonard's to see Father Joseph. She'd decided to beg.

They found the priest sitting in one of the front pews.

"Father Joseph?" Gaetano said. "We're wondering if Mamma could keep Saint Jude just a few days until the feast. It's been pretty hard for her."

"He's gone," Father Joseph said, looking up.

"But I thought you were keeping him in your office?" Gaetano asked.

"Just a little while," the priest said. "I keep him until the others pick him up. The feast is coming fast. The League of Saint Jude will take care of him now."

"What feast?" she said. "I don't want no feast."

"I'm sorry, Mamma," Gaetano said.

"It's going to be nice," Father Joseph said. "The nicest feast we celebrate this year. We have the banners and band all lined up. Everybody will remember it."

Mamma Idelfa collapsed into a pew. All her past sins came flying up at her like dust beaten from a rug. How many times had she missed church? Tithes? Prayers? Was God so unpleased with her? She fell into a trance of Hail Marys and Our Fathers in hopes of conjuring the statue.

"Where is he?" she said at last. "Where is my Saint Jude?"

"If I tell you," Father Joseph said, "you're only going to cause trouble." He stood to go. "You know the feast day," he said. "You see him then."

Mamma Idelfa closed her eyes. She was sure her heart had stopped. She prayed for God to take her home to Him that instant.

God didn't take her home, so she walked to her apartment and lay in bed for three more days. She felt weak with hunger. Her bones ached, and she felt chest pains. One afternoon Death sauntered in and sat in the chair opposite her bed. He wore a plaid tweed suit and had a thick handlebar mustache. He looked like a prankster uncle from the Old Country who'd visited her once as a child. The uncle had told her if she gave him a coin he would make it disappear, but he never gave the coin back afterwards. Death sat across from her with his legs crossed and plucked at his trousers. Finally, he stood and held out his hand to her.

"Would you dance this next one with me?" he asked her.

"Me?" Mamma Idelfa said, quivering. "I hardly know you."

All her life she'd wanted to learn to dance. Salvatore never liked the idea. She feared what he might say now.

Death twirled around and tapped an old song she couldn't place. His steps were masterful and effortless. "I thought this is what you wanted," he said. "Don't be afraid. It's much easier than it looks."

But Mamma Idelfa grew bashful. Death had taken her off guard somehow, and she realized how ill prepared she was.

Death twisted his mustache thoughtfully. "Perhaps another time," he said. He turned to leave, and as he crossed the threshold, he vanished.

Mamma Idelfa went into the bathroom and performed her neglected nightly ablutions. Lingering in front of the mirror, she tentatively lifted the hem of her skirt. She wanted desperately to remember the elegant taps and turns Death had shown her, but, in the end, she resorted to a couple of steps she knew by heart from her favorite Sinatra movie. Her ankles hurt and her toes tingled. It frightened her. It felt nothing like death.

The next morning, she remembered the statuette her son had given her, still on the dresser standing on its head. She went and turned it right-side up. She gathered her saint cards and votive candles and the picture of Salvatore. She burned her finger lighting one of the candles. She lowered herself to the floor and knelt beside the dresser to pray. She shut her eyes tight as she could and tried to conjure up the larger statue. It worked only as long as she kept her eyes shut tight. She shut her eyes so tight her ears rang out like Gabriel's last trumpet.

It was the telephone ringing. Gaetano's voice came on and told her to pick up.

"I found the statue, Ma. Get dressed. We'll go over there together."

Standing on Fleet Street in front of a large tanned brick building, if she squinted, she could just make out the familiar bluish-green garment over the off-white robe on the figure of the saint. Just the right height, just the right girth. Night was settling, the blinds were open, and as they drew closer the saint appeared in all his plastered, painted glory, dressed in Christmas lights. She could make out the folds of his robe, his sculpted hair, even the tongue of fire.

They climbed the stoop and pressed the buzzer. In a few seconds, the door swung open and revealed, not the statue, but a squat, bald man, a potbellied Mussolini.

"Who is it, honey?" said a woman's voice from inside.

"They say they're here to pick up Saint Jude," the man yelled back.

"Oh no," the woman's voice returned. "That statue belongs to the League of Saint Jude. You tell them…just a minute…" A bleached-blond woman in a sequined sweatshirt appeared at the door. "That statue is for the feast," she said, "and my husband's chair of that feast, and the feast's next week. The saint stays right here." She pointed to the floor with both hands. "Now if you want to help, just let me know."

Mamma Idelfa pushed past them. The woman tried to block her, but Mamma Idelfa slipped beneath her outstretched arm. She ran to the statue and cast off the Christmas lights, reached up and grabbed the statue's head, and pulled him down toward her. The blond woman ran over and tried to grab the statue back, but Mamma Idelfa continued to struggle. "Gaetano," she cried. "*Aiuta!*" Finally, the man stepped in, wrested the statue once and for all, and set it upright. In a deep voice he said, "Nobody can own a saint."

Mamma Idelfa grew so furious she fainted. She fell prostrate at the statue's feet. As she looked up from the parquet floorboards, every-thing—the off-white sofa, the small corner bar, the empty bookshelf, the stainless-steel oven (inspiring a quick flash of jealousy)—all of it swirled and faded and blurred. The light from the window burst in upon them and dissolved everything in the room except her and the saint. The statue itself burst into one big, giant light bulb. And in that instant he took on human form. He walked over, lifted her, sat with her in the chair, and put her on his knee.

Mamma Idelfa was elated. She felt like a child again. The saint was hers, and he bestowed upon her preference over all others. He had truly listened to her prayers. She looked expectantly into his face.

But he did not look back with the warm, soft expression she ex-pected. He glared and frowned and shook his head, his lips pursed, his nose squeezed tight, and his eyebrows lowered. He bent her over his knee and spanked her bottom.

The saint held her by her shoulders, looked her straight in her tearful eyes, and said, "Listen, you grow up. Don't be so selfish. I want you to help with my feast."

Gaetano took Mamma Idelfa to the North End clinic. The doctor said except for her low blood-sugar level, which concerned him, she was healthy as a young mule. Nevertheless, Gaetano thought she should stay with him a few days. He installed her in the third-floor bedroom above the Hanover Street restaurant, saying the noise from the street might jog her back to life. But Mamma Idelfa was very despondent. The room was small and dirty, and it smelled like roasted garlic and Gaetano's aftershave. She lay on the safari bedspread, stared at the ceiling fan, and tried turning the light bulbs out of their sockets in her mind. It was no use. The light also streamed through the window, and she could hear the traffic and palaver from the restaurant and the street below—lots of laughter and arguing, people's footsteps, plates clanking, and cars honking their horns. She closed her eyes and tried to re-envision her moment of ecstasy with Saint Jude, but fell asleep in the attempt. It was over. And although she awoke feeling much calmer, she had no idea what to do with herself.

The drums and brass of the North End band, winding up and down the streets, roused her from the bed. She sat up and straightened her skirt. She went and peered out the window, but she couldn't see any of their blue shirts or hats. She wanted to yell down to Gaetano for a pair of binoculars, but remembered he was marching with them. Finally they came. The statue rode on a platform, with four men, Gaetano among them, carrying it on their shoulders. Two or three holding up banners walked ahead. A smattering of tourists followed. Saint Jude's procession was on the small side—nothing like Fisherman's Feast or the Feast of Saint Agrippina—but when it rounded the corner to Hanover Street she felt a sudden surge of panic. Quickly she knelt on the floor and lowered her head out of sight. After some minutes in this penitent posture, however, the music only grew louder. Mamma Idelfa peeked and ducked again. The procession had stopped right below her window. Gaetano, Father Joseph, the couple from the league, all her neighbors—they all stood outside and waited for her. The band played and played their best number—Number 1—while others called for her to poke her head out. They shouted for her to drop down a piece of string with money taped to it in order to stick it to Saint Jude.

"Ma," Gaetano yelled. "Come on out, Ma. It's okay."

Mamma Idelfa stood and slowly pressed against the window. She stretched her stiff joints, took a deep breath, and opened it.

The crowd below cheered.

"Ah!" she shouted, throwing out her arms. She motioned them up to her. "You come here. I give it to you here."

Gaetano opened the door that led up to the apartment and as many as could ran up the stairs. Mamma Idelfa opened her bedroom door to meet them. The statue, which couldn't fit through the door or stairwell on its stand, stayed behind and waved to her from outside. The band ascended, along with some tourists and small children, quickly filling the room. Mamma Idelfa stood on the bed and waved the dollar. She felt her limbs shake and wobble as she bounced. A boy from the butcher's brought in the pig to be roasted; it shook loose and for a brief moment ran around the room and squealed.

My father, my mother, and me, circa 1966, in Dumas, Texas. My mother is twenty, my father twenty-three. They seem so sweet and so young. My father is the inspiration for Neil in "The Man Who Fell from the Sky."

K.L. Cook's first book, a collection of linked stories entitled *Last Call* (Nebraska, 2004), won the inaugural *Prairie Schooner* Book Prize in fiction. His novel, *The Girl from Charnelle* (William Morrow, 2006; Harper Perennial, 2007), was an editor's choice selection of the Historical Novel Society. His stories and essays have been published in journals, magazines, and anthologies, including *Shenandoah*, *Poets & Writers*, *Threepenny Review*, *American Short Fiction*, and *Witness*. He teaches literature and creative writing at Prescott College and at Spalding University's brief-residency MFA in Writing Program.

THE MAN WHO FELL FROM THE SKY

K.L. Cook

On New Year's Eve morning, 1962, Neil and Ben Brewer tossed a duffel bag of clothes and Uncle Jimmy's binoculars into the back of Neil's truck.

"You boys be careful," their mother said. "Neil, you watch out for Ben." She brushed their hair back and straightened their jackets and double-checked the basket she had packed with turkey and ham sandwiches, four big pickles, several cobs of corn, a pan of walnut brownies, and a large thermos of coffee. "I know you boys love your Uncle Jimmy," she said, "and I know he told you where you could get into the most trouble. But don't go tomcatting all over Dallas and wind up in jail. If you do, your father and me ain't coming to get you. You understand?"

They nodded and kissed her, and then Harvey Lee (they'd always called him Harvey Lee rather than Dad or Pop) shook their hands and winked at them, and they headed out of the snow-lined driveway of the farm for the five-hour drive to Dallas.

Neil was twenty and Ben seventeen. It was the first time Neil had been out of Oklahoma since he traveled with his senior class to Washington, D.C. Ben couldn't remember when he was last out of the state, and they spent the first half-hour of the trip pondering this, recounting every one of Ben's seventeen years before coming to the conclusion that Ben had never left Oklahoma, not even as a baby, had hardly even been outside the county. How sad was that?

Both of them were tall and rangy, though Neil had muscled up since he graduated because he'd been working full-time on the family's farm in Reed and gotten extra work hauling bags of grain to and from the silos in Altus. He had black, straight hair that oiled when it grew too long, and his ears stuck out when he was a teenager, but now his face had transformed into something approaching handsomeness. He was happy that school was behind him, and he had no intention of going to college, couldn't see the point. He joked that he'd graduated in the top ten of his class, the punch line being that there were only nine seniors the year he graduated. He did miss playing basketball and football on a team pulled together from all the little schools in Greer County. Neil had had a few girlfriends—mainly summer flings at Quartz Mountain Lake with rich gals from Oklahoma City or Tulsa and even one Spanish girl whose father was a visiting engineering professor at Kansas State University. He'd fumbled through the loss of his virginity with her late one night in the cab of his truck as she whispered a rosary in Spanish, and then she left for Manhattan, Kansas the next day, and he never heard from her again.

Though Neil had not done that well in school, he was bright and funny and quick on his feet, and everyone figured he'd go off—to Oklahoma State or maybe the University of Texas—so there was a sense of palpable disappointment that he'd hung about for the last year and a half, still living with his folks on the farm, still farting around Greer County. But he seemed, in general, oblivious to this disappointment, and felt in fact a lightness, especially driving home from Altus, his body caked in sweat and dust, the cool night breeze blowing over his skin, the taste of a hand-rolled cigarette in his mouth, the thought of the weekend and the almost criminal pleasure of being able to watch women in their bikinis baking on the makeshift beach by the lake, or dreaming illicitly of his Aunt Doris, who was about the sexiest goddamn woman he'd ever seen.

Ben was the brilliant one, or so every one said, including Ben. He liked to read novels and poetry and could quote all of "The Charge of the Light Brigade" and long passages from Shakespeare's *Henry IV,*

Part 1—"Banish plump Jack, and banish all the world!"—and Shakespeare's sonnet about his ugly mistress with her reeking breath and dun-colored breasts, clomping around like an old ugly hag rather than some angel on a pedestal. And the other one that Ben and Neil referred to as the Sugar Daddy sonnet:

> When my love swears that she is made of truth,
> I do believe her, though I know she lies,
> That she might think me some untutored youth,
> Unlearned in the world's false subtleties.

Ben was also good with numbers, so good that he had surpassed his teachers' skills by the time he was in sixth grade. In high school, he had to send off for trigonometry and calculus books. In his sophomore year, Ben had grown ten inches. He was so damn skinny now, his ribs poking obscenely through the skin, that Harvey Lee said he looked like a piece of vanilla taffy that God had stretched lengthwise. He had blond hair with a stubborn cowlick and thick, black-framed glasses, and a face full of freckles. He could play most anything on the piano, and he had a smooth tenor voice, and could beat the pants off anybody in Scrabble and chess. Girls loved him, and yet Ben seemed unaware, on some level, of his own charms, shy with women, rarely even going on a date, preferring to stick his head in a book or work out some complex mathematical calculation rather than ogle the bikinied masterpieces at Quartz Mountain or go to the drive-in in Altus with Neil and a couple of vacationing girls.

Neil loved Ben, not just out of brotherly devotion, but because Ben was pretty damn fun to be around, even though he had his head stuck in books a lot of the time. Neil didn't even begrudge the fact that everybody believed Ben would earn a scholarship when he graduated, maybe even to an Ivy League school. The sky was the limit for Ben. Neil thought he might even wind up becoming an astronaut, orbiting through space like John Glenn, the poster boy of all astronauts with his shit-eating grin and boyish blond crewcut. The only thing Neil really worried about now was that his brother would leave in a year and a half, after he graduated, and then who the hell would he have to pal around with? Greer County wasn't that big.

On the windswept road out of Reed, south to Dallas, Neil's truck swayed back and forth. They shook their heads in delight, and Ben said, "Man, I love the shit out of Uncle Jimmy."

They both agreed that this trip was the best gift that Uncle Jimmy had ever given them—which was saying a lot—and then they both concurred that Jimmy was probably the best damn uncle any two nephews could hope to have. They rode in silence for a while to solemnize their gratitude, and then Neil asked for one of those big pickles. After Ben rummaged around in the basket and unwrapped them from the briny wax paper, he turned on the radio and kept adjusting the knobs from town to town, trying to pick up a good rock-and-roll station, but it was hard to get anything in the Sun Belt except twangy cry-in-your-beer ballads from Wichita Falls, Abilene, and Fort Worth.

But they didn't care because they were going to Dallas for an historic event, and it was all because of Uncle Jimmy's (and Aunt Doris's—let's not forget Aunt Doris) generosity.

How could you not love Uncle Jimmy? Jimmy was twenty-nine, Harvey Lee's youngest brother by seventeen years. He'd served as a paratrooper in Korea, had been decorated many times, including a special commendation from General MacArthur himself. After the Korean War ended, Jimmy traveled the world, working as a cook and bartender in New York and Los Angeles, a bouncer in a couple of brothels in Spain, a ski instructor in Austria, and even for a short while as the driver for a barbershop quartet that traveled through Italy, France, and Greece.

Just after Kennedy won the election, Jimmy returned to Greer County with beautiful Doris, who he'd met in San Diego. Doris was just the woman you'd imagine finding in San Diego. She had long, silky blond hair that moved like a California wave over the side of her face. She had worked for a while as a model in Los Angeles, and her lips were the lips you'd want to see in a cosmetics advertisement, as smooth and delicious as a plum. A mesmerizing kaleidoscopic green spray flecked her brown eyes. She wasn't any slouch around the house or some California complainer, either, which is what Neil and Ben's mother first suspected. She could make a lethal cherry cobbler, sprinkled with cinnamon and spiked with rum, and she could hold her own on the farm without a single whimper, expertly separating the cotton from the bolls and pulling the fruit for hours from the trees in the orchards. Her breasts and hips moved in her dress like small animals, and Neil wished he could stop himself from staring.

"You're gonna get your head knocked off," Harvey Lee said one hot afternoon last August when they were all pulling peaches from the trees. Neil had been gazing in a trance at his aunt, perched on a ladder two trees over, her arms outstretched, revealing a sliver of flesh between her arm and her startlingly white bra. "If not by her," Harvey Lee whispered, "then by your Uncle Jimmy."

One thing Neil admired about Doris was that she wasn't a priss or prude whose delicate sensibilities might be upset by a cussword. Once every week or so, Neil and Ben would go over to Doris and Jimmy's rented house in Mangum, and she'd make a big dish of lasagna for them all, or Jimmy would grill bloody hamburgers and char some hotdogs, and Jimmy's friends would come over. They'd sit around singing, Doris playing the upright player piano that Jimmy had bought for thirty-five dollars. She played with a jazzy relish that Neil thought was as good as Nat King Cole, with Ben relieving her every once in a while. Jimmy and his buddies would sing in four-part harmony, and sometimes Neil and Ben joined in, but mainly they'd sit on the couch or lounge in the chairs and drink beers and listen as they got quietly drunk, grateful to be included in Doris and Jimmy's circle of friends. Doris would make margaritas sometimes, especially if one of Jimmy's friends had been down to Mexico and brought back some mescal, or they'd break out the Jack Daniels and sip the whiskey over ice until it got late, and everybody sat around the kitchen table or in the small living room, or in the summer out in the backyard where they had a picnic table, some lounge chairs, a hammock, and an inflatable pool. Jimmy and the other young men who'd also been to Korea would tell stories, mainly about the tedium and the goddamn trench foot and the goddamn blisters and the goddamn heat, but every once in a while they'd grow nostalgically somber recalling this friend or that fool who got his ass blown sky-high by a grenade or landmine, or some poor fucker who got a bullet through the eye or had his arm burned to goo by a gasoline bomb.

Doris would lounge on the couch with her bare legs sprawled over Jimmy's lap and let her long fingers play lightly through Jimmy's hair, sliding them soothingly across his tan collarbone. Late at night, with all of them sipping their drinks, Neil and Ben pulling on their warm beers, Jimmy would talk a cackling blue streak, recounting his and Doris's private history as if it were something sacred and special, worthy of constant commemoration—how they met at Waikiki Willie's in San Diego where she was working as a cocktail waitress, how he'd begged her to marry him a hundred times ("a hundred and twenty-seven times," Doris corrected) before she finally relented, how he convinced her to move back to Oklahoma last year, reversing the journey of the most famous Okies. And now Doris was working as a hostess at the Quartz Mountain Country Club and Jimmy was a park ranger at Quartz Mountain and gave water skiing lessons on the weekends in the summer and volunteered for the Greer County Fire Department.

"Why did you come back here?" Neil asked Uncle Jimmy one night, after everyone had left except for Ben and him.

"There are two kinds of people," Jimmy said philosophically, leaning forward, an ash-eaten cigarette serving as a pointer, his thick black hair tied in little pigtails by Doris. "Two kinds, I tell you: restless wanderers and homesick pussies. The sooner you find out which one you are, the better. You may have to try to be one before you discover you're the other. Me, I figured I was a wanderer, but the longer I was away from here, the more I figured out that I was just a pussy."

They all laughed at that, and Doris took a long, slow drag from her cigarette and closed her eyes and seemed to contemplate this small pleasure.

"You go out and test yourselves against the world, boys. And don't wait for a war to make you do it. You understand? I saw plenty of the world, and I prefer Reed, Oklahoma and this little piece of paradise."

He reached his big hand over to Doris's thigh and squeezed, making her smile, even though she didn't open her eyes.

"We better get going," Neil said, sensing their cue to leave.

"Be sure and tell old Harvey Lee," Jimmy said, leaning back, "that it's a terrible injustice that I got both the brains *and* the big dick."

Ben and Neil both smiled. This was an old joke, something that they had first heard Jimmy say long ago when they all went fishing. When Uncle Jimmy said it to Harvey Lee, Neil and Ben—who were fourteen and eleven at the time—thought for sure their father would haul off and punch Jimmy. But Harvey Lee just smiled and shook his head, re-hooked the stink bait, and cast out his line. Now, every time Uncle Jimmy would get drunk, he'd bring up the shame and misfortune of this.

Doris said, "Oh, you shut up, you skinny bull." And then, encouragingly to Ben and Neil, she said, "It's not the size that counts anyway. It's what you can do with what you got."

"She's just trying to make you feel better, boys, because the sad truth of the matter is that you two have your father's genes and therefore suffer in comparison to your Uncle Jimmy as well. And I'm sure, Neil, that of the two of you, bookish Ben's got you beat. On both counts."

"Hush, now," Doris said, shaking her head but smiling. "Don't listen to him. It's not about size. It's about velocity and rhythm."

They all laughed, Jimmy too. Doris was from California, where women apparently talked without shame about sex. It made Neil want to go west and find his own beautiful wife with rolling hips and green-flecked eyes and a yellow wave of hair, a woman who could drink you under the table and proffer practical advice about what to do with your penis if it happened to be smaller than Uncle Jimmy's. Though it wouldn't do to have a wife so pretty that every damn guy who saw her wanted to sleep with her, just as Neil fantasized about Aunt Doris—the "aunt" giving the fantasy a little extra kick.

Uncle Jimmy was a great gift-giver, even when he was away in Korea. He'd send them gold-plated chopsticks and elaborate belts with Korean characters on them and intricately decorated fans and silk kimonos

K. L. Cook

(for Granny and Neil's mother), as well as some shell casings and a framed photograph of him on furlough in Japan being held naked, except for a cloth over his crotch, in the arms of eight geisha girls. Five years ago, he sent Neil and Ben packages from Greece, and when they opened them, the packages were stuffed full of currency from all the countries he'd been to. Each package had a hundred different bills—Italian lire, English pounds, French notes—as well as twenty-five American ones. When Ben dumped his envelope, the bills fluttered like confetti in the air, and three of them flew into the fire and crinkled into black ash. It was a wonderful waste—too much, both Harvey Lee and their mother (who'd both grown up and spent their frugal courtship in the Depression) exclaimed, but they smiled when they said it, and Neil could tell his parents were as tickled by Jimmy's generosity as they were.

This past Christmas, Uncle Jimmy wrapped a tiny package, addressed to them both. Neil and Ben didn't expect that much because Jimmy and Doris were trying to get pregnant and were saving money for the down payment on their own house. Uncle Jimmy had said for the boys not to get their hopes up. But when they opened the box, they found a fifty-dollar bill wrapped around two fifty-yard-line tickets for the Cotton Bowl in Dallas on New Year's Day.

"Figured you wouldn't want to miss history in the making," Jimmy said, smiling. The Texas Longhorns were undefeated and ranked fourth in the country and had an outside shot at the national title. They were playing seventh-ranked Louisiana State and were favored to win. Neil and Ben had never been to a college game before, certainly nothing on the scale of the Cotton Bowl.

Later, Uncle Jimmy took them aside and slipped a piece of paper into Neil's palm that had the name and address of a brothel (Jimmy's term—not cathouse, not whorehouse) in Fort Worth run by a classy Irish woman, where the girls had straight teeth and were vigilant about hygiene.

"They don't even care how small your dicks are," Jimmy kidded. "Have a good time on me, boys."

•　　•　　•

Neil and Ben arrived in Dallas by the middle of the afternoon, and they spent two hours driving around in circles before they stopped and got a Dallas-Fort Worth street map. That night they found a couple of bars on the seedier side of Fort Worth where Uncle Jimmy had told them the fun resided. After fueling themselves on beer, they found the brothel. The Irish lady who owned the establishment—a still-beautiful woman with a large platter of shimmering gray hair and a slender, good-postured build—wouldn't let Ben go upstairs with any of the girls. She claimed in her lilting brogue that she possessed a special arrangement with the chief of police assuring her no trouble as long as she didn't cater to minors. She let Ben play Scrabble with the girls in the lobby, however, while Neil went upstairs with a young redhead named Marietta. Marietta inspected and washed his pecker and asked him what he wanted to do, as if he had options. He just said the normal, so she lay on the bed and opened her thighs like a book and Neil gazed stupidly, never having seen a completely naked woman in the light; the image half-nauseated him and half-thrilled him. He leapt on the bed and did what he'd paid for. It was all over much too soon, and now he was fifteen dollars poorer, but Uncle Jimmy would be happy for him.

He went downstairs. Nobody wanted Ben to leave in the middle of the Scrabble game, so Ben told Neil to use his share for a double. Neil galloped upstairs with a blond named Gillian who reminded him of Doris. She let him lay beside her in the bed afterward, and he asked her to stroke his head lightly with her gold-painted fingernails and tell him where she was from. It wasn't busy that night—surprising, considering it was New Year's Eve—and she wasn't used to having men show a sympathetic interest in her autobiography. She poured them both a drink from the bottle of scotch she kept hidden in the closet and unraveled a complicated and tragic narrative that included several cruel Presbyterian ministers from Kentucky and a mother and sister who had died of diphtheria. Gillian proclaimed that she wasn't long for this life, and Neil wondered if she meant life in general or life in the brothel until she explained that she was working her way through the Fort Worth Beauty Academy and then she was going to open up her own shop after she saved enough money, and then get married and have four children, three boys and one girl. Gillian had a slow Southern accent that lulled him into and out of a sentimental reverie. Suddenly, they heard a loud shot, followed by corks popping, and then a melodious version of "Auld Lang Syne." She offered him a freebie for being so sweet and attentive, and afterward they kissed and joked about how much they adored each other.

When Neil and Gillian went back downstairs, Ben was playing the piano and singing "Danny Boy" with three of the girls, including Marietta. The Irish woman sat in the corner, crocheting a bright blue sweater.

"I'm going to have to put the timer on you again, Gillian," the Irish woman scolded, and Neil could tell that there was a history of reprimand and rebellion between them. He felt fortunate to have been the recipient of what might very well be the last of Gillian's talkative indolence and good will.

They slept in the back of Neil's truck, not wanting to waste what was left of their money on a hotel room. They shivered when it dropped into the forties, nothing to keep them warm but their clothes and jackets, baseball caps and horse blankets. They woke scratching themselves, smelling of hay and oats, then found a fifty-cent ham-and-egg diner, swilled some bad coffee to warm and wake them, checked on directions to the Cotton Bowl, and headed over.

Though Neil and Ben had grown up in Oklahoma, they never had liked the arrogant Sooners, and had always rooted for the Texas Longhorns, because their mother's older brother, Uncle Deeb, had been a famous running back in '40 and '41 with the Longhorns, and had even been a finalist for the Heisman his junior year. Everyone had such high hopes for him, figured he was a lock to win it the following year and would eventually go to the NFL and become another Galloping Ghost or Bronco Nagurski, or even a Slingin' Sammy Baugh, since he could not only run like an antelope but throw the ball seventy yards in the air. But after the Japs bombed Pearl Harbor, he enlisted and was killed in the Pacific less than six months later. This was all ancient history. This famous uncle was dead before Neil and Ben were born, but they felt that they knew him, not only because of the newspaper clippings and magazine photos that their mother kept in an album in the den, but because of the way she would get misty-eyed when she recalled the great thrill she, her parents, her six other brothers and sisters, and even Harvey Lee felt sitting in the stands on a Saturday afternoon with thousands of other wildly cheering fans, all decked out in the burnt orange and white of Texas, all of them holding their index fingers and pinkies up—*Hook 'em, Horns!*—all of them shouting Deeb's name again and again as he threaded his way through the slow-footed defenders or launched a beautiful, perfectly spiraling bomb to an orange-jerseyed receiver streaking toward the end zone.

This past year, Neil and Ben and their mother had listened to every Texas game they could on the radio, and they particularly relished the Longhorns' whipping of the Oklahoma Sooners. With each win, the Longhorns climbed higher in the standings until they were undefeated with just one tie and were poised, if the cards fell *just* right with the other New Year's Day bowls, to win their first national championship. LSU was a scary team, however, and not to be taken lightly. They had an All-American halfback, Jerry Stovall, who had already been offered a $100,000 contract by the Houston Oilers, along with a promise of a $50,000 loan to help him start a dentistry practice in Houston after his pro career. *The Dallas Morning News* reported that Billy Bidwell, the owner of the St. Louis Cardinals, would be at the game and planned to rush onto the field at the end with an even better offer to keep the All-American in the NFL rather than lose him to the upstart AFL Oilers. And the LSU Tigers' famous Chinese Bandits defense had shut down some of the best offenses in the country, which worried Neil, since Texas's offense had sputtered late in the season, despite the play of pro prospects Jerry Cook and Ray Poage. The Longhorns had relied too much on their great linebackers, Johnny Treadwell and Pat Culpepper, for key wins that preserved their undefeated record. The Longhorns were favored, but Ben, who combed through each team's statistics and had an uncanny ability to predict the outcome of games, believed that LSU would spoil Texas's season in a defensive stalemate.

When they arrived, the stadium seemed to them a magnificent feast, an enormous concrete salad bowl to be filled with seventy-five thousand people. Neil and Ben had never seen that many people in their entire lives, much less in the same place. They elbowed their way to the concession stand in the cool, shadowed walkway, bought overpriced hotdogs and beers, and then headed for the stairwell.

"Goddamn, this place is huge," Neil said. It seemed to literally swarm with people. He suddenly felt insignificant, a tiny ant on a teeming hill.

Ben led the way down and down the sunlit concrete steps to their seats, which were so close to the field that Neil could smell the newly mown grass, see the bald patches of dirt beneath (the Cotton Bowl was known for thin, slick turf that turned the field into a mud bath on a rainy day). On the sidelines, the players joked and butted helmets and tossed the ball around.

"They're only boys!" Ben said as they squeezed into their seats. He was right. Neil could see their faces, not just the black war paint beneath their eyes but the pimples on their cheeks and chins, the boyish laughter as they chucked the ball to each other. The same age as Neil, maybe just a year or two older. He and Ben had listened as the radio announcers called their names and rendered their exploits in an epic narrative, and yet now it struck Neil as absurd—and somehow wonderful—that all this hoopla was over boys playing a game.

"Can we have your attention, ladies and gentlemen," the announcer exclaimed over the speakers, his voice sounding like a god's. "Please direct your eyes to the sky." Neil watched as everyone looked up, waiting, wondering what would happen. The Texas band's horn section trumpeted and then stopped just as abruptly so that an expectant silence filled the air. A buzzing drone approached the stadium, and then a moment later two small old-fashioned planes skimmed over the stadium's lip and down toward the field. One plane was painted orange and white for Texas, the other blue and yellow for LSU. The planes moved slowly, their wings almost touching. Over midfield, both planes rolled in unison, so that it appeared for a brief moment as if the pilots, who wore long brightly colored scarves that dangled from their necks like nooses, would fall from the planes. The crowd gasped and then applauded.

"That was amazing!" Ben mouthed. The noise in the stadium was so loud that Neil could only read his lips. The planes rose up and up and out of the stadium.

Moments later, a man sang "The Star Spangled Banner," and the crowd stood and took off their hats and held their hands over their hearts and sang along. A gust of patriotism swept through Neil. After the surprisingly harmonious "land of the free and home of the brave," two giant-sized papier-mâché mascots—a longhorn, a tiger—each attached to helium balloons, were wheeled out to the fifty-yard line. They hovered about ten feet above the field, their legs tethered to sandbags. Two men simultaneously cut the ropes, and the mascots floated up and up and up. The crowd fell silent for a strange, magical moment, and then the applause and cheers deafened Neil as everybody watched the mascots rise slowly above the crowd and then disappear into the white marbled sky.

The game, once it began, seemed almost beside the point to Neil, after these pre-game miracles. The first half was, as Ben predicted, a defensive struggle. The Longhorns couldn't get anything going offensively. The LSU defenders were quick and hard-hitting and seemed literally to fly through the air like Chinese acrobats, tripping Poage in the backfield and nearly decapitating Cook in one gruesome tackle that made the hotdog in Neil's stomach flip. Everyone in the stadium expected the Tiger star, Stovall, to have a big day running, but LSU kept passing instead.

"What's going on?" Ben asked. "The Tigers only completed forty passes all year."

LSU looked like the best team through the first two quarters, alternating their quarterbacks, the balls launched beautifully. Neil hailed the beer vendor and after quickly downing another, he felt lightheaded and giddy in the warm January sun. He became mesmerized by the ball's flight, the tight spirals that seemed to float in the air like those mascots. He half-expected the balls to lift and lift and lift right up and out of the stadium.

Late in the second quarter, the Tigers mounted a long drive to the Longhorns' five-yard line. It was only third down, but they'd already wasted their timeouts. The threat of a score brought Neil into focus. The chanting intensified. The LSU and Texas bands belted out dueling songs. One of the LSU quarterbacks, Lynn Amedee, ran onto the field with time ticking down. The ball was snapped, Amedee stepped forward, and Neil heard the thump of his foot on the ball and then watched it fly like a big brown bird through the goalposts. The scoreboard read eight seconds.

"Let's go up there," Neil said, pointing behind him to the stadium's lip. "I want to see what it's like at the top."

They wormed through the crowd, past the concession stands and bathrooms, and then through the cool, shaded cement underworld of the stadium, up the tunnels to the upper section. They came out of the tunnel and then climbed another hundred steps to the last row.

"You can get a nosebleed up here," Ben said.

"Where are Uncle Jimmy's binoculars?" Neil asked.

"I thought you had them."

"Crap!"

The LSU band spread across the field like a blanket. The sun glinted off the horns. Neil could not make out any individual, just the swirled blue-and-yellow patterns plotted out so rigorously by the band for just this moment.

"Look this way," Ben said, his elbows propped on the back wall of the stadium. Neil turned and gazed out over the Dallas skyline, the silver-glassed skyscrapers shimmering. He watched the puffy contrail in the wake of a plane, and he searched the sky for those balloon-flying mascots. Were they hovering somewhere, waiting to float back down into the stadium? He wished they hadn't left the binoculars in the truck. He looked down at the treetops and the sidewalk and the canopied vendors outside the stadium, saw a few people moving like insects. He had the urge, a residue from the two beers, to climb up on the ledge and just leap.

"We better head back down," Ben said. "The second half's about to start."

Neil wanted to stand up here for a while, see the game from this perspective. "Go ahead. I'll be along in a minute."

"You sure?"

Neil nodded and then watched Ben walk back down the steps, his thin figure growing thinner before he disappeared. A few minutes later, the teams returned to the field. The Tigers kicked off. A Longhorn caught it and started up the field. The runner looked like he might break free. Neil could see the gap where he should go; it was so clear from this view. But then several Tigers converged on the runner at once, and the ball squirted loose. Neil assumed it was beneath the heaving pile of jerseys and helmets around the thirty-five yard line. The refs untangled the mass, and at the end a Tiger jumped up and ran around triumphantly.

A few plays later, the Tiger quarterback scampered in for a twenty-two-yard touchdown. Ten-to-zero. The Longhorns were doomed, Neil was sure, but he no longer really cared. It was the wonder of being in this stadium on this New Year's Day that he knew he would remember.

He didn't make his way back to his seat until the fourth quarter.

"What happened to you?" Ben asked, perturbed.

"Got lost," Neil said, smiling, holding out another beer to his brother.

They drank and cheered through the anticlimactic finish. Texas never recovered. They bobbled the ball the rest of the game, turning it over five times in all, and LSU added another field goal late in the fourth quarter. The Longhorns ended the day humiliated, their great season ruined by a shameful 13-0 shutout.

Neil and Ben spilled onto the parking lot with what seemed a million other people. Neil felt again the enormity and absurdity of this event, how exotic to file into this concrete dish with so many other people to watch fifty boys chase a pigskin around for nearly three hours. He and Ben agreed that they were fortunate they lived in America rather than some god-awful place like Africa or Russia where they couldn't stop starving or standing in line for a loaf of stale bread long enough to give a damn about something as magnificently frivolous as the 1963 Cotton Bowl.

• • •

That evening after the game, they wandered the streets of downtown Dallas, ambling drunkenly from bar to bar. Unlike the Irish woman, the bartenders didn't seem to care that Ben was only seventeen. The glasses, Neil figured. Everyone thought you were older if you wore glasses. Besides, Ben charmed everyone. If you acted like you belonged, no one questioned you, unless they happened to have a special arrangement with the police chief that threatened their livelihood. Of course, the bars were so packed with post-game partiers, many of them not much older than Ben, that the bartenders had no time to be discerning about the liquor laws. Neil and Ben moved from table to table and argued the finer points of the game. Neil nearly got punched by an LSU fan when he said that the Tigers were just a bunch of inbred Cajuns, but Ben soothed things over by ordering a couple of pitchers of beer for the table, and they wound up sitting with that group of Tigers and their girlfriends for two hours, until by the end they agreed that Okies and Cajuns were certainly the best damn breed of men and women on God's favorite continent, as well as the rightful descendents of a secret nobility. They all toasted and then belched their approval, and when they parted, they bear-hugged and grunted, and the LSU fan who had nearly decked Neil told him that there were no hard feelings. To prove it, he offered up his girlfriend, a chubby giggling brunette, for a smooch. Neil took her in his arms and gave her a sloppy, tongue-entwined kiss as everyone chanted, "Hook 'em, Horns! Hook 'em, Horns! Hook 'em, Horns!"

Their spirits buoyed, Neil and Ben left, searching for a late-night burger joint but finding instead a thin, ragged little shop with a purple sign dangling from the awning that said *Madame Tsontakis—Discover Your Future.* A yellow light brightened the awning, and the sign on the door said, *Open for Prophecy.*

Ben pointed to the small placard in the window that claimed *Only $2 for the Future!* He laughed. "What d'ya say?"

The smoky parlor had black wood paneling and dark antique tables with gold velvet doilies over the tabletops. Lamps covered in red-tasseled cloths made the room burn. A Greek Orthodox Bible was displayed on a wooden bookstand. Though the room was cramped, it smelled rich and sweet. What was the name of that pastry Neil had tasted and loved so much during the trip to Washington, D.C.? The crust sticky and flaky, the filling made of meat-textured sweets, the only time he'd ever even thought of those words together: *sweet* and *meat*.

Madame Tsontakis. What a complicated sight she was. Frizzy hair the color of red pepper; a burgundy shawl with lace trim wrapped around her shoulders; a thick, floor-length maroon satin dress. Her face was a peculiar mixture of youth and old age. She didn't have a wrinkle on her, but her skin was slightly mottled on her cheeks and around her lips. Her nose was thin and aristocratic, her eyes bulbous and sensuously green and asymmetrical—as if pieces of beautiful shale were lodged in her irises. She could have been thirty-five or sixty, and she carried herself with the grace and feline warmth of a woman who'd had many lovers. Neil was immediately attracted to her. She took his hand in hers, which were surprisingly soft, and caressed it as if she were already foretelling his future. Baklava! Madame Tsontakis's hands carried the name of that Greek pastry.

"Come, sit down, the both of you," she said in a thick, regal accent that echoed musically in the room. She gestured toward two high-backed upholstered chairs, brocaded with red and emerald stitching. After they were seated, she said, "Who will be first to know his future?"

Ben and Neil looked at each other across the red gloom and shrugged their shoulders.

"I warn you. I do not lie. If you do not wish to know your destiny, you should leave now. I will not be offended."

Ben snickered. "Do you vish to know de future?"

Madame Tsontakis clutched Ben's hand and pressed her face close to his and said sharply, "You, little joker. You will be first. Come with me."

She led him through beaded curtains into another room, where Neil could see them on either side of a small table, sheathed with a cloth the shade and texture of Madame Tsontakis's shawl. She held both his hands and made him take off his glasses, and then she ran her fingers over his face slowly, across his forehead, eyes, and lips. She sat down and held his hands and spoke intently to him. Neil could not make out what she was saying, but could hear the low, musical thrum of her voice. After a few minutes, Ben slipped through the beads and sat down silently. He looked shaken.

"How was it?" Neil asked.

Madame Tsontakis said, "See for yourself."

She held out her hand to Neil. He took it and again felt an erotic charge, this time mixed with dread. He passed through the beads and sat at the table. Madame Tsontakis demanded that he roll up his sleeves and lay his hands flat. She closed her eyes and ran her fingers over the backs of his wrists and then traced her fingernails sharply over his forearms to the crook of his elbow, where she pinched his veins. She stood up, circled behind him, clutched his shoulders, and then placed her fingers on his neck and under his collarbone in a way that made him dizzy. He didn't move. She grazed her fingers over his thinly fuzzed jaw line and then circled in front of him and put her face so close to his that he could smell her breath, the faint aroma of something sweet, a Greek liqueur perhaps, or could it be baklava? She put her lips to his eyes. Her breath parted his lashes. Then she kissed him lightly on each eyelid.

"You will soon leave your home," she said, sitting down across from him. She clutched both of his hands. "You will fall in love. But love will not stay rooted in your heart. You will yearn to own a piece of the world. You will fall from the sky. Your friends will die. You will dream of death. Insects will devour you, but you will rise from this feast. You will own the West. You are born for greatness. Your ambition, however, will overreach your humility. Then you will die."

"What do you mean?" he asked, feeling drugged.

She leaned back, smiled, and said, "You have heard what I mean."

"That's all?"

"'*That's all?*' I have warned you of your greatness. Take heed. Four dollars—for you and your friend."

"He's my brother."

"Your brother cannot be your friend?"

The drugged feeling left him. He was suddenly alert and embarrassed, and felt as if he'd been cheated and then called a fool. He paid her, and he and Ben left without saying a word.

They ate a late-night breakfast in silence at a truck stop down the street and looked out the greasy window at the neon glow of the parking lot. Neil finally asked Ben what Madame Tsontakis had told him. Ben fidgeted nervously and then said, "That I will love and kill many men."

"What does that mean?"

"Hell if I know," Ben said, shrugging his shoulders and looking down into the congealed remains of his gravy and biscuits. "What'd she tell you?"

Neil hesitated. He figured that she'd told Ben more than he had revealed, and Neil wondered if he should make a joke of it. "I'm destined for greatness," he finally said. "I'll fall out of the sky. Insects will eat me."

Ben laughed. "You fall out of the barn every week, and the mosquitoes and chiggers eat us both. That's no future. That's your *life*, man."

Neil laughed too, but neither of them could entirely dismiss what had happened to them, nor did they know how to talk about it. Neil thought about their mother, who would also make pronouncements about the future and could sometimes mysteriously tell them what cards they held in their hands when they played Rook or Spades, but she considered these parlor tricks. She would not approve of their visit to a fortuneteller, even if Madame Tsontakis did have a Bible in the room.

They rolled and lit cigarettes, rehashed the sad injustice of the Cotton Bowl, and pretended that Madame Tsontakis and her two-dollar fortunes were not that important. She didn't even know how to read palms or Tarot cards or bones you shake in a magic dish and throw on the table. They went to the truck and climbed into the back. The night was warmer than the last, the stars out, though still chilly. Neil asked Ben if he wanted to sleep in the cab.

"Naw," Ben said.

They pulled the scratchy horse blankets over them. Neil lay awake for a long time, hovering between consciousness and sleep.

"You may be destined for greatness," Ben said just as Neil was nodding off. "But I'll always have a bigger dick than you."

Ben perfectly caught Uncle Jimmy's voice and delivery. You had to love Ben. Even though he was too damn skinny and goofy-looking in his glasses with that smattering of freckles, he'd still been able to win over the whores and bartenders and Cajuns.

Above them, white-blue smoke gauzed the sky. In the distance, a train clickety-clacked over the rails. The air smelled faintly of manure. Neil thought about Madame Tsontakis's prophesy of greatness. Was the woman just full of two-dollar horseshit? What did it mean to fall from the sky? Kennedy nearly blew everybody sky-high last fall in his pissing contest with the Russians over the missiles in Cuba. The man was too young to be president, Harvey Lee argued, would probably wind up getting them all incinerated or send every man under twenty-five into Russia to storm the Kremlin. Uncle Jimmy had been a paratrooper. Maybe that's what lay in store for Neil. He'd parachute into Moscow, falling with a hundred thousand other idiots into a stadium filled to the brim with vodka.

And why would love not stay rooted in his heart? And how would insects devour him? And from what feast would he rise?

The woman was a loon, probably made the fortunes up in advance, crazy crap to spook or intrigue or flatter her customers, and vague enough so that anything she said could be later construed as truth. She was shrewd, though, you had to give her that, and there was something sexy about her, too, that voice and her talk and her fingers on his face and wrists and the crook of his arm, and her beautiful, bulbous eyes, all of it an act to seduce you if you were fool enough, or to make you laugh, as if you were privy to a private joke, which—now that Neil thought about—for two dollars wasn't a bad investment. Hell, he'd spent thirty dollars of Uncle Jimmy's money on a couple of five-minute joyrides, not counting the freebie that Gillian had given him. What was two bucks per fortune? Did Madame Tsontakis believe what she said? Did she did indeed have a gift? Who knew? It didn't really matter. That was the way to sell yourself to the world—with a half-mad sense of belief in your own powers of prophecy and a withering matter-of-fact disdain for those who failed to appreciate your gifts. He'd have to remember that.

The white-blue smoke moved past. Maybe it wasn't smoke after all, just clouds obscuring the stars, but the sky was clear now, and bright and very still, with a three-quarter moon frozen like an ice cube in the night. He examined the sky, imagined falling from the moon, floating through all that cold, black space—like John Glenn, orbiting Earth last February like a canned monkey, but what a lovely sight, and what a tremendous feeling coming back through the atmosphere, burning, burning, and praying that the parachutes held as you swayed in your toy capsule to the pillowy ocean. He'd watched Glenn on a little black-and-white TV set at the VFW in Mangum with everyone else in the county, watched on the fuzzy screen as this beautiful, smiling American man fell from the sky, a modern miracle—ambition triumphing over humility.

I'm the girl in the middle, my brothers, Howie and Steve, on either side of me. When I write, they hover over my head, feeding me lines, working their way into my characters and voice. I might produce the story, but they are the writers and directors. As any good sister would say, "You can blame them."

Sari Rose has received the Katherine Anne Porter and *New Millennium Writings* awards for her short stories. In 2003 she was a PEN New England New Discovery recipient. Her stories have appeared in the *Iowa Review*, *Nimrod*, and *New Millennium Writings*. She is a graduate of the Iowa Writers' Workshop and, at a slow and steady pace, is working on both a novel and a story collection.

AS IN LIFE

Sari Rose (signature)

Sari Rose

When I walk in the door of Schmeer's, the lights are dim and flat, and hanging from round racks, the women's sweatshirts look exhausted. Outside it's raining hard, and I set my wet umbrella in the dark alcove near the front door. On one side of the alcove, bordering the stairs to the second floor, baby clothes hang from a high pole. Occasionally, like now, toward Christmas, a customer might buy an infant gown or a one-piece romper. But otherwise, the baby clothes live here like curled-up bats, sleeping.

On the first floor of Schmeer's, lots of clothes sleep: khaki slacks with elastic waists, embroidered cardigans, robe and nightie sets. Stuart's real bread and butter comes from the Catholic-school uniforms on the second floor. But the first floor lives on—two long aisles like two underground tunnels—for parents who, in the course of buying clothes for their children, have an arresting impulse to buy for themselves something they didn't know they needed.

Schmeer's used to sell it all and sell it like crazy, and our slogan for the past seven decades was, "This, that, the whole Schmeer." This was when the U.S. Rubber Company, Naugatuck Footwear Division, was our neighbor across the street. Before U.S. Rubber closed shop, the rubber workers would rush in on their breaks looking for thermal tees, Playtex bras, Queen Casual pantsuits. My father, his yellow measuring tape around his neck like a second tie, was the Schmeer then. Mr. Irving Schmeer. Now the Schmeer in charge is my brother, Stuart, and he stays afloat by outfitting the children of Mount Saint Mary's, Saint Hedwig's, and Our Lady of Mount Carmel.

Though the store looks closed, it's only noon and I know Stuart is alone, or perhaps with a single customer upstairs. I start up the steps where a bit of light shines down from the second level. On the landing, Stuart has set a bunch of empty boxes, not yet broken down. I climb over some and make for the second set of stairs looking ahead for light. And there is light, but not much. To keep this store fully lit costs more than Stuart can afford.

He's waiting for me at the top of the stairs, a grin on his face. "Thanks for coming," he says. He's holding a box in his hands, and though I know it's ludicrous I think he has a present for me. My heart lifts and I walk up faster, ready to receive it.

"He nearly kicked yesterday," he says, referring to our ninety-year-old father. I stop halfway up the second set of stairs to hear the story through. "He told the physical therapist she had no business working if she's pregnant. Then he told an aide she had no business working when she has a cold. Then he called in the head dietician to tell her the food stinks. After that, he fell asleep."

Stuart puts the box under his arm, like it's a football. He will always look like the athlete he formerly was. "So he sleeps right through dinner and Mom and I can't wake him. But he comes out of it at ten o'clock and asks for a piece of fish! And they give him fish! A piece of scrod! What, he thinks he's on a Carnival Cruise? What is this, the Love Boat?"

Only my father gets scrod at ten p.m. at Harbor View Nursing Home. This is because they're scared of him. "You see a harbor here?" he asks the staff. "There's no harbor here. You got to travel fifty miles to get a harbor view, and that harbor smells like piss. Just like here. Piss View, you could call it." When he is not insulting anyone, his mind is dull. But when he wants to trip you up, he's sharp as a tack. But the staff shot back. They sent him home today, and now he's our problem.

When I reach the top of the stairs, I see Stuart's box is empty—a box previously so full of promise and now it's empty. What would I have wanted? I could use a new winter coat, leather, with vintage buttons. Either that, or my marriage back, but Stuart can't give me that either. "El," he says, holding the box over his head. "Ever hear of the Colorado Avalanche?"

"Basketball?"

"Hockey."

"They good?"

"Like this."

He throws the box down yelling, "Av…a…lanche!" trying to make his voice go from boom to poof, simulating a boulder falling into a faraway canyon. I'd like to say we only act this stupid with each other, but the truth is we act stupid together and apart. It's in our stupid Schmeer blood. The box lands on the others, bounces a bit, and knocks another box down the steps. "What if there's a customer?" I ask.

"You nuts? "

I walk into the open space of the second floor and see what I always see: gray linoleum, wallpaper printed with brown air balloons, and, attached to the outside of the dressing room, the three-paneled mirror where I watched myself grow up. Where my father used to stand and fit the former mayor and rubber executives for sport coats, the rubber workers for their wedding suits and church slacks. The former mayor was jailed, re-elected, then died. The rubber factory moved away, and the Naugatuck rubber workers took office jobs in Waterbury or line jobs on the other side of town, where they made lipstick tubes and safety pins. Schmeer's former salesgirls—Lena, Theresa, Esther, Martha, Barbara, Ellen, Rita—have all died or fallen into unremitting disrepair.

But here on the second floor of Schmeer's department store, Poll Parrot Shoes will always live on, in good health, in a good home, in the back room. Stuart long ago got rid of the tiny shoe department, but even so, the blue parrot still perches on an invisible twig in the display window of the former shoe section. Below the blue parrot, where the seven aqua-covered seats and the fitting stool used to be, sits a 1930s Singer sewing machine. Schmeer's longtime tailor, evicted from his own father's longtime tailor shop, now offers in-house tailoring from his ancient sewing setup. Behind his worn wood counter, Anthony, the son of Anthony, alters the Catholic blazers, the occasional suit for a communion, wedding, or burial.

Stuart goes behind a glass-topped counter where he's set a big carton of child-sized skirts, navy skirts with big box pleats. The carton is wet from the rain, although the small skirts are folded in plastic that keeps them dry and safe. Stuart is also wet from helping the UPS man unload the truck. His forehead, always smooth with good color, is damp, and so is his sporty striped knit jersey. He picks up a bunch of the wrapped skirts and throws them into four piles—small, medium, large, extra-large. "We need you here," he says. "Mom should be able to hire full-time help in a few days, and then you can head back to New London. Dad can't walk and he's down to 115 pounds."

"I dropped the kids with Sam, and I can't stay a full week, but I can help interview a live-in. I have a low case load at work and no one's in crisis."

"Even two, three days would be great. I can go there after work and help him go to the bathroom and get ready for bed, but that's it. If I stay longer, he'll yell at me. He never lets up; it's always, I have too much stock and not enough help. I can't afford help."

"I know. I know."

We stand there for a moment not saying anything, just happy to be sad with each other. I love my brother. What would we do alone?

"I can't believe they sent him home," I say.

"He insulted everyone. It was time to move on. Last night he says to the aide, 'I'm sitting here alone for hours and you're out there talking to some guy with a fat ass.'"

Our father was born without a filter, a brain-mouth filter, and as a result anything that comes into his brain, any disturbing or anxious or mean thought, goes directly into his mouth exactly as it's been delivered to him from his circuits. He doesn't have the cognitive wherewithal to be diplomatic or euphemize. He's been doing this to Stuart and me all our lives; to my mother, all her married life. We'd like to euthanize him.

I look around and notice Stuart has a new display of fleece-lined jackets. He buys anything that goes with the Catholic school uniform; anything the uniform wearer would wear when the uniform comes off; and anything that goes over and under the uniforms. Except for bras. That would require a female salesclerk to help with fitting. And he can't afford to hire a woman, *a good woman*, as my mother would say.

I see a thick, gray-hooded sweatshirt, bright in this one section of overhead light, and I think of buying one for Sam, but we're separated, and I'm not sure of the appropriateness of a clothing gift.

Stuart takes the now-empty carton of skirts, carries it to the top of the stairs, and calls out: Anyone down there? He waits a few second and hurls the wet carton down to the landing where it lands on other cartons. It makes the groaning sound of a man being belly punched, and from the landing we hear the muffled hush and scuff of footsteps followed by the hoarse voice of Anthony. "Hey. You trying to kill me?"

Not on your life. Stuart needs Anthony. Now, killing our father; well, killing our father is a different matter. We would rather he not die; we would rather he be different—rational, kind, appreciative of my mother's heroic efforts to keep him alive. But since this will never happen in our lifetime, we would like to shorten his. Or so we like to say—Stuart and I. In traumatic times, talking this way keeps our spirits high.

I say goodbye to Stuart and Anthony. Together, they keep Schmeer's going, though often Tony is sewing, which leaves Stuart alone to run two floors of a store that may itself decide, some day soon, not to get up one morning.

In the car, I have to shove aside my dog, who wants to drive. The rain has let up; the sun is starting to strain through, and I am so grateful. So grateful for a bit of sun. I am light dependent. I get depressed on dark days and in the dark. Now that it's winter, I put on my pajamas after seven in the evening because I know I'm finished—no light; no nothing. I had nothing for Sam, my husband, after seven. He had nothing for me before seven. Eventually, neither of us had anything for the other, anytime.

Rags has her white head in my lap as I drive up the hill to my parents' house. If my father dies while I'm here, I'll need my dog. Besides, I don't want to leave her alone in Sam's apartment while he's at work, the girls at school. She won't know where she is.

Sari Rose

Going up Millville Avenue in my Caprice I am reminded of my recurring dream of driving up Millville Avenue in my Caprice. The Caprice in my dream can barely make it up the hill, the power or juice has dried up, and my car is at an extreme slant—meaning it's nearly vertical, the hood like a horse rearing up, its snout in the air. I am alone in a car that's tipping backwards, hood first—almost like my father, although he's been falling forward.

His last fall, face first onto the bathroom floor, was the fall that split his nose. My mother found him and called the ambulance. He was ninety; we thought this was it. In the ER, on a hard pallet, he lay for hours and peed in the pants of the four-piece ensemble he'd worn every day since World War II. Not the same suit of clothes, but certainly the same four pieces: dress shirt, dress pants, vest, jacket. And tie. Five pieces really. He wore all five pieces in the winter because he was cold; he wore all five pieces in the summer because he was cold. For the past eight months, he wore all five pieces at night, too. He wouldn't take them off. We thought he wanted to die wearing all five pieces. We could only guess he wanted it said: in death, as in life, he was a gentleman. He was almost there; the words almost spoken.

But from the ER he went to acute care where they told him he had congestive heart failure and he had to take off his suit. They put him in a gown, a white hospital gown with blue dots, and it must have been then and there, in acute care, that he vowed if we wasn't going to die in his five-piece suit, he wasn't going to die at all.

From acute care, he was sent to a nursing home for rehab. Rehab! We thought. Right. Rehab. "Rehab?" Stuart had said, looking puzzled. "I guess it's better than saying *hospice*."

My mother said, "Good. He'll gain some weight; he won't look so bad when he dies." We didn't think he'd last a week. But for rehab we dressed him in a jog outfit and he must have been dead serious about staying alive in a jog suit because he didn't die. In rehab things went from worse to better; he was, at ninety, rehabbed; and as a rehabbed, dying man he was sent home.

Rags recognizes this home—my parents' aqua ranch. She must think to herself, *Aqua ranch, bone on rug.* This is because my mother, in anticipation of a visit by Rags, always leaves, beside her kitchen chair, a bone or a cookie on a small cotton rug. And here is Rags, eating her bone-shaped cookie on a Colonial-style throw rug. As she works on the cookie, pieces fall out of her mouth and she stares at them with steadfast recognition—guarding every tiny bit she has coming to her.

"I almost lost him yesterday," my mother says, sitting in her cushioned kitchen chair. "We couldn't wake him up at the home. Stuart kept yelling, 'Dad, dinner. Dad. Dad.' I felt sorry for him. For Stuart. Seeing his father that way."

"I heard Dad got tired insulting everyone."

"He got tired, but they got more tired. Now I'm tired. I'm exhausted, Ellie. And we need to hire a live-in. The home said so, and I know so. I can't handle him here alone. If I fall with him, that's it. We'll both end up in homes." She pauses and re-settles herself into the back cushion of her chair. She's quiet as she never is, and I imagine her imagining herself falling with him, the two of them side-by-side on the bathroom floor. The closest they've been in years.

"Look at her mopping up every last crumb," my mother says of Rags. You couldn't mistake my mother for anything other than a mother. I adore her down to her bent bones, her balding head, her stretch pants and smock top. She has that mother style—the colorless, formerly green eyes that fall and rest on you as though you're a weary traveler, the prodigal daughter come home after living twenty years in an inactive volcano in the Yucatan. I may look like I've lived in an inactive volcano, I may look like I've smoked pot daily for twenty years, but really I just need my hair straightened and the gray toned down.

"Is he awake now?" I ask.

"Yeah, go see him. He's in the den."

I'm in no great rush. I'm afraid to see him. I've always been afraid of him. And now that he's frail and has received a reprieve from dying, I'm still afraid of him. The customers at Schmeer's loved him, the town loved him: he sat on the Finance Board for forty years. He was Naugatuck's Man of the Year five times, and even when he wasn't Man of the Year, he was man of the year. My fear of him is that he'll yell at me. Since I was born, I was the child who needed perpetual improvement. *Don't*

slump! Don't whine! Be on time! Exercise! You're too thin! Why'd you get a
B in gym?! Why's your hair frizzy? Be a blond! Don't be a slob! Don't say,
"Ya know." Get your taxes in! Eat with gusto!

"Rags, you pig, come on," I say. "We'll say hi to Grandpa."

We go to say hi, but stop at the den door.

I say the *Shema.* I don't know what else to say and I don't think the
Shema is the right prayer, but I know you can say it to mark parts of
the day, especially the passing of day into night. So I say it in the barest
whisper, then knock softly on the door and walk in.

He's sitting in his rocker, a 1970s' Hitchcock with the faux Colonial
pad on the seat and back. He's sat in that rocker for thirty years; listened
to daily dirty jokes from his stock broker in that chair; watched one
million football games and 54,050 re-reruns of Perry Mason; told my
mother 94,060 times that she had a fat ass; told her 206,876 times
that in her eyes he does nothing right; drank 109,080 cups of decaf;
considered 2,056 times that maybe he was wrong to buy on margin;
worried 900,000 times that he should have sold Aetna higher and
Pfizer later. To have lost so much. In that chair, he always wore his
five-piece suit; later, his five-piece, food-stained suit. He still sits in
that chair, hoping to hit it big, even though he looks now like a white
goat, dying in a gray jog outfit.

He barely looks up when I come in. Rags walks over to him, her
tail wagging, not realizing he is mean and dying and worrying about
his falling financial empire and Schmeer's overstocks. He doesn't pat
her, but says to her, "Rags." To me he says with his eyes closed, "I don't
know where I'm at."

"You're home. Harbor View said you were ready to go."

"Go where?"

"Here."

"Where am I?"

"Here, Dad. At your house." I'm standing in front of him; my only
other choice for seating is the hospital bed. I don't think I can sit on
the bed because he always yelled at Stuart and me if we sat on our
beds. "No sitting on beds!" he'd yell. "You want to sit? Sit in a chair!"
Beds were for sleeping. You can nap on the bed, he'd said, or sleep. But

in his troubled mind, if you sat on the bed, you'd wrinkle the spread. You'd leave a crater. The bed, for the rest of its life, would have a crater memory it couldn't forget or smooth over.

"I'm telling you," he says, his voice too weak to rise and register wrath. "I don't know where I'm at."

"Tell me what you mean."

"Money. I need to talk to Ben Rabinowitz."

"Not Ben. You mean Larry. Larry Ruttenberg."

"I didn't say Larry Ruttenberg, did I?" There is a murderous undertone in his voice and I try not to be afraid. "I said Ben Rabinowitz." He sounds like he's growling, but he's really trying to clear his throat. "We have to hire live-in help," he says, "and I don't know where I'm at."

While fifty years ago my father looked dead while sleeping, he now looks dead while awake. His mouth is open at rest, his eyes are closed while talking. He puts his hands over his face, looks down, and clears his throat. He clears his throat so often I have discerned the different tones from his larynx. His voice resonates with ancient music from Central Asia. Tuvan and Tibetan peoples know a form of song, throat singing, where words are replaced by soulful, throaty air blasts. I heard throat singers once with Sam before we were separated. He came home one night with tickets to a throat-singing concert. I wanted orchids and he knew it, but I got throat singers, and, though I wouldn't tell Sam, I liked the throat people. Their music, their songs, were the sounds we all made as kids—imitating an old door being opened in an abandoned mansion. We liked the noises that came from down deep, our voices rich with guttural groans, and we opened those creaking doors over and over, testing what our bodies could do.

"Mom and I can call Larry Ruttenberg. He did your estate planning. He'll tell us." I speak above the throat sounds, using the noises as a bamboo screen to hide me.

He has stopped clearing his throat and looks at me. He is so old he's scary and I can barely look back at him. He is so white, I can barely see him. Could it happen now? Could he be ready to step off the curb and cross over? "You and mother have stopped listening to me. I didn't say Larry Ruttenberg and you know I didn't!"

He takes his hands from his face and sets them in his lap. With one hand he begins rubbing the fingers of the other. He rubs one finger at a time, applying imaginary lotion. When he's feeling upbeat and alive, he'll pump real lotion from a tropical-green dispenser emblazoned with hard-sell words: *painful, cracked, rash, burn.*

"I can't feel my fingers," he says, his eyes closed.

"I'm sorry."

"No, that part I'm used to. Wait, there's more. Come over and listen so I don't have to say it twice." He holds up his hands, and with his eyes closed he seems to wince and grimace as if he's calling upon his entire bodily reserve not to kill me.

He takes his index finger, points it at himself, and bends it over and over. Now, this could be the gesture of a man pointing a gun at his head and repeatedly pulling the trigger. Or it could be Captain Hook trying to summon me with a crooked, creamed finger. In reality, if the real Captain Hook was beckoning me, I could run off the boat and live off forest choke berries. But if Captain Hook is my father, I am obliged to move closer. So I move closer. I move so close I see the moons on the Captain's head, the seas of the moon, even the view of earth. I see on earth, a father seated in a rocker and a small girl standing before him, peeing in her pants.

"Closer," he says. I take a step closer, terrified, and look down. "I said, 'Ben Rabinowitz.'"

"I'll call," I say.

"Good," he says. "Tell him I want to hire live-in help and I want to deduct it from my income tax."

"Okay, Dad." I turn around and start walking out of his den.

"Ellie."

"Yep," I say, waiting. I half turn, my arthritis pain stopping me from a full turn-around.

"You're right." My heart sings. He's never told me I was right. I'm not sure what he's admitting to here, but I'll take it—his recognition that, in all of life, there is one thing I know that he doesn't. "Ben's dead."

"Ben's dead," I repeat.

"Ten years dead. I just remembered."

"I thought he might be dead," I say.

"He was a son of a bitch. He made mistakes and couldn't add a simple row of figures. But I liked him. Call Larry Ruttenberg if you want. At least he's alive."

"I'll call and ask him where you're at."

He doesn't answer and I take that to mean I'm dismissed. "I'll bring in your dinner later," I say. He still says nothing. And after my offer of dinner, I have nothing more to give him. "Rags," I say, and Rags comes. She lives for my commands, my voice, my smell. Sam, however, needs more from me. He needs deeper, more private things that belong to me: my salty prosciutto, my warm artichoke hearts, my marinated mangos, and I'm unwilling to part with them. With two small kids and old parents, I have to keep something for myself.

My mother is in the kitchen looking at notes the nursing home gave her. "They gave me numbers to call for live-in help, but these places charge two hundred a day. Dad will never agree to that."

"We have to lie to him."

"He'll know. He still does the checkbook and scrutinizes every entry. I think it's time to call Mark Manuscz. Mark Manuscz's mother had a wonderful live-in Polish woman. Mark paid her under the table and said she was so reasonable. So much cheaper than a home. His mother loved that woman. She loved the woman so much that when his mother finally had to go to a home, Mark still hired the woman to come sit with her. She was like family."

Mark Manuscz is the last man alive I would call. In my present situation, calling Mark Manuscz is like calling a marriage undertaker.

When we were younger we called him Moose. He hasn't heard from me directly in fifteen years—the fifteen years I've been married. I live in New London, over an hour away, and he stayed here in Naugatuck. He's the local podiatrist and my first boyfriend. My first and only boyfriend in high school, my only lover during college breaks and summer vacations. He works my mother's feet and he works them hard, but he doesn't charge her. For me. In my memory.

In college, we didn't see each other during the school year, but if we were both home for Christmas, Thanksgiving, summer, we started right up again. "He's a little rough," my mother says. "A lot of women have stopped going to him. Theresa, Esther, Lena, Martha, Barbara, Ellen, Rita, they all went and now they don't go. He hurts. But he's good."

I call Mark because he can tell me where to go for 'round-the-clock help. He can tell me, as he used to tell me, where to go for all kinds of things. To IHOP for pancakes; to Breen Field for tennis; to Yale Co-op for albums; to Andrew Mountain to kiss and touch each other. I hope I don't have to reveal I'm separated; he'll tell me where to go for that and I don't want to go there.

"You have to call the Polish Place," he tells me. "They have the best live-ins. Don't even bother calling other agencies. The Polish Place. Here's the number. They get good women. They'll do anything, those women; they want to be part of the family. They'll cook, shop, sweet talk, change diapers."

"He won't write checks."

"They like to be paid under the table. Here's the number. You call and ask for Yvonna. Tell her I sent you. You around for a few days? Come see me for lunch. I know the best place."

I tell him I can't come to lunch and he says he'll come to me.

I know I'm cooked. He has always cooked me, heated me up like a progressive radiator coil. It was the seam on his pants. He had a rough inseam on his jeans which I still remember. I could fondle that seam and it sent me and him through the roof. The seam, rough and almost meaty, stood for something else. Finally we lived out its symbolism. But then I went off to college and fell in love with other inseams.

Since I still have the phone in my hands, I call Sam and the girls. Sam sounds as if he's speaking to me from behind a locked door, as if he's taking the time to say a few words but has no desire to be heard. "How's your father?" he barely says.

Give me a break, Tight Throat, I want to say, but say instead, "Frail, old, and mean. How are you?"

"All right. You didn't pack their bathing suits and I can't take them to the Y."

"What else did I do wrong?"

"I won't get into that now. You want to talk to them?"

I am so mad at him. My father is dying and he won't give me a break. Rae comes to the phone. "Hi, Mommy, is Grandpa still alive?"

"Yes, Sweetie."

"Oh." She sounds a little disappointed. As though she hasn't had enough drama in her life, she needs her grandfather to die. "Daddy's mad we don't have our bathing suits. He's going to take us to J. C. Penney for bathing suits and buy us a cinnamon bun. You want to talk to Jane?"

Jane comes to the phone and sounds weary, depleted. "Hi, Mom," she barely says. "Dad's mad again. You didn't pack our bathing suits and he wants to buy me a bathing suit and I only want a two-piece and he probably won't buy me one."

"It's just for swimming."

"It's just my self-esteem." For a twelve year old, she is a smart ass, but I would never say that to her face. When I was twelve, my father, face to face, and again and again, called me *pain-in-the-ass*. It was his way of expressing affection.

I can't seem to get a break anywhere. After dinner I go outside to the backyard, and because it's too cold and too wet, I can only stand and look out over Hunter's Mountain, where, from this backyard, I used to sit and stare. In my childhood dreams, I used to fly over Hunter's Mountain, over trees and telephone wires. Now in my dreams I fly either to escape people or prove to them how powerful I am. Sometimes, however, I don't have enough lift, can't quite rise above them. Last night I couldn't fly at all. I was naked, couldn't fly, and had to walk to a flea market to buy a robe.

Before I go to bed, I watch television with my father. I make sure I'm completely prone on the hospital bed, so he can't accuse me of sitting on it. He has the TV set to the style channel, and there's a segment on feng shui. With Sam gone, I am curious how I can move my furniture around to create flowing energy. Maybe I'll get more energy. Maybe I can repair my marriage. Maybe I'll find out if I *want* to repair my marriage.

But this show is not your by-the-book feng shui. It's more feng shui with the rich and famous. A middle-aged woman, a real-estate agent who lived in Hong Kong for thirteen years, shows us how she has incorporated feng shui into her California home. A voice-over narrator implies that while in Hong Kong she worked with a feng-shui master. What is obvious is she did a lot of shopping. The camera's quick pan of her lavish home shows many touches from Asia. Outside you see a mountain range which simulates, the real-estate woman tells us, a tortoise. The tortoise theme is carried through to the statuary in her garden—huge sculptures of tortoises, some with wells in their backs to hold water.

"You see a tortoise in the mountain?" my father says hoarsely.

"No," I say, happy to agree.

"What I see is a rich woman who can name her price."

He clears his throat and I'm not sure he can hear me when I say, "Right."

Though he is talking, I can't believe he is talking. He looks too old to talk or even breathe. He has a beige blanket wrapped around his neck and the rest of him looks gray and white. It looks to me like he's evaporating, dissipating into the den, later to fall into the backyard as rain. "I think she's Jewish," he says. "With a big ass."

The camera goes into her white bedroom. "White is bad," says the voice-over narrator. It can promote evil energy. But in the hands of a feng-shui master, white can work." The real-estate agent stands in front of her four-poster king-size bed, piled high with layers of white linens and white embroidered spreads. It's a wedding cake of a bed, fit for a fat king. The real-estate agent holds what looks like a torn red rag in her hand. "I place this," she says, "in between the box spring and the mattress and it wards off evil.

"She gets everything she wants," I say.

"Switch the channel," he says.

"In a minute." I watch as the camera gets close to photos on her bureau.

"Surround yourself," the agent says, "with photos of loved ones. This is a love boudoir. I have no photos of dogs or cats."

"In my bedroom," I say, "I have photos of Rags."

"Better get those out."

We are for now both content and happy with our mutual loathing for the rich feng-shui lady. I switch the channel, and Gary Cooper and Grace Kelly are having a dark argument in which I'm shocked to hear Gary say to her, "If you think I like this, you're crazy." She tells him she is leaving on the noon train. I put myself in her shoes, and I think, too bad there isn't an earlier train. "*High Noon*," I say.

"Leave it," he says. "I don't care."

I say goodnight, offer to help him with anything. I don't think he wears pajamas anymore. His day and night clothes are the same; his days and nights are the same. Always now the jog suit. To ward off death. "No help necessary," he says, but slurs his words and I have to have him repeat. "Mother will help. You're visiting."

He thinks I'm here for a visit, and as I make up the couch in the living room, I imagine I'm a guest, I'm here for a rest; to once again be taken care of. That night, with Rags sleeping on my chest, I lie awake on the sectional and listen for my father falling or dying. He doesn't fall or die, but he does lie on the hospital bed in the den, coughing and listening to Larry King, it seems, all night long. Late into the night, before I finally nod off, I conjure an image of a tortoise at the base of the hospital bed watching over my father, taking over my shift, so I can go to sleep.

In the morning my mother cooks and prepares his oatmeal and toast as though it's a medical procedure. The heat in the house is up to eighty degrees, and I'm wearing gym shorts, a short-sleeve tee, and heavy socks. In this house, you can never be barefoot because my father has a foot thing. A bare foot has always triggered for him anxiety and rage. To him a bare foot is a poison pear laced with arsenic and fungus.

When he has to go to the bathroom, I tie a belt around his waist and hold on to the strap while he leads me with his walker. He walks over the cork floor of the den, each step a shuffle and an effort. He is the pony and I am the cart and the driver. I let the pony enter the bathroom on his own, then I wait outside the door for the sound of a boom or cry. Long before he was a pony, he was wild. He'd rear up and swoop down, spew fire. "Don't sit on the beds!" he'd roar, which we barely heard over his pounding hooves on the hard, cork floor.

After lunch, Rags and I go see Stuart at the store. Upstairs he is with a single customer talking about the history of worsted wool. "Wool was good, but it could feel like tiny pins going into your knees, and some kids, like my sister, had raw thighs from those wool skirts. Now you have the heavy poly-cotton with the same good wear. Only now you got the comfort."

"Huh," the woman says.

Stuart sees me and Rags and says, "El. Rags." Then goes back to his customer. She looks familiar. But I can't remember her name. I forgot lots of names when I left Naugatuck. Five minutes later he's done and walks over to me, to where I stand near the BVD display.

"Sam called me last night," he says. "He wanted to know how you were."

"He didn't call me."

"He was probably afraid you'd blow him out of the water." I think Stuart means this as a compliment to me, but I'm not sure. Am I meaner than most people? More angry?

"He didn't say much except the girls missed you. I think he misses you, too."

"Yeah, but when he's with me, he doesn't miss me."

"You giving him a chance?"

"To do, what? Find fault with me? Yes, apparently I'm giving him many chances to do that."

Stuart leans back against the counter with the leather wallets and fleece gloves. "I feel bad for you guys."

Stuart himself is childless and divorced, but in Naugatuck still finds enough women to date, enough sports teams to exercise his identity.

"He seems angry at me all the time," I say.

"Men," Stuart says.

"Men," I say. I stand there looking at Stuart, at his lowered head, his sympathy, and I want to cry. You live and die, you wash dishes, have kids, put thousands of miles on your car, belong to discount-buying clubs. Your husband thinks you've fallen short and you thought he was short when you married him. But he was nice then. And your poor brother. He is alone because he's a flawed man and you're alone

70   *Glimmer Train Stories*

because you can't live with one. "Gotta go," I say. Stuart knows I'm choked up, and lets me leave. I start down the stairs, but when I'm close to the landing, he calls out to me.

"You interviewing help today?"

"Yes," I say, barely able to talk.

"Good luck."

Downstairs, the baby clothes look a bit brighter with the sun out today and blasting through the storefront windows. I'm reminded that thirty years ago, when my mother worked here, she hung infant dresses in the long, silky plastic from the wholesaler. A row of baby dresses, draped with their floor-length plastic capes, looked like tiny, bridal superheroes.

I get back in my car, and Rags relinquishes her seat behind the wheel and goes to the passenger side. She looks out the window, happy to see anything. I sit in the car for a few minutes trying not to cry, to think of reasons not to cry. When I was young my father seemed to like me best when we worked at the store together—when there were customers observing us being father and daughter. He'd call me his *asthma baby*, his highest compliment, even though I never had asthma. I had the bad posture; Stuart had the asthma, but he outgrew it. "She's my asthma baby!" he'd say to the long line of rubber workers waiting at the cash register. And to answer their puzzled looks, he'd sing: "*Yes sir, that's my baby / No sir, I don't mean maybe / Yes sir, 'at's ma baby, now.*" Is it wrong to have wished, as I sometimes did, to be asthmatic?

I go back home and when I walk in the front door, my mother says, "Mark Manuscz is here. He's in the den with Dad."

It sounds like she's saying, Mark Manuscz is dead with Dad. I wish I were dead. I look like hell, my hair is frizzy and gray, and I want Mark to think I've done well, that I'm happy with my permanent inseam; with what I have.

She offers Rags a biscuit from her hand and Rags accepts it gently. They are like two queen mothers, gently extending their gloved hands to each other—reaching toward each other but, because of propriety, barely touching. "Mark knows you're here? That's right, you called him about getting a Polish woman. I didn't tell him about Sam and you. I'm sure he'd be very interested."

I can tell my mother is interested too: having a long-time family friend, a podiatrist, still pining for me. She has always liked Sam, but, just like laughing at bad news, Dr. and Mrs. Mark Manuscz has a forbidden thrill. "The first Polish woman is coming at eleven o'clock. I hope Mark is gone by then; he'll want to run the show." She nods toward the den. "He's trying to push orthotics on Dad, but Dad," she whispers, "is yelling about the money. Go on in."

Rags is searching my mother's open hand for another biscuit, in that way dogs have of thinking magic and good fortune happen to them, to serve their purposes. "All gone, Rags," I say. "Come on." The den door is open and we walk in.

"Ellie," Mark calls out and comes over to kiss my cheek. "Rags," he says, bending down and petting Rags hard behind the ears. I don't think that's Rags's favorite place, but everyone seems to think that's her favorite place. People are always trying to figure out the pleasure points of dogs. Mine is the top of my head, the back of my hand, but no one thinks to look there.

"I'm trying to tell your dad he walks on his heels and an orthotic insert would balance him. He'd be steadier on his feet."

"Your orthotics are a bunch of crap," my father says. "Stuart had two of your orthotics and they made him worse."

"Stuart has bad stenosis."

"You gave him worse stenosis." My father's voice, while weak and raspy, is spirited. His anger, as always, is causing new buds to grow. He's a study in nature. "You gave Stuart things he didn't have before. Look, you want to visit, visit. You want to say hi to Ellie, say hi to Ellie. But leave my goddamn feet out of it." He is in full bloom.

"So how are you, Ellie?" Mark asks.

"Okay. Trying to get my father what he needs."

"You want to help me? The two of you? My big toe is sore. Can you help that?"

"Let's see," Mark says.

"Oh, sure, you'll look and say, 'Orthotic.' Three hundred dollars for a sore toe."

"Shut up and stop being a fart. Show me your toe."

My father almost smiles. He likes that no-nonsense talk, but if I talked that way to him he'd kill me.

"It's circulation, Irv. Part of your condition. You need to put your feet up. Your ankles are swollen, too."

"Good. Goodbye. Nice seeing you, Mark. Take Ellie and go."

Mark is happy to take my arm and we walk out of the den. "So how are you?" he asks again.

"Okay." The crook of my arm, I'm thinking, is another pleasure point. And I'm thinking, Mark looking at me is another pleasure point. His face is dark. Dark eyes, dark eyebrows, a smooth, high forehead. Sam looks a lot like him. But Sam's high forehead is usually scowling at me. His curly hair is diminishing, but from time to time a stray curl pokes out from the receding pack and winks at me. His hair remains playful even though he, most of the time, is not. For this reason—not for looks or youth—I want Sam to keep the hair he has.

It is a short walk from the den, down the den steps, through the small, narrow hallway to the kitchen. We pause outside the kitchen door, where two steps away my mother is sitting on her kitchen chair listening to everything. "How's Sam?" Mark asks.

"We're separated. But who knows. Maybe with some rest and separation we can reconnect."

"That's what I said about Mary Ann. Maybe it will work for you."

"Ellie!" my mother calls loudly, knowing I am two steps away from her. "The Polish woman will be here any minute, and I need you to do some things for me."

Mark and I pause, look briefly at each other, then walk in the kitchen. "Hi, Mark," she says. "I'd love to offer you coffee and a piece of Entemann's, but the Polish woman will be here soon, and I need to make more notes and talk to Ellie."

"Good luck. If Yvonna comes with her, tell her I said hi, and I'll call her soon. And remember, you can negotiate price a little."

"Thanks," my mother says. "You know, I need to come see you soon. The big toe again. The nail is pressing in. And I like the pens you give out."

"I only give out to you, Mag," he says, giving my arm a squeeze. He kisses her goodbye, he kisses me goodbye, and he's gone.

The doorbell rings and it's Yvonna, the owner of The Polish Place, and the woman Yvonna wants us to interview, Diva. Yvonna looks a little like Ivana Trump and a little like Leona Helmsley. Diva has a face like Meg Ryan and a torso like Madeline Albright. We all sit around the kitchen table. Before us, against the wall, is the wallpaper mural we've had for fifty years. We should have an anniversary for this mural. It's a Paris street scene with vendors, organ grinder, and monkey. My mother has always said the mural represents the Schmeer family and, for the benefit of Yvonna and Diva, she points out our Parisian counterparts: a man and woman sitting at a bistro table, a boy running with a loaf of bread, a girl with a balloon. And there we are.

"*Diva*," my mother says. "Like Dee-va?"

"Like Dee-va."

My mother gives a verbal overview of our house. "It's a big house and yet it's not a big house, if you know what I mean, Diva. It seems big but when you think about it, it's just the kitchen, the dining room, the living room, the master bedroom, my little room off the kitchen, and his den, where he spends just about all his time—you know, his TV, his papers everywhere, his phone, he calls his stockbroker."

Diva looks at my mother and then looks at Yvonna and says, "Yes? House broken?"

My mother goes on. "Okay, maybe the house *is* big, but we won't ask you to do any major housecleaning. Just him. Just Irv. You take care of Irv. Irv ring bell, you come."

Diva looks at my mother and I get the feeling she would like to put her fingers in my mother's mouth to get a handle on what the hell she is saying. "Yes? Irv, bell?"

Yvonna and Diva leave and a half hour later, Yvonna's associate, Tina, and another applicant, Marguerite, come. Tina looks like Ivana Trump at seventy-two with a long, blond ponytail. "I Yvonna's helper. Anything you want tell Yvonna you tell me. Is okay." Marguerite, the applicant, looks like a strapping Margaux Hemingway, and I wonder why she wants to live here, bathe, feed, and change my father's wet clothes. Tina introduces Marguerite by saying she's learning English and she likes to paint on big canvases.

My mother nods, as though this is exactly what she has asked for. She starts in again.

"Marguerite, it may seem like a big house and it is maybe a big house but your job will be Irv. You take care of Irv period. He needs help walking, you help him walk. He needs help going to bathroom, you help him go. Getting dressed? You dress. Have you done that before?"

"Yes?" Marguerite pauses and continues to look at my mother as if looking for clues.

"He has congestive heart failure," my mother goes on, "and he's weak, and he doesn't sleep. He, Irv, weak. So you may need to catch some rest during the day, if you're with him at night. Do you drive?"

"Yes? I can?"

"Say, if we needed you to go to the CVS for medication, could you drive?"

"Yes?"

"You have license?"

"I think it's okay." She looks over to Tina and then down at her own lap and swallows. I can hear her swallow.

My mother cups a hand over her mouth and says to Tina. "Tina, I think we're having a communication problem. Tina, you hear me?" Marguerite stares at my mother. We're all staring at my mother. "I don't think we're understanding each other."

"She's learning," Tina says. "In Poland, she's engineer."

My mother sighs and goes on. "Marguerite, if you want to paint, we set up canvas and easel in your room, and you can paint. What you like to paint? You paint trees? A man?"

"I paint. Here, there. I big colors."

"You color hair?" my mother asks her, and points to her own hair. "The roots. I see you have roots. You color hair?"

"Mom!" I say and I clutch Marguerite's forearm.

"Is okay," Marguerite says, patting my arm.

My mother doggedly presses on, putting her fingertips into the scalp of her own hair. "I've colored my hair for fifty years. I still use the same shade I used back then. I mix Autumn Maple Glade with Harvest Ember. Maybe Harvest Umber."

"No, I...No," she says to my mother.

Rags is under the table, at my feet, and I pat her, let her lick my fingers. By mistake I stick a finger in her eye, but she doesn't care. She's forgiving and interprets all touch as love, unless I hit her hard under the chin.

"Okay," my mother says. "Just woman talk." To Tina, she says, "I just don't know, Tina."

"We try again with someone else," Tina says. "What you want?"

"Fluent isn't necessary, but she should at least understand me and speak fairly well."

"They get more."

"Like, for example?"

"A hundred and fifty dollars per day."

"We're on a limited income."

"Everyone limited. But okay. I bring you tomorrow." They leave quickly by the back door next to the washing machine. I give Tina a handshake, then return to the kitchen table. "I can't believe you asked about her hair."

"What, I thought it broke the ice. But I don't know. One loser after another. Let's see what Yvonna can bring tomorrow."

My mother and I make dinner and I serve my father in the den. "I hate chicken," he says. "Everything with her is chicken. She's trying to kill me with chicken. I had chicken last night."

"That was scrod."

"Well, it tasted like chicken. Tell her I want fish tomorrow." I don't say anything, but leave the den and start doing dishes. The doorbell rings.

"Oh, it could be Brandon," my mother says. "I owe him for the last snow."

It's Sam. And the girls.

"Ellie," my mother calls out. "Go down to the basement refrigerator and bring up an Entemann's."

Rae comes in the door, gives me a hug, and says, "Na, Na," which is her babyish, affectionate form of *Mama*.

Jane says, "We miss you."

Sam says, "How's your father?" He's scowling as he walks through the washing-machine alcove. His body looks as if it's attached to a rigid, steel outline of a man. "Girls, come on," he says, leading the way into the den.

"What does Dad know?" I ask my mother, who is sitting on her chair. "About Sam and me."

"Nothing. Stuart and I weren't going to tell him Sam has his own apartment. You want to tell him, okay."

"No!"

"I hope the girls don't say anything to Dad," my mother says.

"They're afraid to say anything to him."

"Then I think you're safe."

The girls come out of the den in two minutes, then go into the living room to watch TV.

I follow them into the living room. "You give Grandpa a hug?"

"Kinda," they say, looking at the TV, not me. My mother lets them eat their Entemann's in front of the TV in the living room. I never let them eat outside the kitchen; I learned that from my father. The girls know they'll see me tomorrow evening so they don't need to be with me now. Instead, they apparently need to watch *The Simpsons*, where they can take comfort in Homer's latest fall from grace. It must reassure them that someone so stupid manages to say alive, episode to episode.

Sam is still in the den with my father when the back doorbell rings. I look through the Venetian blinds in my old room and see a car I don't recognize. Still, I have a feeling, and when I open the door Mark is standing on the porch steps. He is wearing a navy, down jacket, which falls high on the hip. I walk out on the porch to see him. It must be thirty-five degrees, but I don't put on a jacket; I won't be out long.

"I came to say go and have a good life. Try to mend things with Sam."

"Really?" I say.

"No, not really," and then we are kissing. I'm not sure I'm kissing him, but he's kissing me. Now he's hugging me, and while I'm not hugging back, I'm standing there allowing myself to be warmed. His arms are buried beneath the sleeves of his puffy jacket, but I know his arms are under there, just as I know the inseam is still there. This isn't love; this is a tiny inlet where I can pull over and rest my oars.

Finally, I pull away. "It's cold and Sam's inside," I say.

"Jesus! Sam's inside? I'm out of here. I don't want to get us shot. I'm really trying to do the right thing. I'm gone. I've left."

"Go. That would be the right thing."

He gives me one last kiss. A soft, slow one, and he's gone. Without another word, because I think he doesn't have any words to say. Even *bye* would be wrong.

I go back in, and as the warmth of the house hits my face I'm suddenly freezing. I open the coat closet, put on my red ski parka, and go in the kitchen where my mother is sitting in her chair.

"Who was that?" she asks, then mouths the word, *Mark?*

"Yes."

"Don't ask for trouble," she whispers.

I open the refrigerator to get some Coke or cold chicken or anything to change my dreamy mood. Mark's smell is still in my nose. He had the same smell twenty years ago. These days Sam is odorless; I can't smell him anymore. He keeps it to himself.

While I'm rummaging behind the refrigerator door, poking a finger into a tiny dish of leftover egg salad, I hear Sam come into the kitchen. I kneel down low and open the fruit drawer. I just don't want to see him right now. "Okay, quick visit," he says. "The girls have school tomorrow. Where's Ellie?"

"Right here," my mother says.

"Right here," I say, coming up with an apple.

"Why do you have on your parka?"

"I was going to take Rags for a walk."

"I'll come, too."

So we get Rags and start off. "Your father seems okay," Sam says. "I mean, he looks tired and old. He has no strength. But he said to me, 'Nice to see you, Sam,' and I think he meant it."

"He always liked you."

"What's not to like?"

I don't answer.

"What's not to like?"

"You always seem mad."

"Because *you* always seem mad. You always seem to have a bad word for me. I'm a slob. I eat too fast. I mumble. I feel you don't appreciate me."

"I feel you don't appreciate me, either."

"I said it first."

"I do appreciate you, Sam. I do.

"Can we try to be nicer to each other?" he asks. "Can we just make the effort?"

"Can *you* try?"

"Can *you* try?"

"Yes," I say. I'll try. I really don't want to try, but at the moment I smell wood smoke, a smell that always makes me hopeful. So I dig deep to find something about Sam that makes me hopeful, and I think, the smell of his scalp. It used to have an earth smell: earth, oil, soil.

"Can I smell your head?" I ask, and he lets me. He takes off his knit cap and lets me. And there we are, Rags by my side, and I'm all nose, trying to bring back an old scent. What I come up with, however, is more cold air and the strong smell of wood burning.

That night, after everyone is gone, I put on my pajamas and robe and go into the den to watch TV with my father. "You like that hospital bed?" my father asks me.

"Yes."

"I hate it."

Apparently my father is watching the feng-shui channel, for here we are again. We're seeing the home of a Dr. Marcus and the doctor is wearing a navy blazer and an ascot.

"Dad, he's wearing an ascot. I didn't think men wore ascots anymore."

"He's a jerk. With too much money."

My father dozes on and off—he floats in and out; I'm not sure what he sees and doesn't see. If he even registers that the TV is on. The Dr.

Marcus segment includes scenes with the doctor's grown son, a thirty-year-old man, who is showing the feng shui in Dr. Marcus' bathroom. The old son sits fully clothed in an empty, dry jacuzzi. "This is a gold-and-marble-inlay jacuzzi," he says, the camera catching all the candles lining the shelves of the marble backsplash. "It's my favorite place," the son says, "when my mom's away on business."

I am repulsed by the psychology here: a thirty-year-old son, waiting for his mother to leave so he can light her candles and soak naked in her jacuzzi. I look over at my father, who seems to be watching, but I'm not sure he's taking it in. Still, I play the daughter asking her father questions: "Doesn't the son have a job?" I ask. "Why's an old son in his mother's bathtub?"

"You've done well," he says. "Not everybody does so well. You've got your own tub."

"I've done okay," I say. But I pretend to be modest so I can take in what he's said to me: *You've got your own tub.* He has actually paid me a compliment. He's paid me. My father, who thinks he's got nothing, has paid me. *You've got your own tub.* And I do. I have a tub, a house, a family. Rather, I might have a tub. Right now, I don't know what I have.

He's getting sleepy again. "Turn the channel," he says. I turn it to some old movie in which I recognize no one. He closes his eyes, folds his hands in his lap, and says, "Leave it there," so I leave the channel just where it is and we say goodnight.

That night I listen for him falling, and he does fall. I hear a crash and go into the den, and there he is on the floor near the TV. "I was trying to get to the bathroom by myself," he says, "and I didn't make it." I try to lift him up, which is stupid. I'm tired and go for the dead lift. I put my arms under his and just pull with all my might. This gets me nowhere except on the floor with him. Suddenly we're eye to eye.

"You're good for nothing," he says to me.

"So are you," I say to him. He starts laughing and I start laughing. We are on the cork floor, side by side, looking into each other's eyes and laughing.

• • •

The next day, first thing, nine o'clock, Yvonna shows up with another applicant, Vivka. "She just came off another job," Yvonna says, "but the man not need her," by which I take to mean the man died.

Vivka looks about fifty, but fifty long years in Poland.

"She speak well and she take care of men. She good."

We sit at the kitchen table.

"Vivka, what's your experience taking care of people?" my mother begins.

"I take care of doctor's father for a long time and doctor here write me letter of introduction."

My mother holds the heavy piece of writing paper and we both read the doctor's letter. Vivka took good care of his father. She was strong, caring, uncomplaining, and diligent. She drove, she cooked; she treated him like a king. "The doctor's father was a big man," she says, "and I do everything for him. I wash him and dress him and help him walk. I change diaper. I also cook, clean, whatever you want me to do, I do." She doesn't look at Yvonna, she looks at my mother. "You have nice house. I don't need much space. You have bed for me here, I fine. I have my own apartment in New Britain, which I keep, where my mail come, and if I can go home once a week, once every two week, I fine with you." She pats her left breast to show everything is fine with her if everything is fine with us. It is. She wants to be paid under the table; we are fine with this. She wants to go home once a week. Fine. She will start right away. She has food and clothes in New Britain. She'll get her clothes and be back in two hours; bring to my parents the pierogies and cake she has already made, not expecting she would be taking a job today.

"Irv might eat a nice pierogi," my mother says, which we all take to mean the deal is sealed.

We take Vivka to the den to meet my father. I stand in the doorway of the den with Rags at my feet. My mother takes Vivka halfway into the room and the two of them stand before him. He's sitting in the rocking chair watching TV with the volume up high.

"Turn off the TV," my mother says. Emeril is cooking a veal stew.

"Go away," he says. "I didn't ask for anybody."

"I want you to meet Vivka. We want to hire her for you. Turn off the TV."

He picks up the remote, makes a big deal of looking down at it and pressing a button.

"Nice to meet you," he says, his face still looking down at the remote. "Now leave me alone, if you don't mind. I don't feel well." No one budges and he looks up. "You look like a nice woman. But no thank you to your help. I've got something else in mind." To my mother he says, "Leave it to you. She's got a *tuchus* as big as a train."

"He doesn't know what he's saying half the time," my mother says to Vivka.

"She doesn't know what I'm saying, but I know what I'm saying, and what I'm saying is she has a big, fat…"

"Dad, cut the crap," I say loudly from the doorway. "We have a nice woman here." Rags starts barking just then. She goes into the middle of the room, looks at me, and starts barking. "It's all right, Rags," I say. She comes over to me and barks and then goes to my father and barks. "If your plan is to work Mom into the grave with your demands and insults, I won't allow it."

"The dog's upset," my father says, with disgust and weariness.

"You're a pain in the ass," I say, walking into the middle of the room and patting Rag's head. "Dad, it's Vivka or Harbor Hill. Since your insurance ran out, Harbor Hill is $260 a day. Vivka is $100. And you get to stay in your home. I have to get back to New London. What's it going to be?"

"Vivka. Vivka? Her name is Vivka?"

Vivka says, "Viv-ka or Viv-ki."

"I'll call her Vicki."

"It's all right," she says. "You call me anything."

"Vicki, then."

"Okay," she says, and the deal is sealed.

In the hall, walking toward the kitchen, my mother says, "Vivka, this is what he's like. You've seen it. Can you handle it?"

"None worry. I take care of him. He not feel good."

"Thank you," I say, holding her arm. "Thank you."

I pack my things, then go to say goodbye to him. I'm scared to death to face him, to open the den door. But I have no choice.

He's sitting in his rocker, but he has a ledger on his lap, where he is recording numbers. "Ellie," he says when I first walk in, "bring me my sport coat. Mother put it in the hall closet."

I rummage through the closet. "It's still in the plastic from the cleaner. Mother cleaned it on me, when I was in Harbor View." He starts coughing and, because of the throat singers, I recognize the sound. It begins as the sound of a wineglass being clinked, then changes to the growling of a wolf. I find the coat and bring it to him. I have to put his hand in the sleeve, and then he can manage to push the arm through. "I'm always cold," he says.

"I know," I say. "I'm sorry. You want some coffee and Entemann's?"

He shakes his head. "I have a big mouth. I know it."

I don't say anything, my terror resumed. I was lucky once, but I won't test it again.

"I know you and Sam are separated. He told me. Why didn't you tell me?"

"I was scared."

"Look. You work it out. Whatever it takes, you work it out. You got two kids. Look at mother and me. We stay together for you." He starts to laugh, but is interrupted by some coughing. "A parent will always be a parent. Your kids will always need you."

"I know," I say, and start to cry.

"Don't cry. Go and do as I say. I told Sam the same thing. So go and set things right. Next time I see you, I want it straightened out." He takes a roll of bills from his pocket, the ancestral, father's money roll. It's part of his uniform, like the stained jacket, like the vest. He peels off some tens, some twenties. "Buy something that looks nice. You look like hell. And one more thing."

I'm sure he's going to say the thing I can carry with me, the good word.

"Next time I see you…"

He coughs a cough, a low guttural sound that simulates the battering of horse hooves. I wait.

"…I want you to be a blond."

I stop to see Stuart at the store on my way out of town. It's cold and overcast, though the clouds look like there's some light behind them, like an x-ray film on the doctor's light board. I bring Rags into Schmeer's to say goodbye to Stuart. It's four o'clock and he has some customers who have stopped by after their shift at Risdon, after picking up their kids from basketball practice. He's with a teenage boy talking about running. "Your problem is, you run on your toes. And your stride is hard. You should think about having an easy stride, easy stride.

"El. Rags."

"I don't want to interrupt you, but we hired a woman. She seems good, she speaks English, and I told off Dad. Now I have to get back."

"No, no, wait. We're finished here." He turns to the boy and extends his hand for a handshake. "Ray, good man. It's just some mechanical things you need to work out."

If the day comes when the Catholics stop wearing school uniforms, Stuart could hold formal workshops at the Marriott, and his old customers would pay to attend. He's that good.

"You hired someone and told off Dad?"

"I did it all."

"I'd never have the nerve to tell him off. You're my hero."

"Likewise." I blush, and I can feel it—the rush of blood to my cheeks. "And the woman seems good. If you go over there in an hour, you can check her out and have some pierogies that she went home to get. She's keeping her apartment, and probably wants a day off here and there, but otherwise she's game to live in."

"She going to stay tonight?"

"Yep."

"Good work, El. My little sister. I'll walk you to your car." He calls out to the few customers. "I'll be back in a minute."

We walk out to the Caprice, parked in front on Maple Street. "How many miles on this?"

"A hundred and fifty thousand. Sam wants to get up to two hundred thousand."

"You gonna let him?"

"Maybe."

"Men are tough," he says.

I look at him, and he doesn't seem tough. He is a likeness of me, with less gray, even though he is older. His skin is fair, his eyes are fair—a little Danny Kaye around the eyes and brow, a little Bono in the nose, a little Madonna around the mouth. And so am I. We could be in movies or on stage, but instead we are here.

I lean against my Caprice and wrap my worn, red parka around me. It's cold, but Stuart is just wearing a sweater with big geometric designs on it. And his running shoes. Always his running shoes. If he thinks of running this store as an athletic event, he can keep it going—it's an act of imagination that keeps the store afloat.

I look at the storefront window, packed with clothes, silver tinsel, and fake presents wrapped in red. He's got big paper snowflakes floating among the sweatshirts and the Lee jeans, the navy slacks, the box-pleat skirts. I'm remembering that twenty-four years ago at Christmastime, my father wore Christmas ties and put on a good mood for the customers. He massaged the big bull necks of the rubber workers as they clustered around the cash register. He'd call out, "Deck those halls with matzo balls!

"El," he'd say, to get my attention, as I stood before the cash register, ringing up sales in my own wool skirt, not a uniform, but a kilt. I'm remembering his Christmas cheer. "Ellie," he'd say, again, and I knew he was pulling me into his cheerleader routine. "Matzo, Matzo!" he'd call out.

"Balls, balls, balls," I'd say. It was my line. It always got a laugh.

"That's my baby," he announced to the customers. "'At's my baby. Asthma baby." Then he'd sing, loudly: "Yessir, asthma baby. No sir, I don't mean maybe. Yes sir, asthma baby, now."

It was our song.

*Me, age three or so. I'm wearing my grandmother
Jennie's shower cap. I loved to play dress-up.*

Jennifer Moses is a fiction writer and essayist whose work has appeared in the *Gettysburg Review*, *Commentary*, the *Antioch Review*, *Fiction*, *Ontario Review*, and elsewhere. She is the author of the memoirs *Bagels and Grits: A Jew on the Bayou*, and *Food and Whine*. She writes regularly for the *Washington Post* and lives in Baton Rouge, Louisiana, with her husband and three children.

CHILD OF GOD

Jennifer Moses

Jennifer Moses

When Gordon first laid eyes on Lucy he didn't think anything of her, skinny little white girl with a limp and that spaced-out, sideways-looking look of a newly clean junkie, which is what she was, he was sure of it. Just one more white girl with a bad habit trailing her around and maybe, too—who knew—she'd done her time on the streets, going out to Airline Highway and turning tricks for thirty, forty dollars, more if she blew them, less if she was desperate; who cared just so long as she got her next hit? Had the look: the shuffly walk, the squinty eyes, the raggedy hair, not that he put much mind on her. Mainly she just stayed in her room, anyway. Stayed in there, all curled up in a ball like a baby. Didn't even watch TV. Didn't even turn the lights on. Just stayed in there, in the dark, curled up into a ball like a baby.

Well, he'd seen them come and he'd seen them go, and this one, he predicted, wouldn't last long: wouldn't last more than six months, and then she'd disappear into herself, shrink and shrink until she was no more than skin and bones, and then one day there'd be a lit candle in her room, and Miss Dolly would call them all together to tell them that there'd been a death in the family. That's how she put it, Miss Dolly: "Bad news, there's been a death in the family." And the others would all nod and shake their heads, wondering if they'd be next, praying (if they had the sense to pray) that they wouldn't, counting their lucky stars that they were still among the living, even if all they did at St. Jude's Home was sit around, smoking and watching TV.

Not that he was complaining: he liked the place just fine. He liked having his own room, all clean and private, all to himself, and no one could come in unless he said they could. He liked having hot running water, a toilet that always flushed, and three meals a day, thank you very much, though some of the other residents complained about the food all the time, saying it was bland. He had friends in the place, too. Louis, whose room was right across from his: before he'd taken sick, he'd been a welder. Martin, who'd done time in Angola, Gordon didn't know for what, but had served his time and come out clean, and then, *wham*, it turns out that he's got the virus. The social workers, the nurses, the cleaning ladies, even the volunteers. They were all just fine with him; better than fine. They were caring, decent people, didn't matter if you're black or white, a pimp or a whore or whatever you once were, or if you liked to do it with boys or girls, now you were at the place and they were going to take care of you and that was just fine by him; it was a blessing, yes indeed, it was a state of grace.

Praise Jesus.

They'd picked him up off the side of the road, is what had happened. Literally. That's how low-down he'd become. Picked him up off the side of the road like some dead animal, like roadkill, and hauled him off to Earl K. Long. Pumped out his stomach. Shaved his face. Pumped him up with medicine, with antibiotics, with Norvir and Fortovase and Viracept. Fed him on cherry Jello and Pedialite until his stomach was strong enough and they could switch him to real food.

His sister Ruthie came and said, You're nothing but a junkie, but the good Lord done saved you anyway, and now you gonna fall down on your knees and thank your Savior Jesus Christ for all he's done for you on this very day. His sister Martha said: I need to tell you now that if you're going to keep killing yourself, if you're going to keep living this way, then I have to say goodbye to you, because I can't just stand here anymore, watching you killing yourself. It isn't natural. I just thank the good Lord that Momma and Daddy have passed on so they don't have to see you like this. His sisters—both of them—were school teachers.

They lived in fine brick houses up past the airport, and drove nice clean cars. And every day, it was the same thing: You gonna fall down on your knees and thank your Savior today for saving your sorry butt? Because if you don't, you are lost for good. And on and on they went, hectoring, haranguing, talking at him like he wasn't even there, and then one day, just like that, it happened. A nurse was telling him that he'd gained weight, and was even beginning to look human again, and just like that, *Boom*, Jesus came into his heart. Only it wasn't a *boom*. It was more like a flash. Yeah, that was it: a flash of brilliant, warm sunshine. Something he could feel in his entire body. *I'm here!*

And Jesus hadn't ever let go, no indeed, not one time since.

But Lucy: he was pretty sure that Lucy didn't know Jesus, and what's more, that she didn't *want* to know about Jesus. Some people were like that. They just couldn't take the Lord's blessings; they weren't ready for St. Jude's, and it was sad, but it was the way it was. They weren't ready for God's love, and no amount of talking to them helped, either. He knew that for a fact. After all, how many years had people been telling him about Jesus, and yet he'd stayed doing what he *had* been doing, which was sticking a needle in his veins, stealing money from his own kin, and for what? For drugs. For that next pure high. For a death in the gutter.

Skinny white girl who stayed in her room, curled up on her side, in the fetal position, no bigger than a kid. He figured her to be about thirty, thirty-one, the daughter of some kind of no-count rednecks, the kind that seemed to flourish like cotton in South Louisiana, white and black, it didn't make no difference if your father was a drunk and your mother was a slut, maybe hit the kids, or called them names; and then the father came home and whapped everyone around, or maybe even did it with his own daughter. Yup, he'd heard that that could happen too, more in white families than in black families, the father doing it to his own daughter. Made you sick just to think of it. Made you want to grab a gun and do some killing. Because there was evil in the world and then there was *evil*, and as down and out as Gordon had been, as much as he'd used people, and done dirty, and lived for the needle, he never did take a life away, or harm an innocent person. Because—and this is where his sisters had him—his parents had taught him right from wrong. From the very beginning, they'd told him never to take anything that you can't give back. His father had sat him down and drilled him, saying: What couldn't you ever give back? Until Gordon had finally figured it out and said: A person's life.

What else?

Their, I don't know, their arm or something like that? Like if you got into a fight. A knife fight or something. And you cut some guy's arm off.

What else?

I don't know. What else, Daddy?

A person's happiness. Don't never let me catch you being cruel, taking a person's happiness from them. Understand, son?

Yes sir.

No, he couldn't blame his parents for what he'd done all by himself. Drugging and drinking and whoring around, scaring his wife and kids off, losing his job, losing everything, his wife taking the kids all the way to Detroit to get away from him, telling him that she'd gone to the judge and he'd lost custody, that was that. Telling him to his face that he couldn't see his own kids, no sir, not now, not ever.

But Lucy, he thought, Lucy probably had been abused as a kid, and then went out and abused herself. She had the look, right down to the rabbity eyes. She had the look of a girl who was trained to be a whore by her own daddy, the look of a girl who couldn't die fast enough.

Which was why he was surprised when her folks finally came to visit, and it turned out that they were just as nice as nice could be. The mother brought cookies; the father looked nervous, pushing his hands deep into his trouser pockets, but saying hello and how-you-do like he was visiting a bank, and not just visiting his junkie-whore daughter and her junkie-whore friends at St. Jude's. Dressed all nice, the both of them; looking just like any ordinary couple, the kind you'd see at a shopping mall or the movies, the kind that go their own way, mind their own business. Drove in from Lafayette and when Lucy saw them she said, "Mom! Daddy!" and threw her arms around them. Happened right out front, in the common room, because that's where she'd been, watching TV. Watching *The Price Is Right*, because by then she didn't spend all day sleeping; she'd started coming out of her room. The mother passed around the cookies and the father looked at his feet, and finally all three of them went outside, out to the little closed-in patio area where there were chairs and a couple of potted plants—pretty plants, too, ferns and whatnot—and sat and talked. It was summer, hot as blazes. Gordon could see them from inside, could see the way their lips were moving, and how Lucy sat way up front on her chair, all squinched up to the edge like an excited child, waving her one good arm around.

St. Jude's wasn't all ex-whores and junkies; not really, though at first, when he'd first arrived there, that's what Gordon had thought: he'd thought it was a place for ex-whores and junkies to die in when they didn't have any other place to go. But it wasn't true. They didn't all die, even. Some of them even got better, and left. Louis was his best friend, and he was about as straight-up as you could be, doing welding at the big plants—Exxon, Geismar—that would have been until he got sick. Funny thing, too, that you could have a friend in a place like that, a real friend who you could shoot the breeze with, and tell stories; but there you had it, grace coming upon him like dew on the grass. When Lizzie, the volunteer, came, she'd drive them all over in her minivan, drive them up to the K-Mart on Florida Boulevard for socks and undershirts, things like that, or to the discount CD shop that Gordon knew about off Gus Young, he and Louis laughing like crazy when Lizzie fussed at them to put their seatbelts on, or bawled them out about minding their language. It was all in good fun, though: Lizzie didn't mean it, she was all right; rich white woman coming in once a week to drive a couple of niggers around, lecturing them to eat right and treat women good. Fellow across the hall, a fellow named Tommy who moved out a month or so after Gordon had moved him, he was a math teacher: went back to work, is what he did. Moved to New Orleans and got a job in the Orleans Parish school district, teaching seventh graders how to find the common denominator, and figure out the y factor when two plus y equals nine. And then there was that white boy, the one whose walls were covered with pictures of half-dressed men, and Miss Dolly fussing at him just about every day to take the pictures down, they were too provocative, they disturbed the other residents, there were *rules*, and if you can't abide by the rules, well, then, they'd just have to see you to the door. But everyone knew that Miss Dolly wasn't about to kick Alvin (that was the white boy's name) out; Alvin had been living at St. Jude's for years already; he'd lived there longer than any of the other residents, longer than a lot of the caregivers and nurses, too; he could practically run the place by himself if he had to, and what's more, he knew things before anyone else did, including who was bringing weed in and smoking it in the bathroom, and who was getting some of what they shouldn't be getting no more, fraternizing within the walls, and who had a wine bottle stashed in his coat pocket, and who was going to die before they even really understood that they were sick.

That was another thing: some of them were so young, so young and so lowdown, that they didn't even know what they had. That was what Gordon was telling Lucy the first time, ever, that the two of them ever really sat down and talked. By then she'd put on a couple of pounds and had lost some of her rabbity look, but she still walked with a bad limp, and was too skinny, leaning on her cane, her right arm hanging by her side, all bent up and useless from the stroke she'd had—which was another thing the virus could do to you: give you a stroke, a storm in your brain, leave you all bent up, unable to walk, or worse, with half your face caved in like a fish, the other half alive and twitching.

It's sad, but it's true, he was saying, that some of them come in here—hell, I've seen 'em myself, and that was even before Jesus gave me the strength to walk again—and they're no more than babies. Kids. It's sad. They laying up there in the bed, don't know what's hit 'em. And when you talk to them about the virus, you know, use the word right out, they're in complete denial. Either that or they just too sick to know what's what. They look at you like you're from another planet. Or they start talking about faggots. You know: that only faggots get it, and they're all white. It's sad is what it is. A damn shame.

She'd looked at him then with shy eyes from behind her eyelashes, and he saw, for the first time, that her eyes were blue, and the lashes black and thick. And there was something else about her, too, that he hadn't noticed at first, not all those weeks when she was curled up on her side in her room, or even all the weeks since, when she first started coming out to the common room for her meals and to watch TV: there was a certain innocence about her, a certain way she had of holding her head cocked slightly to one side, which made her small chin look like it was pointing somewhere, or perhaps asking a question.

Gaud, she said. That's just gauddamn awful. He laughed then, hearing the Cajun inflection in her voice.

What's so funny? she said, and he could have sworn she was blushing, if only ever so slightly.

After that, he told her stories. Stories about growing up in Scotlandville, before drugs hit, and how it was back then; stories about the Gold Coast, which was what black folks called the neighborhood right around Southern, the area where the professors and the administrators lived in proud brick houses surrounded by myrtle trees. Stories about his crew; stories about his wife—or rather, his ex-wife, because he wasn't going to deny it, he had driven her off. Driven her off, her and his two kids, too, with his drugs. There wasn't anything he didn't do, either, back then, back before he'd been picked up from the gutter by the hand of the Lord, delivered back to the light of day. Heroin. Marijuana. Cocaine. Crack. Speed. Hell, he was a virtual laboratory of chemicals, a walking chemistry set.

Never did finish school, neither, he told her. My sisters, they both went on to college, earned their degrees. But me, I was too busy for that. Too busy getting high.

Ain't that the truth, she said.

She was easy to talk to, was what she was. Easy, and she didn't judge him. Unlike the black sisters, who looked at him like he was dog meat, like he was something they'd scrape up off their shoe. Or maybe that was just his wife, before she left him, before she finally got so disgusted that she took all her things and packed up the kids and got in the car and kept driving north until she couldn't drive any farther, driving all the way to Detroit before she finally stopped. Then had a lawyer write him a letter, demanding that he give up custody. Too high to even know what he was signing away. Didn't care. Didn't care about nothing, just so long as he could get his next fix. But Lucy wasn't like that: she'd sit beside him, nodding and laughing, and every now and then she'd give him this sideways kind of glance from underneath her eyelashes, making Gordon feel like he was special, like he was somebody, like maybe there was a reason he was still alive, when so many others were gone, track marks in their arms and the air around them stinking of death.

He told her this story: What finally made me scared? Well, you see, I had my friends—the fellows I called my friends, that is. You know how it is, when you're into drugs, you don't really know it, but your friends, the people you call your friends, are really your enemies, because they're the people you're doing drugs with. Let's see: there was Willy, I knew him from all the way back, from when we was kids, coming up. Me and Willy and his brother, Joe, we used to steal the girls' underpants and their brassieres from their mammas' clothing line, parade up and down the street with it on our heads, then we'd run like crazy, you know, when their mothers found out. Got a whipping anyway, but that was the way it was back then. Then there was a fellow named Craig, never did learn his last name. He held up a liquor store, ended up in Angola. Bunch of us, really, all of us in and around Scotlandville, just getting by, though honestly I don't remember it. I couldn't go to sleep in those days, thinking that if I had a single dollar on me, I'd get killed for it. But that's just the way it was, living the life. She nodded, and her hair—which was straight and brown and cut straight across, like a boy's—shimmered, catching the light.

Well, I'll tell you, because this is what happened. Willy? He was staying at his family home, you know, the same place where he came up. Ain't nobody else living there because the whole neighborhood, it went downhill. All the respectable people, the parents with kids to raise, moved out. Willy's brother, Joe, he moved out, too—moved all the way to Texas, if I remember correctly. The whole neighborhood ain't nothing but a place for junkies to shoot up and to get killed. But Willy stayed, because where else did he have to go? Stayed in the family house even after the plumbing and the electric had been turned off, and there wasn't nothing in it but maybe a mattress on the floor and a broken-down TV, because everything else had either been sold or stolen. So anyway, one day, we all kind of look around and realize that we haven't seen Willy for a while. For a week maybe. Go looking around. No one's seen him. No one's heard from him. Go knocking on his door, but the place is locked and ain't no one home. A few more days go by, and then I heard what's happened. All the dogs in the neighborhood? All the stray dogs, that the pound doesn't catch? They hanging out in Willy's yard, just standing around, barking, barking like they going crazy. Turns out that that's because Willy's in the kitchen—what *used* to be the kitchen before he sold all the appliances—dead on the floor, a needle in his hand, cockroaches the size of your fist crawling all over him—and the smell! And that's when I said: I had enough. I don't want no one to find me lying dead with a needle in my arm.

I done some pretty bad stuff, too, Lucy said.

She was, he learned, thirty-five years old. Never been married. Had no kids. Spent time on the streets, just like he thought. Started using young—twelve, thirteen—because, she said, she wanted to feel good, wanted to be liked by the popular kids at her school. He had a hard time imagining that, what the popular kids at her school must have been like, because she had grown up in a new subdivision near Lafayette, in a three-bedroom house with air conditioning and a swing set in the backyard, and she was supposed to have gone to college, too. She was supposed to have followed her big sister to LSU, and gotten a degree, and made her folks proud. But instead she fell in love with the life and ended up on the street, spreading her legs or opening her mouth, she didn't care, just so she could get enough money for the next high, and before she knows it, no one's talking to her anymore: not her older sister (who became, of all things, a social worker); or her maw-maw, who had cancer, only Lucy was too strung out to go see her to say goodbye before she died; or any of her cousins; or her parents. She didn't blame her parents, though: they were Catholic. They went to church and prayed for her soul.

I just about did kill them, is what I did, she said.

They were sitting out back, because by now it was getting to be late fall, and the weather was cooling down some, especially at night, when the shadows fell, and everything got all soft and dreamy. That was the first time he noticed, *really* noticed, what she looked like. Not like before, when he'd seen her as a compilation of parts: round face, pointy chin, shiny hair, hips as narrow as a boy's, and not much in the way of female softness up top, either—all of that, no doubt, all hollowed out of her, all stripped away from her years on the street. But now, as she reached over to tap her cigarette ash into a glass dish, adding her ash to the heap of ash and butts already in it, he saw how long and delicate her hands were, even the hand that didn't work right anymore; he saw how graceful and lovely was her body. She was like some pretty little animal; like a pretty animal you'd see in a forest, the kind that would run away from you, scared. Not that Gordon knew a thing about pretty animals, or really any kind of animal, not to mention forests. Where he'd grown up, they'd had one park, that was it, and it only had a couple of trees; as for animals, the snakes and the lions and the tigers in the zoo were enough for him. He didn't much care for the animal kingdom, although once he'd had a dog, Barker, whom he'd loved like it was a child. Whatever had happened to Barker, he wondered, and then realized that he'd lost Barker around the same time that he'd lost Melinda and the kids, all of them gone, all of them as far away from him as was possible in this lifetime, making tracks, putting up a wall of miles.

Lucy was dressed as she always was, in loose cotton pants and a T-shirt, with flip-flops on her feet. No makeup, of course, because what was the point of putting makeup on when the highlight of your day was taking your morning meds and having the caregivers fuss at you because you weren't drinking your juice at breakfast? (Actually, he thought, that wasn't quite true either. Some of the women—particularly the sisters—put on makeup every day of the week, didn't matter how sick they were, laid up in the bed.)

I don't know, she said, exhaling a thin blue spool of smoke. I just don't know.

That's when he noticed that the insides of her wrists were threaded with spindly blue veins, a whole map of veins just there, just inside her pale white skin.

Did he love her? Sometimes he thought he did. Other times he just thought he was crazy. Crazy, or desperate, or both. He hadn't had a woman for a long time, and that was the plain truth, but now wasn't the time to be correcting that situation, not here, not at St. Jude's. Plus, right around the same time that he had that thought, a terrible thing happened. It was his friend, Louis. Louis, who he used to ride with, riding around in the car, every Tuesday morning when Lizzie, the volunteer, came. Riding in Lizzie's mini-van, with Louis and sometimes another resident or two, going up to the video store to get Louis a whole bunch of horror videos, weird shit with titles like *Blood Friday* and *Evil Comes at Midnight* and *Satan's Crossing*, because Louis could sit in front of the TV, hour after hour, and watch that shit.

Louis, like Gordon, was a good-looking man, the flesh still on him, his face still shiny and bright. Had had him a life, Louis had, and from the looks of it, was on his way back to that life, back to life on his own, get himself his own apartment, get his job back. He was doing that well. But then—*wham*—Louis ends up in Earl K. Long, with a runaway fever, and the next thing you know, he's on a respirator.

That's when the volunteer drove Gordon over. Drove him over to see his buddy Louis at Earl K. Long. Drove him and drove one of the caregivers, too, a real nice woman, name of Judy. Because, the volunteer said, it would be awful not to say goodbye to him, it would be awful not to have a chance to say goodbye to your best friend. Talking the whole time, *blah blah blah*, about how he had to say goodbye to his friend.

When they got to his ward—ward 5C, intensive care—they were given masks to wear. But Gordon didn't want to go in; no, he truly did not. He didn't want to see Louis like that, all hooked up to machines.

The women went in first, while he waited in the hall.

I just can't, he said when they came back.

He needs you.

I just can't see him like that.

He's unconscious, but he'll know you're there.

By this time, both women were crying: the white volunteer, the one who came like clockwork every Tuesday morning, talked too much but otherwise was all right, and how many rich white ladies are willing to hang out with the brothers to begin with? She was crying. Judy was crying, too. Women and their tears. Made him uncomfortable, seeing them crying like that. Made him feel like scratching himself all over, like walking down the long windowless hall, walking and walking and never coming back; no, he did not want to see his buddy all laid out and breathing on a respirator, or watch women cry.

Just for a minute, he said.

He put the mask on and crept in, and at first it was hard to tell what was going on, whether his friend was alive or already dead, that's how weird it was—his friend's big strong body laid out, as if on a slab, and his rich brown skin, the color of dark caramel, covered with what looked like powder. His feet sticking out from under the sheet, and, up top, his big chest covered by no more than one of those throw-away bright blue coverings that they make out of synthetic materials. His eyes half-open but glazed over, and his chest heaving with the effort, straining against the machines. And his hands, upturned on the bed, the palms a whitish-pinkish color he had never noticed before, and the nails grown long from disuse. He was Louis, but not Louis. He was like a statue of Louis.

I've just got to take the bitter with the sweet, he told Lucy, afterwards, after he had returned from the hospital in the backseat of Lizzie's minivan, gone into his room, and had a few private words with Jesus. Just got to take the bitter with the sweet.

I'm sorry, Gordon, Lucy said. I really am. And she leaned forward, and with her one good hand she touched Gordon's knee.

I am too, baby, I am too, he said.

If he *was* in love, which he still wasn't sure of, it sure didn't feel like anything he'd felt before. Not like with his wife, Melinda. He'd been crazy for Melinda, and that had been the God's honest truth: that woman had made him crazy: crazy with desire, crazy with jealousy, and just plain crazy. First time he laid eyes on her, that was that: he had to have her. Big-boned woman with a generous behind and a quick, big smile, a smile that made her eyes dance, and her hair all teased up into one of those crazy dos like she was trying to be Angela Davis or something—women still wore their hair natural in those days. She'd only been twenty, maybe twenty-one when he met her, and he wasn't much older, but he'd gone after her like she was his own personal treasure; he was a treasure hunter and she was his gold, and by and by she agreed to marry him, laughing that she must be crazy to marry a crazy colored coon like him. But that had been way back, back when he still had his habit under control, back when he was still driving a truck, making a good living, too, driving those big babies, eighteen-wheelers hauling everything from factory parts to tulip bulbs, driving all over the continental United States, then coming home to Melinda. But no sooner had he walked in the door than it was: Honey, will you see if you can fix the sink? It's all backed up. Or: Praise Jesus, you're home, I got two sick babies and I feel like I'm coming down with something myself. She changed, too. What was once generous flesh became fat, and what was once a joyful laugh, a kind of crazy pride in how outrageous he could be, became a frown. So yes, he's not proud of it, but he did it: he had other women. It was easy, out on the road. He met them everywhere. At bars. At clubs. Bought them a few drinks, and if he got really lucky they'd invite him home with them, and sometimes, too, they came back to his truck, and they made love right there in the sleeping compartment of his cab.

There weren't that many of them, but each time he did it, he knew it was wrong. But he was young, young and stupid and horny and lonesome. Didn't know a good thing when he had it. Didn't know enough to leave things alone.

But with Lucy, things were different. He felt tender toward her, like he wanted to protect her. He wanted to put his big strong arms around her and breathe Jesus right into her mouth, so Jesus would flow down her throat and fill her heart and her lungs and her veins and her bones, so she wouldn't hurt anymore. So she'd never cry again. So she could go home to her mother and her daddy in Lafayette, and say: *Momma, Daddy, here I am, I've come home.*

When the word came down that Louis had died, dying there in his bed at Earl K. Long, surrounded by people who didn't know him, people who didn't know enough to hold his hand or touch his brow, Gordon felt a blow, as if he'd been hit in the guts, as if there weren't enough oxygen in the room. He went to Lucy, to tell her, and she looked at him with big eyes, eyes like a fawn, and stood there, nodding. But she didn't touch him, or do much of anything other than reach for the pack of cigarettes that she always kept in her right hip pocket, and offer him one. He prayed for guidance, but Jesus didn't answer him either, and then he had to pray for patience as well as guidance. And then, *boom boom boom*, things started happening at St. Jude's, like they sometimes did, real fast. A brother and a sister moved in together: Loretta and Laurence were their names, and when they weren't squawking at each other, they were squabbling with everyone else. Loretta was one of those big-boned women, tall and somehow raw looking, with lips that always looked shiny and puffed up, like the inside of a plum, and with hair sticking up all over the place, shuffling around in slippers; and what do you know, no sooner than she had moved herself in, gotten herself comfortable, she's coming on to him. Sliding her big-assed self right on up to Gordon and saying and doing all manner of things, all leading to the same one thing. Doing it right in front of Lucy, too, saying, You sure are one good-looking nigger, which was not only offensive, but embarrassing, too, talking that way in front of white people. Wiggling her big bottom in his face when he's having his breakfast, sliding her tongue around in her mouth. And the brother, if anything, was even worse, one of those poor souls who you don't even know how to start understanding, with a big head and enormous feet and hands—but what does the man do? He parades around in his sister's clothes, wearing her bright pink fuzzy slippers, her bra and skirt. Then another resident, a black boy who never did do nothing but listen to music on his headset and eat bowl after bowl of Lucky Charms, he wanders off one day and never comes back. It was downright confusing, and in the meantime, there was Lucy, always Lucy, hovering on the other side of the window, a hair's breadth away, a breath away. Lucy, who came to him now in his dreams, entering him in his sleep like a wind.

It was hot again outside, when he and Lucy smoked, summer coming, and already all the scrub woods around St. Jude's looked like they were about to catch fire, everything on fire: the houses, the buildings, the billboards, even the pavement of the parking lot. Shimmering with heat, contagious, and day after day, no rain.

One day she told him a story. The two of them were sitting under the awning at the side door, looking out at the driveway, and there in front of them is the flower garden that some former resident had planted, planted and then died, because that's what happened here: they came here to die, everyone knew it, wasn't no secret. Came here to die because they either didn't have families or because their families didn't want them no more. His own sisters had given up on him which was why he was here, and as for Lucy, her parents had had to turn their backs on her, too, what with her whoring around, her drugs, the men she took in, her stealing, her cheating, her lying. Yup, she'd told him all about it, down to the last ugly little detail. Everything, or at least everything that she could remember, which left some stuff out because she was blacked out or nodding off or beat up and unconscious and in a hospital or beat-up and bleeding on some mattress somewhere; didn't much matter, she didn't care.

But this story wasn't about those days. This story was about a friend of hers that she'd had when she was young, when she was still just a little thing coming up in her parents' house, before she'd gone bad. This friend, she said—her name was Mary—was closer to her than her own sister was. She was her best friend, and that was a fact, the kind of friend that she did everything with, and told her dreams to. We were pretty much the same size, too, so we could borrow each other's clothes and everything, she said. When we grew up, we were going to go to college together, share an apartment, everything. We were going to be in each other's weddings, and name our children after each other, and live next door for the rest of our lives. That's what we planned.

Plus, after college, we were going to join the Peace Corps. We used to talk about it, how we were going to go to Africa, see the lions and elephants. Oh! I just loved those elephants. I probably spent the night at her house a thousand times. And you know what happened?

Gordon shook his head, no.

Ain't nothing happened except that Mary—I don't even know where Mary lives anymore because when she grew up, she left town, left Louisiana even, and every time for, I don't know, for ten years, every time I called her house, talked to her mother, her mother wouldn't tell me a damn thing, and then her mother, Mrs. Batiste, starts hanging up on me. Saying, I'm sorry, Lucy, but I can't talk to you, and then, click, she hangs up. Then the phone number gets changed so I can't call there no more anyhow. And Mary? She was *beautiful*. Just beautiful, I tell you, with these real big old brown eyes and crazy curly hair, and I just loved her. I did. I loved her so much.

You really loved that girl, Gordon said.

I did. I really did, Lucy said, sniffling a little, sniffling into her hands, because all this time, all this time that Lucy had been getting slowly better, slowly beginning to walk right, slowly beginning to put on weight, she had never cried or carried on in any way, leastways not in front of Gordon. But now a terrible thought came to him, and he didn't know why he hadn't thought of it before, that maybe Lucy preferred women, that maybe that's why she'd never opened up to him, not really, or at least not in any womanly way, not even when she'd seen Loretta go at it, switching her big behind back and forth. It was almost as if she were in love with this old girlfriend of hers, this friend from before all the bad things happened, like she could never want no Gordon, not all this time, not with her wanting Mary. Pain blossomed within him then, blossoming inside and spreading out through his veins and capillaries, his nerve fibers, his bones, until finally he was shimmering with it, aglow. He looked at her real long and slow then, looking at her in a way he'd never looked at her before, with wide-open eyes, with eyes that begged, taking all of her in, not caring if she was uncomfortable or self-conscious before his gaze. Taking in every little bit of her, from her small, sharp nose to her wispy straight brown hair, her narrow hips, her slightly pink, slightly freckled skin that stretched down from her neck and plunged under her blouse, encompassing her soft, wet, secret places, and when he saw the blush spreading across her neck and face, he kept looking at her, because he had to, because he had to know who she *was*.

Will you pray for me, Gordon? she said.

He took her by the hand then, her small pale hand in his, and right there, right on the patio outside the side door where the caregivers let themselves in, right there overlooking the parking lot and, beyond it, St. Stephen's Home, which was for oldsters, hundreds of them in there just drooling and nodding off in their wheelchairs in the sun, Gordon and Lucy got down on their knees, and began to pray. Jesus, Jesus, Jesus, Gordon prayed—aloud, because Lucy had asked him to—Lord God, come into this woman's heart, come and heal my sister Lucy, bring her closer to You, fill her with Your love, heal her broken wounds. And on and on he went, praying to the Son, coming to the Father through the Son, praying for Lucy, but praying for himself, too, praying until he couldn't hear himself pray anymore, praying until the words were so deep inside of him that they leapt out of his throat before he knew what he was saying, praying without thought of time passing or aware- ness of his own body, his own breath, his own skin; and when he was done, his face was wet with tears and Lucy's eyes were closed and her lips were moving, her hand still in his, and he knew, right then, that Jesus was with him, that He was with the both of them, that Lucy, too, was a child of God, that she had been redeemed. And that's when he married her—because that's just what he was going to do, marry her and make her his wife—because he knew that Jesus was with both of them, working through them and in them, forever.

Praise God, he said.

Praise God, she whispered by his side.

When I was four, the world was full of wonders. It still is.

Rolaine Hochstein has published two novels and more than thirty short stories. Two stories won the O. Henry Prize, one a Pushcart Prize and the Seaton First Prize of the Kansas Arts Commission. She gratefully accepted fellowships from the MacDowell Colony, Yaddo, and the New Jersey State Council on the Arts. She has a mid-life MFA from Columbia University and currently works face to the wall at the Writers Room in New York City.

DON'T TELL THE CUZZINS

Rolaine Hochstein

On the point of noon I rush into the super-sized revolving door that takes people with walkers and I.V. stands. David is waiting for me, plopped in the middle of a row of chairs like he's giving an audition. I thank God I'm not late and for reminding me to wear the big earrings that David picked out for me. David, legs spread, leaning on his cane, looks me over, and I think I pass, but just barely. He consults his gold wristwatch before he gets up.

David is still fat, even with half his weight gone. His clothes swim on him as he moves toward me, glaring angrily at the steep cement walls of the outpatient waiting room. I can tell he's been fighting with the people upstairs—the illiterates, he calls them—the physical therapists who keep trying to get him to take the surgical cork out of his neck and make an effort to talk. He has been waging this battle every Tuesday and Thursday morning since he was released from the hospital, brought in by his home help aide who keeps herself scarce.

"So hello," I say with a quick click of a kiss. David grabs my arm with his free hand and steers me to the door that says *No exit.* He holds it open and pushes me through.

It's a mild day and the whole city is out, coats flapping and mouths running in a dozen colorful languages. David, no fan of the masses, moves through like an ocean liner. (I'm waving from the deck.) He hands me a sheet of his engraved white stationery with our agenda printed in pencil. As usual, he has everything worked out. As usual, he can't spell. First we stop at the *Daery Queen* to pick up a *Vanila milkshak*, which will be David's liquid lunch. Then we step around the corner to the *Chink resterant*, where I am to keep quiet while he deals with the personnel.

A second sheet, lined yellow paper torn from a writing pad, is addressed to our waiter-to-be. It explains David's milkshake and insists that the lunch check be given to him. Once we're seated at a discreet table surrounded by bamboo and large ferns, David pulls out the yellow pad. He scribbles and pushes it across to me. I read: *Don't insult me by ordering cheep.*

I uncap my pen and start to compose a snappy reply. *Okay. I'll eat for two,* I start to write. But David snatches the paper from under my hand.

I can hear, he storms in inch-high letters with three exclamation points.

"Sorry," I say as pertly as possible. Adding insolently, "I forgot."

David punches me with his eyes. *Take the Lachez,* he writes. He wants me to take all his art—the Lachaise, the Rouault, the Picasso drawings, the Whistler pen-and-ink, all the beautiful male nudes and portraits of him and his gay friends.

I don't want anything. I just want him to get well and stay alive. Regardless.

David was my husband's cousin, not mine. We had met long ago, once, at a wedding, and then he moved out of the family picture. It was my husband's family, heavily airbrushed to soften the sharp edges of their immigrant origins. The cousins were as breathless in their rush for respectability as their ancestors had been in their flight from Europe to escape the Czar, and also, of course, the attentions of everyday anti-semites. My parents had arrived later than my husband's, so I had to work hard to win their acceptance. My husband kept saying how much his family loved me, but I knew I was still under consideration when, after a long absence, Cousin David came back.

His point of entry was the funeral of his father—my husband's Uncle Morris the butcher, who died suddenly, but not unexpectedly. David turned up in a sober suit, acting as if he'd been with us all along. He had gained a lot of weight in the fifteen years since I'd last seen him, but he still had that dark, rakish look—very handsome, I thought he still was. The cousins greeted him coolly, and tried to keep a disapproving distance while they poured their solicitude over the bereaved Aunt Bea, who was cushioned by his arm, leaning on his shoulder.

After the service, David approached my husband, the easiest one, and my husband embraced him, exchanging memories of a shared childhood. They talked for a long time. "I've got to move in with the old girl," David said. "She's not as healthy as she looks. She needs more than an eye to be kept on her." He hoped we'd stay in touch.

David stamps his feet under the table till I give in and order the over-priced Chef's Special, the Sun-kissed Scallops on Shimmering Red Peppers with Tangy Glazed Orange Rind. For one thing, I don't want anybody—myself included—to think that my attachment for David is shadowed with any taint of designs on his possessions, any touch of greed.

Tak the art, he writes furiously. *Bring me a truk. Tak snuf boxes. Tak amerilluses. It would giv me pleasur. Fuck your pride. Tak something from me.*

It took him a long time to get me to meet him in the City, the first time for lunch at the Museum of Modern Art. He was waiting for me with his gold watch, a big ruby ring, and a membership card, so he could take me in as his guest. "You really must get yourself a *vendeuse* at Saks or Bergdorf," he told me as soon as he stopped fussing over my late arrival, he with his trouser legs the size of oil tanks. "If you have no taste, as seems to be the case, let someone else choose your clothes for you."

Why, if he hated me, was he always wanting to get together? I was up to my neck in laundry and car pools, didn't have time to comb my hair, let alone dress in style. What David did with his days, I had no idea. He would take a long, disgruntled subway ride from low-rent

Brooklyn to come to the City and irritate me. All I had to do was speed through the tunnel, pay a fortune for parking, and be home by three o'clock to pick up my daughters from school—an effort that earned me one of David's mighty shrugs.

He was no less contemptuous of my taste in art. In the big white lobby of the Modern was a huge, primitive-looking painting full of figures and squiggles that looked to me like directional signs. "Calling it *semaphoric* is soporific," David said, to put me down.

Now I had him, Mister Malaprop. "Could you possibly mean *sophomoric?*"

David gave me a wicked oeillade. "You'd have to be asleep to miss the eroticism," he said. Then he pointed out shapes that at once became what he said they were. "How could you not see them?" he insisted. "Unless you don't want to see."

At lunch, lapping over the sides of his chair, languorously eating a chicken-salad sandwich, David made sure I wasn't overlooking the facts of his life. "The only way to experience Rilke is to hear it read by a gorgeous German who is petting you." David's German, he loudly announced, was a male dancer he had met working in some mysterious capacity on a production of Bernstein's *Regina*.

"Blitzstein's," I said. We were seated by the window wall. Outside was the sculpture garden.

David leaned back, his belly rising like a bubbledome. He cocked an eye out to the statue nearest us. "You like that Lachaise?"

Under the cold March sun, the molded bronze was as shiny as a basking seal. But it was a standing woman, a nude, monumental, chest and belly defiantly outthrust, splayed hands on her wide, strident hips. "Formidable," I think I said.

"I've got a drawing of it." I didn't believe him. "You must see my collection one of these days." I nodded agreeably. I thought he was one of those arty people who feel free to dramatize themselves and make up stories. Nothing that day altered my opinion.

Knowing full well that I had to get home, he excused himself during coffee and left me sitting there. I went to look for him. On cold, sunny days the museum glittered like an iced-over pond. Surfaces were clean and even—no alcoves, no crevices. I found him leaning against a wall near the escalators. In those days David was obese and ornate, with lustrous black hair worked into a high wave above his smooth, tanned face. His head was tilted at an imperious angle that freed his jaw from its pillow of fat.

I said, "You are cruising on my time."

David looked at me unruffled, unrattled. I looked at him and saw why his hair, though he was in his forties, had not a touch of gray. His hair was dyed. His eyes were lined with fine dark pencil. It was makeup that produced his flawless complexion. He flashed his pirate eyes.

"The world," he informed me, "is full of chubby-chasers."

In the Chinese restaurant my plate arrives and David sets up his milkshake container and pokes a straw through the hole in the lid. He tucks a napkin under the turtleneck that covers his bandages. I concentrate on manipulating my chopsticks, pretending not to notice his struggle to suck up the milkshake and gargle it down.

The genius at Mt Sinai wants to bild something with membrane and springs that will work like tongue extenshun.

"So then you'll be able to eat?"

Talk not eat. Sed he was physician not magician.

"Leave it to you," I remarked, "to get cancer when everybody else has AIDS."

This brings a smile, but he still can't finish the shake. He sets the container aside, no hard feelings. I do my bit, eat with brio, with sighs and chirps and ecstatic appreciation of the Chef's Special. I'm also prepared to do a lot of talking, but David cuts me off with a poke of his pad. *He* wants to talk, so to speak. He wants to revile everybody, from his doctors (*the gestapo*) and his home-health aide (*the Abyssinian princess*), a recent winner of the Pulitzer Prize for musical composition (*a real shit*) and my daughter's new boyfriend, a foreign-exchange student (*French phony!! 1 lectur at Sorbon and everybody is a philosofer in a Sartre café*). Finally he wants me to bring him up to date on events in the suburbs. I report on the social and educational progress of my daughters. And my husband, his cousin's, grim fancy that this progress depends on nothing but the application of his nose to the grindstone.

Be greatful not catty, David scolded me.

Not long after the museum meeting, an interesting postcard came in the mail. It was from David, parchment paper, printed in Florence, Italy, with a pen-and-ink drawing of a priapic centaur making eyes at a youthful Apollo. David was inviting my husband and me to Friday-night dinner at his mother's house. "Please come," he PS'd. "Keeping Bea happy expends more energy then when I played Ariel with gosmer wings in *The Tempest*."

My husband shook his head. He was surprised the card got through the post office. My husband didn't approve of David, but family was family and he remembered the little kid with the smart mouth, whose father always brought along a package of rib steaks. No doubt my husband was also glad to have someone, a man whom he considered no kind of a rival, to take my mind off housewifely malaise.

So we drove to Brooklyn at the end of a long spring Friday, fighting traffic until we found the right little street, and then the right little bungalow among its look-alike neighbors, and then a tight little parking place. David opened the door grandly. He was in a slightly soiled blazer with a pocket handkerchief immaculately fluffed, as was his brilliant hair. He ushered us in and the look-alike was gone. He had put his hand to Aunt Bea's décor. A lamp here, a footstool there. A knowing touch that changed the place, in my eyes, at least, from tasteful to spiffy. A small watercolor, signed *Picasso*, hung above the old living-room couch.

We sat down to dinner at an oval table covered with china, silver, and crystal gleaming in the light of a palatial chandelier. On the other side of the room divider was Bea's kitchen—tiny, belligerently clean, smelling of intense cooking. Bea, stately in a flower-printed apron, used a fluted silver ladle to spoon chicken soup with egg noodles into translucent china bowls. Her cooking was low-salt but her table talk was spicy, running down all the relatives who, now that Morris was gone, couldn't be bothered to pick up the telephone and see how their aunt Bea was doing.

David reclined in Hamlet-like moodiness at the foot of the table. He had his own objections to the cousins. "Who wants them? Who needs them?" he enounced fastidiously. "Is there an ounce of charm or humor among them?"

After Bea's heavy dessert he finally took us downstairs to see the pleasure dome that he called his den. He'd been telling the truth. He had an art collection. Hanging from floor to ceiling. Stacked on the floor, leaning against walls and furniture. Art stars. Museum names. There was the Lachaise drawing of the master-woman, taking it all in stride. David was explaining to my husband in the matter-of-fact voice he used for cousinly confidences, "I go through dealers' back rooms. I've always had an eye for a bargain." To me, in his Oscar Wilde voice, he described a different mode of acquisition. "I was often called upon," he said, "to sit beside some important art faggot and keep him distracted from the bad food and mediocre company."

He took down a lovely gouache by a famous painter, "This I got for a pinch on the ass." Beside it on the wall was a pen-and-ink drawing of a husky young man, nude, belly flaccid, beautiful face. "Me, when I was a wild, good-looking kid. If signed, it would be worth a fortune."

There were sculptures, small ones on tables, bigger ones standing on the floor, many male nudes, some in quite unseemly postures. In this room, on a convertible couch upholstered with some shiny plaid fabric with a Scotchgard label, David conducted his affairs, including a current one—he told me with great satisfaction—with a fireman who lived up the street. It was hard to imagine Dionysian revels taking place down there while Aunt Bea sat up in the kitchen polishing silver.

He repeated his offer to give me the Lachaise, and completely misunderstood my hesitation. "The price of this drawing," he warbled, "could get me a seat at *shul* for ten years of High Holiday services, or, better still, a subscription to the Metropolitan Opera." It was a beautiful picture, and I appreciated its value. That's what made it hard for me to accept. Besides, where would I hang it, a drawing so big, something so blatant and overbearing, so frontally nude? David rolled his eyes. He threw up his hands for the heavens to witness such philistine stupidity.

Tak the Lachez.

"Where would I hang it?"

Hang in bathroom. Hang over kingsiz matrimonial bed. Have orgy for once. Give my cuzzin a treet.

My daughters adored their cousin David, who listened with interest to what they had to say, treated them with deference, and took their side against me in any conflicts that arose in his presence. His presence was not a rarity. Naturally, Aunt Bea was included in all family occasions—weddings, baby namings, bar mitzvahs, and so forth. David, as her escort, had to be invited, too. Portly, polished to a high gloss, he arrived with his mother on his arm, her devoted servant while she played her part like royalty, Swan Lake-ing it up in décollete, jeweled splendor. David put on his best avuncular behavior—no flash, no swish, a small but elegant gift, polite but cool greetings to the party hosts and surrounding family. When the festivities got going, he stayed in low gear, mostly hanging out with my husband and me, our daughters and, as time went by, their invited boyfriends and partners. When he was not with any of us, I could find him, seemingly comfortable, settled in a roomy but unobtrusive corner, with a prideful eye on his mother being fussed over by the rest of the family.

Don't tell the cuzzins wen I croke, David scribbles at the secluded restaurant table. *Insulted me wen I was alive. Cant cum to cheer at my funeral.*

I learned he was sick on the afternoon of the first night of Passover, the first Seder that took place after the death of his mother. I was cooking the undeviating traditional dinner as usual, but this time there was no Aunt Bea to be picked up at her door, so David found his way to our house on his own. He arrived exhausted after the short walk from the bus stop. I thought he was giving me a guilt trip for not picking him up at the station, but I was wrong. He had been to the doctor. "There is something," he said, "about learning that you are not only no longer decorative but also nonfunctional, that makes one feel completely *de trop.*"

The brisket was in the oven. I was making matzoh balls, and I stopped and wiped my hands. I looked severely at David. "Don't get sick," I warned him. I didn't even correct his grammar. "Please don't do that to me."

The next time I saw him was in the hospital, getting tested, getting his future laid out. I followed my husband into the sunroom, which was cloudy and smelled of the yellow vinyl that covered the furniture. A giant TV tilted overhead and never shut up. David looked strangely ordinary with a day's growth of beard and serious, smoky eyes, and he gave my husband his undivided attention. Speaking in a low, down-to-earth voice, he thanked my husband for the two new belts he had brought, one black, one brown, each several notches tighter than the old ones. He told my husband how to dig up tomato vines from the backyard in Brooklyn and plant them carefully in ours.

It seemed like forever till he addressed me, and then it was as if I had just entered the room. "Please forgive the wrinkled pajamas," he said with a face. "The Ethiopian harpy must be out celebrating her emancipation."

In fact, his put-upon home-health aide—a young Jamaican woman named Corlie—was unaccountably giving up a paid assignment in order to wait for David. She visited him at the hospital. She was there in his house when he returned, silenced after surgery, to Bea's old bedroom, now full of medical apparatus, opera tapes, and David's outrageous amaryllis plants—brought indoors and put in little pots, lined up on a coffee table, row on row, jungly, gaudy, indecent shades of red and orange, pushing enormously out of their protuberant bulbs.

It was Corlie who kept in touch with us and phoned to tell me when she would bring him to the City for outpatient treatment. It was Corlie who would be waiting for him when he and I finished our Chinese lunch.

In the restaurant David manages to summon the waiter, request the check, and also, against my will, to have my unfinished Chef's Special wrapped for me to take home.

"I've got an appointment uptown," I yell at him. "What will I do with a bag of leftovers?"

Throw in garbaj. Giv to bum on corner.

I give in, give up, as usual. I tell him that my husband and I will be out to Brooklyn next weekend. I ask what he wants us to bring for him.

A beautiful Wop to take care of me. Black bitches aint fun.

I take a deep breath and look past him at a scroll with a drawing of Chinese mountains. I scoop up his yellow pages to take home and burn. "You are obnoxious," I tell him sincerely.

David claps his hands with glee.

My husband will keep his promise. He and I and our grown daughters will be the only relatives at the funeral. Along with Corlie, David's dentist, and presumably the rabbi, we will be the straight group at the graveside service, separated from an only slightly larger gay group, including the fireman and David's friend John, who is the executor of his estate. They will look at us curiously as we exchange our common feelings. We will all be sure that David would have enjoyed the spectacle of his friends and family, standing under umbrellas with our shoes in mud, while the summer sun went into hiding and the rain poured down. Corlie will be wearing a jade pin, a gift from David. "He was like a father," she will tell me, crying as hard as the rain.

The first time I saw David was at Cousin Shirley's wedding. The caterer had spared nothing. The round tables were crowded with filled plates and bubbling goblets. The flowers in the middle were set on stands, so the diners could see each other across the table. Evening bags and diamond rings sparkled on the periphery. On a platform under a canopy the bride and groom sat in twin thrones at a table banked with food and flowers. As soon as the bread was blessed, the band began to play.

David rose from his place at the singles' table and came over to where I was seated for the first time among the married cousins. He was terribly dashing in a slim tuxedo, burgundy jacket with a white jabot

114

and ruffles at the wrist. He had courtly manners, as well. He made a fraternal bow toward my husband, and then he asked me to dance. My husband, who was not a dancer, said, "Go ahead. Have a good time."

And how we danced! In a whirl. My skirts flew. The band stepped up the beat. Other dancers stopped to watch us. We did the Lindy. We did the waltz. David's eyes flashed. He was sure of his lead, and light on his feet, and every chance he took, I was right up with him. The band kept playing for us, and there was applause at the end of the set.

Cousin Harriet gave me a fish eye when David returned me to my place. "Your entrée is getting cold," she said, though my husband had considerately put a cover over the plate.

One day, far in the future, Cousin Harriet, visiting her aunt's grave, will notice that David is buried nearby. She will be furious with my husband for not contacting the family, and will come right over to tell him. The brash, naked lady will be hanging in my living room, over the couch where my husband will apologize and explain that he was honor bound to obey David's last wishes. On the same wall, next to the lady, will hang the torso of David, which Harriet will ignore, but which will be generally admired. "That's my cousin," my husband will say, quite grandly, in response to comments. "But my wife," he will invariably add, "is the one who was really close to him."

David lost his speech but he kept his persona. In my story I used (distilled, abridged, modified, sanitized) many of the real David's spoken and written words. The story David is a fictional character. The man he is modeled on and named for was truly a character.

—*Rolaine Hochstein*

it is all but over—

There are still some nice things in the house, It would give me great pleasure if you would take somethings home to New Jersey, as gift from me now so I can enjoy your having them—
"Things" are getting nasty I dont know when I shall see you again—
NO will not make me happy,

I don't need anything any
more,

They took me off Chemo
because I was so enervated
Enervated
Exhausted.
Take the VCR

it they can
build something with membrane & Springs
that will work like tongue extension
So I may be able to make some Vowel
Sounds that now I cant even fake.
About eating regular food they don't
think they can help. He said he
was a physician not a Magician.
Any way I work at stretching the
Tongue and it touches, parts of my
mouth that it couldn't a month ago.
So I work on,

I will pot up some
geraniums for you
it
or rip them up now
and plant them
in Boston —
Take pots
buy ~~them~~ potting
soil at 5 ⚬ 10 —)
take geraniums
Now if you want
Them.

I could call — but it would
~~it~~ would distress her
what else would ~~they~~
Like to have.
I gave John the house

have nice Wedgewood
pisspots — would you
like some
not to eat on
Jasper were decorated

"Just Friends"
he was to stupid to
be gay but he was
a beauty
N.Y.C.

SILENCED VOICES:
NAWAL EL SAADAWI

by Sara Whyatt

Early this year, Nawal El Saadawi, the renowned Egyptian feminist writer, left her home in Cairo for Belgium, leaving behind her the threat of a court case on charges of disrespect to religion and apostasy for her most recent work, a play entitled *God Resigns at the Summit Meeting*. Her website carried a call to academics, writers, and institutions worldwide to send protests and petitions to the Egyptian government against the campaign by religious authorities to ban her works. It carried a particularly alarming message that "To

Nawal El Saadawi

bring a writer to trial before a court relying on dangerous accusations of this kind is a license for her assassination and can encourage any

Glimmer Train Stories, Issue 65, Winter 2008
©2007 Sara Whyatt

mad man who might cross her path to kill her." (www.nawalsaadawi
.net/news/07/petition07.htm) Speaking to the press from Brussels,
she said that she plans to stay away from Egypt for six months to a
year, for her "peace of mind," and to take up teaching positions and
offers to attend conferences. Yet she is adamant that she will return to
Egypt to confront her detractors.

Nawal el Saadawi, age seventy-five, is no stranger to book bannings
and censorship, having been a controversial figure throughout her
long career. This latest attack on Dr. El Saadawi came in January 2007
when she and her daughter, the author Mona Helmi, were called for
questioning to the prosecutor general's office. It was her publisher,
Mahmoud Madbouli, who, shortly afterwards, decided to withdraw
the book from the Cairo Book Fair, held in early February, telling the
press that he had done so of his own volition and not under orders
from the authorities. He is quoted as saying, "We do not normally read
all the books we publish. But on learning that Saadawi's book…of-
fended readers' religious sensitivities, we decided to withdraw it." This
extraordinary move is particularly surprising in light of the fact that
Madbouli had already published over a dozen of Saadawi's works.

In March, the Islamic Research Council at Al Azhar University,
one of the world's leading Muslim research centers, announced that
it had filed a suit against the play on charges of "insult to Islam." Dr.
El Saadawi retorted, "Since when do men of religion pass judgment
on plays? That is something for theater critics to do, not them. It is a
piece of fiction, and fiction has no limits." She describes her book as
being a comment on the current socio-economic and religious issues
in Egypt. On the withdrawal of her play from the book fair, she said,
"I feel worried about the future of Egypt, whose young people are
denied a real chance to be educated and exercise their minds. Con-
fiscation provides a breeding ground for extremism."

Dr. El Saadawi is one of Egypt's best-known writers, who has become
renowned at home and abroad for challenging taboos around, among
others, women's sexuality, female circumcision, and the wearing of
the veil. She is a prolific writer, having written over forty books, and
has had her works translated into thirty languages. She graduated in

medicine in the mid 1950s and worked as a psychiatrist, later becoming the Director of Public Health before being dismissed from her post because of her political activities. She spent a brief spell in prison in 1981, when she was among a large number of people arrested for their opposition to President Anwar el Sadat, and who were released after his assassination. She herself stood for president in 2005, pulling out of the race citing harassment from the security forces. In the 1990s she was among a number of writers and intellectuals who appeared on terrorist groups' death lists. Among them was the Nobel laureate Nagib Mahfouz, who was subsequently stabbed in a Cairo street. She left Egypt in the mid 1990s to take up writing residencies in the U.S. In 2001, not long after her return, there was an unsuccessful attempt to force her to divorce her husband, Sherif Youssef Hetata, also a doctor and writer, on the grounds that as an "apostate" she could not be married to a Muslim.

This is just another instance of what has been a series of attempts—some successful, others not so—by Egypt's religious leaders to ban books. An attempt to ban Iqbal Baraka's *The Veil: A Modern View*, published in 2002, has so far been thwarted. The book criticized the growing tendency of young Muslim women to take up the veil, and asserts that the hijab is not prescribed by the Koran. The editor of a leading women's magazine, *Hawaa*, and president of the Egyptian Center of the writers organization, International PEN, Baraka is, like Dr. El Saadawi, a prolific writer and a feminist, not afraid to speak out. In 2000, the publication of Syrian author Heidar Heidar's novel, *Banquet for Seaweed*, led to riots in Cairo and a call for it to be banned. What had caused apparent offense was a phrase that described God as a failed artist. That one of its characters lays blame on the religious authorities for the existence of despots leading a number of Arab states may well have added to the ire of institutes such as Al Azhar.

Nawal El Saadawi is a controversial figure, who has been a consistent and powerful proponent of women's rights. Frequently fiery in her rhetoric, in her writings, at the podium, and in interviews, she attracts criticism from academics and the media in Egypt who accuse her of being egocentric and attention seeking. Some dismiss her recent flight to Brussels as simply a media stunt. Yet others have stood up in her support. One writer recently quoted in the independent *al-Masri al-Youm* says, "I never thought that one day I would find myself defending Nawal El Saadawi, but the first blow against her would mean an Islamic state has become reality."

Dr. El Saadawi is unlikely to be imprisoned, yet to be singled out as an "apostate" is, as the appeal on her website points out, to become a target for extremists. It is the individual—sometimes acting entirely alone, other times in concert with small groups of other fanatics—who can wreak the greatest havoc. Assassinations of writers worldwide are, thankfully, extremely rare, yet the impact of those few deaths, coupled with almost constant threats and the triumphant posturing of extremists, is certain to make others think twice before writing on controversial issues. Who knows the extent of self-censorship, what goes unwritten and unsaid? Saadawi says of herself, "I've always been threatened, I live in fear—it has become a part of me." She is a strong woman. Others may not feel so able to live under such circumstances, and so keep silent. It is therefore imperative that writers such as Nawal El Sadaawi, who continue to challenge and put themselves almost literally in the firing line, need all the support that the international community of writers can give.

For more details and an update of the case against Nawal El Saadawi, visit her website at www.nawalsaadawi.net.

Appeals protesting the continuing threats against Nawal El Saadawi and judicial actions taken against her works and that of others in Egypt should be sent to:

His Excellency Mohammad Hosni Mubarak
President of the Republic of Egypt
Heliopolis
Egypt
Fax: 011 202 390 1998

Sara Whyatt is Program Director of the Writers in Prison Committee of International PEN, the writers' association, in London.

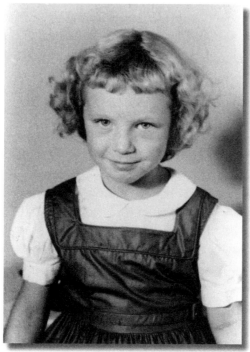

First grade, and quietly pleased about the kiss in the cloakroom.

Patricia Foster is the author of *All the Lost Girls* (memoir) and *Just Beneath My Skin* (essays), and the editor of *Minding the Body* and *Sister to Sister*. She's working on a book of stories and hoping to finish a novel. She teaches in the MFA program in nonfiction at the University of Iowa, and lives with her husband in Iowa City.

BEST PLACE ON EARTH

Patricia Foster

While his friend Jed Hargrove talks about percentiles and variable interest rates, Dr. John Connelly thinks only of the crisp bacon Martha fixed this morning. He remembers picking up two crunchy pieces, feeling a surge of appetite as he plopped them in his mouth, but before he'd finished chewing, he gagged. He'd barely gotten to the sink in time. To preserve his dignity, Martha pretended not to notice as she casually set his plate of eggs and buttered rye toast, cut in triangles, on the linen placemat. Just as nonchalantly, he wiped his mouth with a fresh dishtowel and walked back to the bathroom to gargle, pretending not to notice the plate. There would be no breakfast today.

But what he misses most is his cup of coffee. He looks at the maroon mugs on the conference table, the pyramid of cream substitutes, the stirrers, the napkins, and Jed Hargrove and Marvin Peevy and the other seven members of the Board of Directors at Southern First Bank sipping like old ladies. He wants to grab a mug and swill it down like booze. Might perk him up. Get his innards going. Start the engine. Exhaustion now grips him, and he has to concentrate hard on the other men—staring at Jed's shaving nicks and the tight collar around his thick, rounded neck, and Marvin's stiffly starched pinstriped shirt—so he won't sink back in his chair and fall dead asleep.

"Do I have an agreement on raising the rate on checking accounts by half a percent?" Jed asks, pen poised over a document. Everyone nods. John does, too.

But he has no idea what he's agreed to, what silly things they're talking about. He stares blankly at the headline on the report in front of him: *Gateway to Self-Sufficiency*. If anyone asked, he'd admit freely that he's come to this meeting only for the benefit of his grandchildren: Becca's boys, Todd and Donnie, and Rachel's brood, Denise, Melissa, Rodney, and James. After each quarterly meeting he parcels out fifty-dollar bills to the kids as if they're dimes. These are modern children, raised in the lap of luxury, anticipating, even expecting, money just for breathing.

"Not having money sucks," Rodney, a tall, emaciated kid with a ponytail, said the first time he pocketed the fifty.

"What?"

"*Sucks!*" Rodney shouted, as if he were deaf.

"What's that mean?" He wanted to tell Rodney to cut off his damn ponytail and start acting like a gentleman. And why didn't he yank up his pants and start working out with weights? But Rodney was already talking.

"Means it's shitty."

"Don't *curse* in front of me," he roared, but Rodney merely shrugged, indifferent, and asked if he would drive him to the video store.

Mostly, he doesn't understand his grandchildren. They look like drifters or hobos in their baggy jeans and ragged T-shirts that cost, Martha told him, just as much money as nice, sensible clothes. They mumble when they speak. Sometimes they walk away in the middle of your sentence or stare at you with their mouths hanging open. Catching flies, Martha calls it, sighing. But the day he complained about their belching and farting as if they were ruffians bred for the street, Martha had only laughed. "Just cut them some slack, you old bird." She sounded exactly like them, as if she'd shunned her own generation and joined theirs, dressing now in sweatshirts with upbeat slogans and faded jeans and tennis shoes.

Frustrated, he'd stabbed his mashed potatoes. "These are cold. Get me something hot."

And like a good woman from *her* generation, Martha had done just that.

"We are obliged," Jed Hargrove says, "to do what is prudent. A cautious but, let me say, calculated response to the community." He's talking about redlining what they call the Bottoms, a low-lying acreage five miles from Jed's new subdivision. The Bottoms flood nearly every year. The only people who live there are scrap dealers, drunks, and a few old sharecroppers—all on welfare—who work for Smoky Dillard. What he's really doing is redlining Smoky Dillard, who always votes Democratic. "It's not politically correct to call them sharecroppers anymore," Martha told him yesterday. "They're truck farmers now."

While Jed talks about the acreage, John wonders if he's had his eyes closed or if he's just been daydreaming, staring at the light shimmering through the pale green curtains, making them seem thin and gauzy. He honestly doesn't know. He thought he was huffing and puffing just to get here this morning, but now the energy's draining out as if there's a leak inside him that he can't find. He stares intently at his friend, Jed, who, at age sixty-seven, looks like a basset hound with his long, sad face and sagging jowls. Jed's describing something about the redlining, but to John he looks flat-out bored, as if he'd just as soon lie on the floor and gnaw a bone. This surprises him. He'd always thought of Jed as ambitious and cunning and fierce. Maybe he's here for the three hundred bucks, too.

The thought of the money pleases and calms him: money is the immutable immunity, the force, the glue that holds families together. Just stay the hour, he thinks, pass Go, and collect your three hundred bucks. Today he's not worried about actively participating in the board's concerns (he's spent years being an alert critic), but he does fret about the appearance of participation. Does he *look* wide awake? Is he still sitting up? He glances down at the floor, sees his feet in the black leather Florsheim shoes he bought at Pfaff's Shoes last fall, small, tidy feet set side by side on the flat, gray carpet. These feet have walked everywhere in this town, stood by too many sick beds, rushed in and out of Linn County Hospital, marched in every parade down Church and Main. Staring at his feet and trying to remember the last time he had the stamina for a parade, he's surprised to see a roach darting down the curtain, its hard, shiny body scurrying across the floor. For the first time today he feels desire: he wants to crush it. He wants to smash it dead with his shiny black shoes. But he can't make his feet work fast enough, can't coordinate desire and enactment. By the time the roach scurries away, he's no longer daydreaming at a bank meeting in Rose Hill, Alabama, but lost in memory, lying on a lumpy double bed in Gretna, Louisiana, listening to the whine and thump of insects skittering in the swamp grass.

That morning in 1947, heat shimmered like water on the pavement when he and Martha stepped off the bus from Tuscaloosa and walked hand in hand down Dauphine Street. Still dressed in their very best, he carried the one suitcase between them, a small blue valise with plastic lining and a cranky zipper. All around them were city sounds: the clanging roar of the trolleys, the repeated cries of vendors selling violets, aphrodisiacs, fortunes, pralines, cigars, beignets, and the honking, squealing joy of cars. *Annual Mullet Festival*, a red banner waved in the distance. A little black girl sat on an overturned crate selling strawberries piled up in paper sacks. From around the corner a fat man with filthy hair rushed by them. "Pagan!" he yelled at the riverboat docked serenely in port. "Ignorant pagan whores," and pointed to the women in colorful dresses idling on the dock. John turned Martha away from the man, squeezing her hand. They had only two days for a honeymoon, two days of relief from jobs and school with a free place provided by his Aunt Louise and her Cajun husband, Emil, who owned a motel in Gretna. As it was, they could barely make ends meet, even with his mother sending twenty dollars a month for rent from her work at the bag factory in Pascagoula. Of course, they'd promised *not* to marry until he finished medical school, but here they were, giddy and unrepentant and hot.

"Ya'll just come on," Aunt Louise had said when he'd called to ask the favor. "Bring that little miss on down here. Stay with us in Gretna. And I mean that."

"We don't want to put you out—"

"Get your patookis to Gretna," she said. "I got me a pot of gumbo cooking every day, got crawfish and shrimp with your name on it."

Now he and Martha—sweating in her pale pink linen suit—were waiting for Aunt Louise and Emil to pick them up. John had never been to Gretna before—for all he knew it was as exotic as Hong Kong—and didn't really know Louise except that, in the family, she was known to talk up a storm and stay up late smoking and playing gin rummy.

"Your Aunt Louise thinks you're a big shot," Martha teased, hugging his elbow, "because you're gonna be a doctor." He was in his third year of medical school.

"And you don't?" He pulled her to him, felt her breasts through the wrinkled suit, could barely wait to get to the motel, get through the niceties of visiting in Aunt Louise's kitchen, eating her gumbo, yakking about nothing, and then skedaddle to their room. He imagined white bungalows and a big double bed with clean white sheets and little wrapped bars of soap in the bathroom like he'd seen in Dean Salter's office. His thoughts were rocky, flooded with sensation, his body like a clock wound too tight. He had no idea what Martha was imagining, but she gripped his hand with such urgency he wanted to push her into that alley behind the bus station, the world be damned. Pagan to the core.

When Aunt Louise and Emil honked and waved from the corner, he and Martha jumped in the backseat, the big windows down, a timid breeze blowing in as they started out of New Orleans, past the medieval cemeteries and the end of the trolley tracks, crossing the U.S. 90 Bridge to West Jefferson Parish.

"You're starting the right way, Johnny, coming to the land of plenty." Aunt Louise had a thick pelt of dark hair pulled low on her neck and a spray of wrinkles around her mouth.

In the backseat, Martha looked at him and smiled. *Joh-nnnny*, she mouthed.

"Best place in the world. Nothing but water and fish and pelicans and saw grass," Louise said, as if she were a realtor selling her land.

"And *insecte*," Emil said in French.

"Hush now."

"What's that?" John asked.

"Nothing but Emil shooting off his mouth." Louise bopped her husband on the back of the head, and he turned to her, smiling, making little pinching motions with his fingers.

"Well, nothing's gonna bother us," he said, looking at Martha. "We'll be fine."

The relief of cool air invigorated him. All he felt was appetite. All he wanted was sex and sleep and food. For the first time since this morning, he closed his eyes and thought of nothing but the immediate future. No worries about grades or rent or exhaustion. No fear that Professor Nesbin would test him on antibiotic-producing microorganisms. No biting his nails over getting that weekend ambulance job. When he opened his eyes, they had crossed the Mississippi, and he could see the beginnings of Gretna: patches of saw grass and cattails on a low, flat sweep of empty land. Pelicans rose from the water, squawking. A shimmer of moisture hung in the air. They passed a string of cheap motels, pastel paint peeling from the walls, the salt air etching itself into the wood. The sun shone white and milky, a stark blaze of heat boiling the air. Aunt Louise talked the whole way, telling them about some chicken-necked man who'd been peeking in her window, "eyes as dark as some burned piece of toast." After about fifteen miles, they turned into the Southern Breeze Bungalows, and he could feel Martha's held breath, the air taut and unforgiving, suspended between them. Gone in his mind was the little cabin surrounded by rhododendron and bougainvillea and a trellis of wisteria. Gone was the mahogany double bed with the clean white sheets and the individually wrapped bars of soap. Gone was the dusty, futile dream of luxury and privilege he'd stroked and petted and dignified into reality. Here were four dilapidated cabins, the white paint so faded and peeled that the cabins looked to be made of bark. One scrawny cypress tree grew twisted near the first cabin. A stunted pine stood like a lone sentinel guarding the motel from the highway. When John turned his head, he saw brackish water lapping at the shore thirty feet across the road, heard what he thought must surely be the drone of mosquitoes.

"Home sweet home," Aunt Louise said cheerfully, turning to him in the back seat, grinning. "Best Place in the World, Johnny. Gretna, Louisiana."

Their room was so small, the double bed took up almost every inch of available space. The mattress, lumpy and thin, caved in in the middle, the bedspread puddling in wrinkles of cloth. John could reach out from one side of the bed and touch the wall, just as Martha could do from the other side. For about twenty seconds, they both sat silently, stupidly on the bed, trapped by ugliness. Along one wall there was a chest of drawers with a lamp and a faded pink lamp shade. The bathroom was the size of a big closet and included a shower, toilet, and sink, all squeezed together with no room for movement. But what did it matter? "Needs a jazz band," he whispered, already squeezing and touching Martha, alone finally in a room that was theirs.

That evening, they left the windows open in hopes of a breeze, though mostly they heard the big trucks accelerating down U.S. 90, gears grinding, brakes wheezing, and, in between, the sounds of the surf and some fisherman calling out, "Let's go, Mama. Nothing biting. Only us getting bit." But it didn't matter. Martha's skin felt like velvet, damp and soft, her body slowly and then not so slowly becoming his in every way, as his was becoming hers. They made love with a passion built from stolen caresses and brooding confinement, then slept in peace and exhaustion, curled around each other in the low spot in the bed.

In the middle of the night, Martha woke him. "Listen." She half sat up, leaning on an elbow, her attention like a fine, quivering wire.

"What?" He didn't want to wake. Sleep was as precious to him as food.

"There's something…"

And then he heard it; a rustling, something light and fluttery. A swishing sound.

When he snapped on the light what he saw was an army of cockroaches—palmetto bugs, they're called down here—flying toward them as if in formation, a buzzing crackle just above their bed. No, they weren't all flying. Some were crawling around the walls, marching or circling, darting to the center of the ceiling as if regrouping, and then dropping like bombers with a whack to the dresser and the tiny moat of floor around the bed. A few landed on their pillows.

"Aeeeeee!" Martha screamed, as one crawled across the bed. Incredibly, he laughed.

"Best place on earth," John said, jumping up and shaking the bedspread, slapping the pillows, grabbing his shoe to begin a counter-attack. "Gotcha!" he made his own dartlike thrust, slapping the walls, the floor, the dresser. He was Mad Max on a mission, twisting his upper body until he got caught in the narrow space between the wall and the bed, and had to jump on the mattress. "Gotcha!" he grabbed Martha, then released her to smack his shoe at the ceiling. The rest escaped through holes in the walls, cracks in the floor, tears in the screen, waiting slyly, he knew, in their hiding places, for silence and darkness to return.

Martha pulled the sheets over her head.

"It's okay," he said, climbing back in, wrapping his arms around her.

"Noooooo." Her voice was muffled. Only with coaxing did she pull the sheet off and look at the walls and ceiling. "I've got to get outta here," she whispered, her breasts shielded by her folded arms. "I can't stand it."

They dressed quickly and wandered out into the darkness, the dank smell of brackish water mixed with the stink of gasoline. They ran across the highway and then through the saw grass to the water, which was flat and still, almost eerie. Lights from the boats far out in the Gulf twinkled in the darkness. A fish splashed near shore. They stood together and watched the water, holding hands, silent and still.

"Paradise," Martha said, making a face.

"Our own corner of Eden," John laughed.

Martha moved closer to him. "I don't ever want to be poor," she said softly. She didn't look at him. Her gaze was fastened on the water. "Please," she said more softly.

"We won't," he said, squeezing her hand and pulling her down on the coarse, damp sand—everything was damp in Gretna. "I promise." To pass the time, they talked about what they'd buy when they made their first hundred dollars. "A dining-room table," Martha said, drawing an oval table in the sand. "Something beautiful."

"A new suit," he said, thinking of how important he'd look in a navy blue suit, single breasted, two button, notch lapel, one that actually fit.

They talked about the things they wanted, the modern brick house with a nice curved patio, their own driveway, new shoes, a big double bed, and then, at first light, they rushed back across the highway to their shabby room, certain the roaches would be sleeping, certain they could do again what they did best.

"The overdrafts for the month are predictable," Jed says. "Our old favorite, Martha Connelly, leads the pack."

The men applaud and look at John, waiting for his laugh.

"John?" Jed's voice swims through the air, pushing against him. He hears Jed, but he doesn't want to leave his honeymoon, those magical hours of surprise and ecstasy, that stolen pleasure. He wants to see Martha kneeling on the bed in her lacy white slip, brushing her dark hair back from her face as she tells him about growing roses and delphiniums, and where she'll plant them around that first brick house. "John, are you okay? Do you need me to call Martha?"

At the mention of Martha, he looks up, sees her pulling all the sheets off their bed in Rose Hill, bundling them into piles, washing and drying and then folding them into clean, neat stacks. She always looks preoccupied and happy when she folds the sheets, as if such purposeful acts please her, as if, next to money, cleanliness is the most coveted sign of success.

"Did you know I had surgery?" John asks suddenly, glancing around the room at these men who have all been to his house for parties and dinners and to watch ballgames on TV. He closes his eyes because he can't remember the surgery. He can't remember even being in the hospital, though every morning he sees the scar, a long fishtail of red flesh, narrow at one end. He wishes he could lift his shirt and show it to Jed, a slash of puckered skin, puffy at the edges. He wishes he could tell Jed there's someone in his bathroom at night, someone who pushes at him from the other side of the door and tries to stop him from getting in. Though he doesn't see who it is, he knows he's there.

"I know, John," Jed says. "I know about the surgery. That's why I'm worried about you. You've got to take care of yourself now. You've got to go *slow*."

"Slow," John says, as if he's not sure what this word might mean. Slow as in *stop*, he thinks. Slow as in turning onto his right side and wishing he could turn to the left. When he looks around, the other men are staring at him, their faces embarrassed, perplexed. Quickly, they look away. "Guess I better get my three hundred dollars and go." Now he laughs as if he's back to his old joking self. "I make a motion that this meeting be adjourned."

When Martha pulls up in the Lincoln Continental, John gets in slowly, holding onto the door for support. He's got to get his strength back. He's always been a sprinter, impatient, relentless, rushing wherever he needs to go. Early Bird, everyone calls him, because he's always thirty minutes ahead of the game. Grasshopper, they say, because he leaps ahead. Now he moves like a weak old bull, testicles dangling, penis shrunk, body ambling along as if he's dragging an invisible weight. Often he has to stop to catch his breath.

"I've got your lunch all ready," Martha says, barely glancing at him. She's looking in the rearview mirror, wiping lipstick off her teeth. She's just been to the beauty parlor, and her hair is dark and curled close to her face. "Fried fish and okra and crowder peas and cornbread. Doesn't that sound good?" Now she looks at him, straightens his twisted sport coat, tells him to put on his seat belt, and then barrels out of the bank parking lot.

At home, the table is set, and Martha puts the plate of food in front of him. He doesn't have the heart to tell her he's not hungry. His appetite, always hearty, is on strike. But he knows he's got to eat to get well. Steam rises from the crowder peas. The cornbread is cut in a wedge. He decides to take a bite of flounder, the butter swimming on top. Martha's always been partial to butter. The first bite tastes so good, he remembers why gluttony is a sin. The second and third bite he barely notices. He tries a scoop of peas. Martha's telling him about some special organic turkey she's ordered for Thanksgiving. "You know Becca will want me to do the cooking, not just the turkey but the candied yams and the green bean casserole and—"

Before she's finished the sentence, a disaster happens so fast inside his throat a horrible mixture spews out of his mouth, a thick, liquid explosion. It rises in its own erratic arc, splattering the yellow table-cloth like rain.

Embarrassed, he wipes at the mess before Martha can. "It tasted good," he says, surprised at the sour taste in his mouth.

Martha stops eating, and then, as if making a conscious effort, she picks up her iced tea and drinks solemnly.

He takes a sip of water, tries another bite, but this time the gag is immediate. He gets the napkin to his mouth in time. He leans back in his chair, suddenly exhausted, too tired to do more than sit.

For the first time since he's come home from the hospital, he and Martha stare at each other across the table as if they've both found the dark place inside where there are no more words. He watches her stricken face, sees her jaw tighten, her shoulders stiffen. They could be wandering together in a basement room crammed with the discarded and yet precious things of their lives. Here is the picture of their first brick house. Here the double-breasted charcoal suit he wore to a medical conference in Washington, D.C. Here the cracked glass bowl that once held watermelon balls for an Easter party that ended in rain. They gaze at these things, but dare not pick them up, these reminiscences of their lives.

Outside a soft breeze flutters the leaves. A squirrel sprints across the deck, and then stops to gnaw at an acorn. Their silence is finally interrupted by the arrival of their oldest daughter, Becca, who comes in noisily, letting the screen door slam, her kids in tow.

"Stop that!" She's in the breezeway, slapping at Todd and Donnie, who sprint past her and run laughing into the kitchen, reaching up to whack the door frame while asking Martha for a Diet Coke and a 7-Up.

"We're *dy-ing*," Todd says, clutching his stomach and pretending to be ill. He makes wrenching movements, pretending to puke, then as suddenly, he stands by the refrigerator, panting as if he's been stranded on a desert island without food or drink.

Martha gets them drinks. Becca leans over and kisses John, sees his plate, then steps around him and takes Martha's spoon to eat some crowder peas. "Wow, these are good. Can we take them home? Did you have some, Daddy?"

Todd smacks Donnie on the head, and Donnie's 7-Up splashes onto the floor. "Stupid!" Donnie yells, and moves closer to John.

"I've got something for you," John says to the boys, trying to get their attention and simultaneously reach into his pocket for the money. This, he thinks, is the least he can do. But the boys aren't listening, and he wonders if he's even said the words out loud.

"You only got that score 'cause you were jacked up on Mountain Dew, stupid," Todd jeers at Donnie about some video game.

Donnie laughs, saying, "Uh-huh, but sixty was still higher than you, jerk."

John struggles to get the money out of his pocket, but his pants are twisted against his thigh, and it's hard to get things coordinated. His hands feel clumsy and stiff, as if they belong to someone else, someone old. His pants, too loose now, are bunched up by a belt, the pockets folded into pleats.

"I've already *ordered* it," Martha is saying to Becca. "Every year you *say* you want to do the dinner, but you know you hate to cook turkey, so don't pretend you're going to do it this Thanksgiving." She's laughing, but Becca's mouth goes tight. Her nostrils flare. She hates to cook, John knows, but won't admit it. Instead, she swears her mother needs to direct the show, keeping them dependent on her super-charged carbohydrate meals.

"Hey," John tries to say, focusing again on the boys, but the word slips back inside his throat. He tastes bile, but he must give them the money. That's what he's still good for. That's what they'll remember him by: his generosity, his ability to give. Money is the glue. Money is what holds the family together. He must give it to them now. He puts his hand back into his pocket, tries to slide it into the twisted, folded cloth. He doesn't know why he thinks about Aunt Louise, but as he wiggles and yanks at the cloth he remembers the morning he and Martha walked up from the water, hurrying toward their slovenly love nest. He caught sight of Aunt Louise standing at the window of her kitchen in the motel, staring out at them. She wasn't grinning now. She looked pensive, sad, her hair spreading out in a wiry mess. Maybe she was remembering her own young love. Or maybe she was thinking about the eggs and crayfish she'd just cooked, knowing they wouldn't show up in her fading green kitchen with its loud ticking clock. And just as suddenly, he remembers the hospital: the same dour green walls and slick linoleum floors, the tick-tick-tick of an instrument connected to his body, a tube down his throat, an exquisite pain in his belly that felt like a huge electrical fire.

He gets up as quickly as he can. "Bathroom," he says when they glance at him. They seem to forget him when he's sitting among them, but watch ardently his comings and goings, his shuffling to the bathroom, his fumbling for light switches. He starts toward the back room, but he doesn't go there. Instead, he lets himself out the side door and walks slowly toward the little park across the street. For a few steps, it's like walking on air. He's being transported by a cloud. Then it seems like the park is miles away. A mirage. He walks and walks and walks. He notices every pine tree—the tall one with the broken branch, the neighbor tree with its wide wingspan—the pine needles carpeting the ground, the leaves of the magnolia trees in the park, dark and green and voluptuously shiny. There's the familiar low spot, still damp from last week's rain. He steps in it, feels the water seep through his shoe, a baptism.

He walks toward a woman swinging her two daughters on the swing set, one squealing in joy, the other stoic, stiff-legged. "C'mon," the woman says to the resistant one. "One-two-three, wheeeeee." But the child won't play, and the woman steps back, puts her head in her hands and whispers, "*Please*, Carly. Try to have fun."

He walks past them to the middle of the park where there are wooden picnic tables with stiff, hard benches beneath the tall pines. His wet shoe feels cold, his sock clammy. Now that he's walked this far, his pants are looser, the pockets clear. When he reaches inside and feels the money he longs to think of what it might buy. Such a soothing power. Instead, he thinks about Dr. Jamison, the bulky surgeon with large hands, leaning over and telling him he'd do everything he could. "Everything, old boy." He thinks about waking up from the anesthesia and saying to Martha, "Find out what she's doing and what I'm doing and what we're gonna do." He doesn't think about how his grandsons will stare at him, squeamish and troubled, wondering why he looks the way he does, his face gaunt, his eyes glassy, his skin ashen. He doesn't think about how the hospice nurse, smelling of wood smoke and sweat, will walk into his house and bathe his face with cool fresh water, soothing his brow and letting him suck on the edge of the cloth while she croons about coming home to Jesus. He doesn't think about the final explosion that will rise from his stomach, surging through his esophagus and throat and out of his mouth, leaving him so empty he's floating, floating.

What he thinks about is Martha's table. He bought her a beautiful table. A solid mahogany table, big enough to seat an even dozen. He can see it with the lighted candelabra and the silver epergne, the pale, linen napkins, and the ornate silver. He can almost taste the peeled shrimp piled up in a crystal dish, the lump crabmeat in the Bayley's West Indies Salad, the olives and the cheese and the stuffed celery, the champagne poured into fine crystal glasses ready to be drunk.

He reaches into his pocket and pulls out the money. It comes out easily. Six fifty-dollar bills. He fingers the bills, then drops them on the picnic table, watches as the breeze lifts one and carries it away. The other bills scuttle like leaves. What he feels as he turns away is lighter, his step easier, his pockets empty. From here he sees his big brick house and the two cars parked in the garage, a Lincoln Continental and a Buick Riviera. He sees Becca's Taurus under the shade of the mimosa tree. And beyond that the dogwoods and lilacs, the azaleas just bursting into bloom. In summer the roaches will return to Rose Hill.

They always do. Even in a well-tended house, even with extermina-tors and maids, a few will persist. And Martha, he knows, will see one scurrying across the floor one morning in early June. She'll want to turn to him and say, "Can you believe!" with mock dismay, but he won't be there. He'll have finished with "going slow." And then, no longer squeamish, Martha will pick up his shiny black shoe and do what she has to do.

INTERVIEW WITH CARYL PHILLIPS

by Kevin Rabalais

Born in 1958 on the Caribbean island of St. Kitts (population 40,000), Caryl Phillips moved to England as a child, was raised in Leeds, and later educated at Oxford University. In 1985, Phillips published his first novel, The Final Passage, *which received the Malcolm X Prize for Literature. His other novels include* Cambridge; Crossing the River, *winner of the James Tait Black Memorial Prize, and shortlisted for the 1993 Booker Prize;* The Nature of Blood; A Distant Shore, *which received the 2004 Commonwealth Writers Prize; and* Dancing in the Dark.

Phillips's nonfiction includes The European Tribe, *winner of the Martin Luther King Memorial Prize, and* The Atlantic Sound. *He is also the author of plays and screenplays.*

In 1993, Phillips was named one of Granta's *Best Young British Novelists.*

Kevin Rabalais interviewed Caryl Phillips in his home in midtown Manhattan.

Caryl Phillips

Glimmer Train Stories, Issue 65, Winter 2008
©2007 Kevin Rabalais

Unlike your more recent work, your first two novels, The Final Passage *and* A State of Independence*, were traditional narratives, linear in structure. Did you have a model in mind for those early books?*

In retrospect, compared to my later books, they appear to be linear and relatively straightforward in terms of narrative chronology. But in the early eighties when I began *The Final Passage*, I was conscious that the very first words I wrote were "The end." So even then I was conscious of playing with time and narrative chronology. I knew that you couldn't really tell the story of those Caribbean characters using a traditional, nineteenth-century, Dickensian, naturalistic narrative. As soon as you have characters who migrate, who cross water and become culturally plural and lose something, their dreams and their whole sense of themselves is thrown out of kilter.

What were you learning as you wrote those first two novels?

Like most writers, I didn't have any money. I kept having to break off and write a script for television or do some journalism or something else to make money. So it took a long time. But in that process of taking time off from the novel, I was reading a lot—American novels, British novels, and, specifically, Caribbean novels, because I wanted to get the atmosphere, the flora and fauna, correct. Having grown up in England, I wasn't really able to name the Caribbean trees or describe the sunset properly. But none of the novels I read seemed to give me a structural model. I was stumbling to find my own way to something that suggested a coherent narrative, some kind of structural movement that reflected these people's lives.

What role does reading play in your writing now?

Like most writers, if you write enough, you lose the innocent pleasure of reading. It's a very extraordinary book that shakes you into some world that you remember, perhaps, from before you were a writer, a time when fiction was magic and could transport you. You're too often aware of the scaffolding behind the story. The type of writers that I read then and the type of writers that I return to now are, for want of a better term, the engineers, people like Faulkner and Márquez, Twain and Conrad. In terms of nonfiction, I return to Baldwin for the narrative attack in his essays. These are not always people I want to read for pleasure, but I read them to try to understand how to move a story, how to get four wheels on a narrative and get it moving. It's very rare that I come across a new book that has something inside the narration that interests me or whose structure interests me.

Are there any writers who have surprised or shaken you lately?

I think that W. G. Sebald is the last author who surprised me. He surprised me because he articulated something that I feel increasingly not just in my own writing, but as a reflection of where I think we're drifting as readers and writers in the early twenty-first century. This is the collapse of the difference between fiction and nonfiction. Sebald seemed to articulate that confusion around fiction and nonfiction and find a form that synthesized the two. The writers that I tended to look at who influenced me when I was beginning and, to a certain extent, still do now, are people like Baldwin, Naipaul, Bellow, Mailer, and Graham Greene, writers whose careers exist in fiction and in nonfiction. These are writers who seem to place an equal weight upon their nonfiction and fiction. In some cases, like Baldwin, they will probably be best remembered for their nonfiction. But Sebald surprised me because here was someone whose career you couldn't really divide between fiction and nonfiction. J.M. Coetzee's work is also like that, to a certain extent. I think his autobiographical trilogy is a pretty carefully calibrated piece of nonfiction by a fiction writer. In some sense, I think that Coetzee is probably the last writer of pure fiction who surprised me with how he positions himself as a writer and how he negotiates that issue of fiction and nonfiction.

As a young man, I was very attracted to the form of the Polish writer Tadeusz Konwicki's books. His work, like the work of many Eastern European writers and artists, employed narrative strategies that made sense to me. These were writers, artists, and filmmakers who lived in a world where they never knew what was happening from day to day. It was like a bizarre, surreal dream. One minute they were German. The next minute there were tanks in the street and they were Russian. Within their lifetime, they had no idea how to combat this bizarre series of transformations. That's like being a migrant, basically. One minute you're hot, sitting in the Caribbean, and then the next minute you're cold and sitting in London.

After The Final Passage *and* A State of Independence*, your work took a new direction. The structure of your novels changed drastically. Do the experiments in structure of these later novels have to do with this drifting that you mention?*

The structures grew out of the subject matter. To be honest, looking back now, I don't think I would have had the confidence to write books such as *The Nature of Blood* or *Crossing the River* as a first or second novel. With *The Final Passage* and *A State of Independence*, I felt like I had done something that was reasonably conventional in terms of chronology. After that, I didn't want to mimic the form. I wanted to push at the edges of how you tell a story. To find a contentment with an ability to tell a story and then repeat that form, just pour new characters and new plot points and situations into it—it just seemed a little too premature to have found a solution to how to tell a story. I wanted to keep pushing at the boundaries. Luckily, the subject matter that I found myself dealing with kept demanding that I address the issues in the stories with something that was formally more challenging than before. I got a couple of books done, and maybe it was time to spread my wings a bit. But I'm not sure that I would have had the wherewithal or the courage to have done that initially.

In that sense, in terms of the technical problems that each novel presents, does one book grow out of the next?

I always feel that the biggest challenge for me is not "What's the story?" or "What should I write next?" but "How am I going to tackle the next piece of work?" I've been very lucky in that I've always known that there's a rich reservoir of stories and people floating around that I want to write about. Some are purely imaginary. Others are based on fact. Rather than have a sort of template that I can go to and say, "Okay. This is how I tell my story," and then pour the new ingredients in, to me it's always been a challenge of "How are you going to tell this one? How are you going to approach this?" Maybe some people are constantly searching for character or plot or subject matter. But I've been lucky. I've always felt that I've had subject matter that I will get to eventually. It's always there.

How does structure develop for you?

It grows organically. I always ask myself, "What is this book going to look like? What is the shape of it going to be?" I have an idea of what that shape will be, but I never really know until I start. A very concrete example of this comes from the book I'm writing now. To all purposes, it's comprised of three essays. The central essay is about eighty pages long. It's based on the life of a boxer who lived and died in Britain in the mid-twentieth century. I first came across his story twenty years ago and have spent a long time thinking about him. I finished the essay, and then about four weeks ago I realized that the place he said he was always happiest is a holiday resort in north Wales that he owned for a short time. I knew instinctively that I had to go there. I didn't want to have to go there. I was busy with other things. But I knew I had to write something about it. I didn't know if the trip there would produce just a few lines of color in the piece or if it would spawn ten more pages, but I went there instinctively. While I was there, I realized that the boxer had three daughters who are still alive. I knew that I had to interview them. That's the real story. Now, the book has been held up because next week I'm going to fly to London and interview them in the hope that it will provide a deepening of the story.

This is pretty much how my fiction goes, as well. My plan with the essay was to write eighty or ninety pages about this boxer's life. But in the writing, you begin to uncover new ideas. Even in nonfiction, the same thing happens. The form of the essay changes. I become restless. I begin to just sense the form. Either you submit to this instinct to further develop and further refine the form, or you stick to your original idea and work within certain parameters. In the case of *Crossing the River*, *The Nature of Blood*, and several other of my novels, I began to trust my instinct and submit to it. In other words, if I discover something in the journey, then I'm prepared to tear up the original template and follow to see where it leads. With the development from my first novels to the later works, the one thing I learned in that journey is not to be afraid to follow your instinct. And you must make the reader follow you. In my earlier books, I had a much more conservative sense that I must serve the reader. After that, I decided that shouldn't be the case. If my instinct tells me that I need to do something, then I follow it.

Each of your books brings its own demands and teaches us how to read them in their own way.

The British writer Margaret Drabble said to me not long ago, "The thing about reading your books is that with each book I learn how to read the next book, because you're teaching me how to read them." I knew she meant it as a compliment because she's a generous, spirited person, but it took me a while to figure out exactly what she meant. At this time last year, I was in Dublin, and Roddy Doyle was introducing me at a reading. He said, "The thing about your books is that they're not easy. Can't you make them easier for us? We want to read them before we go to sleep, but we just can't because we're not going to slide into them. Why are they so hard?" Again, it took me a while to discover what he meant. But yes, he's right. Why are they complex? Why are they so challenging?

Why, do you think?

I think it has to do with that transition that I tried to articulate earlier, realizing at a certain point that I wanted the reader to follow me. I always had a reasonably cogent idea that the books in themselves constitute a body of work. I always figured that if the reader sees the bigger picture it will become clearer. If you follow book by book, maybe they are difficult individually, but based on Drabble's point, if you manage to stumble through one, then perhaps you're not so surprised when you get to another one. From one book to the next, you begin to realize that certain conventions will be ignored and certain counter-conventions are prevalent.

The way you speak of a body of work is similar to something that David Malouf once said. He compared the arc of his body of work with the shape of a story collection.

I'm not sure that I'd make a statement as confident as David's, maybe because I'm not as far on in "the collection of short stories" as he is. What I would say is that I am reasonably sure of what the collection will look like at the end. Writers are a bit like dogs in a sense. As you go on, you stop at this tree. Then you move on and stop at another tree. You are always marking your territory, but it takes a while, if you are thinking long term, before you're actually aware of what your territory is. Again, I was lucky in that from quite early on I had a sense of the themes I was grappling with. I had a sense of territory that would recur and that I would want to cover again and again. I've always had a sense of one or two books down the line. I know where one book is leading. I'm not finishing a book and then twiddling my thumbs. I'm usually finishing and thinking, "Okay. I have a sense of what the next one will be." As far as a collection of short stories, as David Malouf has suggested, well, I'd like to think my body of work has that kind of coherence and planning, but I don't know yet.

When did you first read about Bert Williams, the Caribbean-born entertainer at the center of Dancing in the Dark?

A few weeks ago, my assistant from ten years before was in town and I gave her a copy of *Dancing in the Dark*. I said, "You *did* do research on this, didn't you?" She said, "Yes. I dug up all of this stuff for you." I laughed. She said, "I wondered what took you so long to write this novel." I said, "I had other things to do." That, actually, is quite typical of what I mean by planning.

I remember talking to somebody in 1998 about the first essay in the collection I'm writing now. I remember saying, "Listen, I'm going to write something on so and so." I sent him a draft recently, and he said, "I thought you had forgotten about it." I said, "No, no, no." It was bubbling all along.

You really do have a backlog.

Sometimes you have an idea for something, and it doesn't get to the front burner right away. Anything can happen. Somebody else can bring out a book on the same subject, or, as happened to me once, I was talking to another writer who was passionately concerned with a certain area, and I took all of my files of research on that area and handed it to him. I said, "You would be better at this than I would." It felt good that somebody else wanted to write about that character.

Are you working simultaneously on projects?

In the past, I've started something and broken off to do something else, and then come back to it. Maybe it's just a function of an addled brain. These days I try to focus on just one thing, although, for instance, when I finish this book, I know that I'm going to write a play based on

146

somebody's book. I've been working with the writer and the director. In the past, I might have tried to do a draft of it in between these essays, but now I tend to try and get one thing out of the way before moving on.

Do you think of the books in aural or visual terms?

Music has always been important to me. I hear it, and I then know how I want the narrative to move, when it should go from quiet to slightly more turbulent, and then to a moment of suspense. As a kid, I loved the straightforward pop songs of the sixties and seventies. So many of them were narratives with a beginning and middle and end. I'm thinking about people like Stevie Wonder and Marvin Gaye. Their songs all had a story to them. But I was a bit of a weirdo, as far as my teachers were concerned, because I also liked Beethoven's symphonies. One minute I would listen to Marvin Gaye and the next to the Sixth Symphony. It made no more sense to me than it did to anyone else, but in retrospect I can now see the larger movement. With the symphonies, I was learning something about pacing and movement, and in the smaller, pop songs, I was learning about how to tell a story.

That's the larger scale of structure, but how do you work on the level of the sentence?

I hear sentences completely, before I write them. That's the thing which annoys me most about reading contemporary fiction. I can't read most of it. I'm always complaining to one of my good friends, the British poet Glyn Maxwell, "Why can't people hear music in words?" He laughs and says, "Because they're not poets. They're novelists." But novelists should be able to hear music in words, too. They should be able to hear the way words flow. When they can't, it's the kind of thing that stops me reading dead in my tracks. If I come across sentences that are just clunky, then I don't really want to pursue the work. The author must have a reasonably well-attuned ear. I wouldn't say that I sit there and the words flow naturally. Sentences must be worked over. I have to go back and rework and rework, but the ultimate, driving impulse for me is, "Does it flow? Does each word move within the sentence, and then from that sentence to the next sentence with a certain elegance?" If it does, fine. If it doesn't, I need to drag the whole thing down and begin again.

Does your inability to read contemporary fiction have anything to do with your decision to write, primarily, historical fiction?

It has been an issue for me in the past because of the subject matter I was dealing with. I felt like I had to do historical repair work. It was not on people's radar. People didn't fully understand the connections my work was making, and they weren't really aware of what I felt was the contemporary resonances of understanding the way the past feeds the present. I felt obligated to write about the past. I was always trying to write about the present, too, but I had no problems refracting it deeply through the past. I feel less of an impulse to do that today because people in the past ten to fifteen years have written about contemporary relations in Britain, raising an understanding of issues that have to do with nationality and belonging. We now have a much better sense of how this is rooted in the British past. I don't feel the same necessity to do that historical repair work, which is perhaps why a novel like *A Distant Shore* has a contemporary setting. The next novel I will write is also contemporary. I wouldn't say it is over, but it's not as pressing on me. Even a novel like *Dancing in the Dark* didn't really feel historical. Obviously it did in terms of certain nuances and period research. But I always felt as though I was writing about a character who could be alive now. I felt I was writing about what it was like to live in a celebrity culture.

In that way, Dancing in the Dark *is much more of an emotional history of the time and characters than a historical novel.*

That's what I was trying to get at, I think. It's certainly not a biography, and doesn't prevent anybody from doing the nuts-and-bolts research and try to produce a more detailed and scrupulous biographical study. My novel is much more of an emotional portrait of celebrity, a man who was an exploration of the words *celebrity, notoriety, race,* and *belonging.* That, to me, seems to be the story of what happens in America time and time again. But in that sense it's all contemporary. Though many of my novels have been historical, I felt they were necessary because there wasn't anything else like them. If I was going to make whatever point I wanted to make about a contemporary world, I had to at least introduce some of the past.

As someone who writes nonfiction and fiction, did you ever consider writing a biography of Bert Williams? Do you think that we can understand his character better through the novel?

I obviously think you can understand the character better through fiction because I'm biased. That's my job. I'm not a biographer. I respect proper biographers and people who know how to immerse themselves. And there are a few people who are good at doing both. Peter Ackroyd is terrific at doing fully fleshed-out biographies and writing fiction. I don't think I have either the patience or the skill to immerse myself in a character's life without my imagination kicking in. Ackroyd came under some criticism years ago when he published his Dickens biography, because he began to imagine certain passages. I understand why he wanted to do that, but he was offending the purists, who wanted to know why they were having to deal with imaginative interludes in a biography. Well, they were having to deal with them because Ackroyd's a novelist and he can't think about a character for a long period without wanting to speculate. I suspect some of that would happen were I ever to try to write a biography, so I've just gone straight for the imaginative speculations.

How does the process unfold for you?

The internet has changed everything sporadically. Ten years ago, my assistant would have had to do a lot of legwork, interlibrary loans, photocopying. These days, it's a bit easier in terms of pulling things off the internet. The one thing that hasn't changed with research is the basic nuts and bolts of it. What would generally happen is that I would say to the person I was working with, "Bert Williams. African-American theater between 1870-1900." My assistant would get books from the library. I would look through them, though I wouldn't read them all from cover to cover. I would put Post-Its in the pages that seemed most relevant and photocopy them so that all of the books could go back to the library, and I would then have a pile of three- or four-hundred pages of photocopied material. I would read those pages and mark what was relevant. The assistant would type that material onto a disk, which I would label something like *Bert Williams* or the name of a location. In the end, I always have a file that runs between one hundred and two hundred pages. I keep that as a research bible before I start to write the novel. When I start to write, if I get stuck, I'm able to look up something—modes of transportation in New York—and I will know when the subway was dug, when the El stopped running, when cars replaced horses, things like that. All of this stimulates your imagination. If you write about Bert Williams walking through New York City, you want to know whether he would get splashed by a horse and carriage. These are minute things, but they keep my fictional mind alive because I'm able to keep fact-checking. Then other things would crop up along the way. I would have three or four questions each time I met with my assistant. I would say, "Can you find out if a gentleman would wear a frock coat in New York in the 1890s? Were there ashtrays in bars or did people flick their ashes on the floor?" Small details usually stimulate larger points. These are all backup things to sort of assist me as I write the fiction.

The language in your novels also stays close to the period about which you are writing. What kind of research does this require?

I spend a lot of time checking words to see whether they were in usage at the time I'm writing. There's one website, etymology.com, which I find very helpful. For instance, in the eighteenth-century essay I'm writing now, I describe one of the characters as having an interracial marriage. I was reading it yesterday, and I thought, I don't know if they'd have used the term *interracial*. My assistant is in Israel on holiday at the moment, so I had to go and look it up myself. It took about twenty minutes, trying to find out if that term would have been used in the late eighteenth century. In terms of the actual voice of the characters, though, that comes down to imagination. You can't research that. But in terms of the accuracy of voice, you certainly can check and double-check.

That accuracy is present in your fiction, as well.

Words betray. It's one of the things that any writing workshop will teach you. Words betray character. It's not only what a character does, it's not only what happens to that character, it's how the character expresses himself. He must have a nuance and a weight different from other characters.

Earlier, you mentioned your admiration for J. M. Coetzee's work. In a New York Review of Books *essay, Coetzee wrote about the structure and polyphony in your work "as imaginative forays into a single body of work, the history of persecution and victimization in the West." He proposes that your work has a single aim: "Remembering what the West would like to forget."*

At this stage, if I were to say what the aim of my work has been, I think it's increasingly an exploration of the meaning of *home*. That's obviously connected with what Coetzee is saying. Home is connected to persecution and memory and loss. But it can be as simple, or as vague, as loneliness or isolation. If you looked at my work toward the end of the nineties, you may have seen large historical themes played out, small lives coming into contact with large historical themes. But I think these days, either as a progression or development from that, I'm much more concerned with lives, loneliness, isolation, and grappling with the meaning of *home*, not necessarily on the grand, global scale, but often on the domestic scale. I spoke earlier of the case of Bert Williams. Here was the pure, profound loss of a man sitting at a bar in Harlem, with drink after drink, being thoroughly unmoored despite being at the center of the culture because of his celebrity. There's no great global persecution in that, but there is, I think, a preoccupation with home and loss and belonging.

You've mentioned that you have a problem with the terms loss *and* home*, noting that "Any Diaspora involves a sense of guilt and loss." Is writing a means of trying to combat or understand that loss?*

Certainly I've tried to understand what it means. I think of the modern condition at the beginning of the twenty-first century, and I see a certain displacement and cultural plurality that involves having a multiple sense of the meaning of home. I try to write about this, and not just in a contemporary sense, but historically as well. I don't know if you can combat or compensate for the loneliness, or for the sense of being unmoored, adrift and bereft, simply depressed in one's life. I don't know if reading a book, let alone writing a book, can ever repair that degree of damage.

Kevin Rabalais is co-editor of *Novel Voices* (Writer's Digest Books), conversations with award-winning American novelists.

I look at this photo, still, and I think:
that's *what I look like, that's the* me *of me.*

Thisbe Nissen is the author of the story collection *Out of the Girls' Room and Into the Night*, the novels *The Good People of New York* and *Osprey Island*, and co-author and co-collagist of *The Ex-Boyfriend Cookbook*. She's at work on a new novel, *The Screen Doors of Discretion*, and a collection, *How Other People Make Love*, in which this story will be included. A native New Yorker and graduate of Oberlin College and the Iowa Writers' Workshop, she is currently the Fanny Hurst Writer in Residence at Brandeis University.

AND THE NIGHT GOES OFF
LIKE A GUN IN A CAR

Thisbe Nissen

"He came to me last night." My mother jerks her chin at the orderly and dislodges her oxygen tube. I lean to nudge it back up her nostrils, and she grabs my blouse, pulls me close. A button pops. The woman is seventy-eight, with the grip of a barroom arm wrestler. "He's a fei-sty lit-tle rab-bit…," she sings, her shudder nearly orgasmic.

Behind me, Ken—my mother's feisty rabbit of an orderly—laughs. "You're too kind, Mrs. Russakoff." He's setting out her dinner.

"In the gable…in the…tuffet… The storm broke…" She is reliving something behind her eyes. "Lightning struck as he entered me—"

"*Mom*—"

The light glinting through the nursing-home window is the grim golden-gray of city dusk. "Oh, he was vast!" she marvels. I turn toward Ken's laughter behind me and, unfortunately, awkwardly, meet his eyes. We're both red-faced. He shakes his head. My mother paints the mental images, and we're the ones who get stuck with them, like an attic full of god-awful amateur acrylic and oil canvases we can't throw out for fear of hurting her feelings. Ken busies himself at the sink. In a world of tubby health-care workers in cartoon-print scrubs, it's just like my mother to wind up with a nursing-home orderly who might as well be a Calvin Klein model. And only my mother has the power, through mere implication, to make me feel precisely as embarrassed as if I'd just lured Nurse Ken up to a sky-lighted turret in the old wing of the Riverview Home for a squalid, rutty tryst, thunder shaking the windows, the very walls around us trembling as we climax, simultane-ously, and then crumple, spent, into each other.

My mother is—*was*—pseudonymously—Scarlett Beech, author of sixty-seven novels of wanton lust and ribald copulation. During her ten-year decline, she's stopped writing stories and tells them instead, from an ever-weirdening Alzheimer's-addled fishbowl. Which might be amusing if she didn't always manage to push buttons in such a way that her tales hit—freakishly, disturbingly—a pulse point of arousal, like the accidental brush of cloth against a nipple at just the time of month when that's all it takes to send a quiver through your pelvis, fallopian tubes fluttering like waking eyelids. Sitting at my mother's bedside I feel myself go appallingly, thrillingly wet—a warm drop, like the pop and drain of a clogged ear—as though I'm ready to be thoroughly fucked by this attractive man in scrubs fussing nervously with my mother's boiled carrots.

When my father died this spring I wanted to find a home for Mom near me, in California, but she refused to so much as discuss it. She said, "I will slit my wrists, Millicent." This was maybe six weeks ago. She wanted to stay in the apartment, on the Upper West Side, where I grew up, in Manhattan, where she'd lived her entire life. *Slit her wrists?* How was I meant to take that?

"So you're going to insist on being three thousand miles away from the place where I have a job and a life, a fiancé…?"

"Such drama, Millie!" My mother never called me Millie. "We'll have *lunch*…"

"We can't *have lunch* if you live three thousand miles away."

"Irredeemable," she said. I think.

"Did you just say 'irredeemable'?"

Distracted by something at her feet, she folded herself down to whisk at the wheelchair footrest with a spotty, swollen hand. "Damn cuttlefish! Bottom-feeders…"

"The cuttlefish are back?"

She turned her head up at me in annoyance: what the hell did I think that *was* swimming through the carpet if not cuttlefish?

"Time for a little Zyprexa?" I suggested.

"They won't let you have it."

"Let me see what I can do." I went to the kitchen for her pill.

"I do so look forward to the wedding," she said when I returned. I pushed the tablet through her lips, held her chin, lifted the glass, and tipped water in.

"Swallow," I said.

She swallowed.

"So now you're looking forward to it, huh?" I asked.

"Davey is a wonderful man." She grew moony. "So virile…very plum."

"Plump? I'm not marrying Davey, Ma. I'm marrying Kirk, Ma. Do you remember meeting Kirk?" Davey was a childhood neighbor. I last saw him when I was still in Underoos.

"Oh, it's vague…Vaguely plum. Davey's a man like your father." And then, Zyprexa be damned, the cuttlefish seemed to return, and she bent forward again, swatting. "A broom, Millicent! Something! A shovel…spoon them like…a net! Where is that net?"

"Why don't I bring Dad's fishing rod up from storage and we'll make an evening of it."

She snapped up. "Oh, Millicent…" She'd had it with me. "They're absolute shit." The ankle flicking resumed.

"Ma, you know where there's *great* fish…remember that market in Berkeley…?"

"Millicent," she said, lifting her face, eyes narrow, jaw set, "I will slit my wrists."

When my mother is fed, washed, pilled, settled, and sleeping, I head for the bus stop. The dusty sunset has mutated into another summer-evening storm: premature darkness, the streetlamps like giant shower-heads. Weather lends a humility to this city, and it's not unbecoming. The streaked neon of lightning, industrial silhouettes revealed in each flash. Also flashing—these in my mind, unbidden but hardly unpleasant—are images of furtive, urgent, lightning-bolt-lit turret sex with Nurse Ken.

And as I make my way down the wet Riverdale block—in this section of the Bronx that's hardly the Bronx, just up the Hudson from our old apartment, now sold—who's waiting under the bus-stop shelter at the nursing-home corner but Ken, who, from the look of his bumblebee shirt, is some sort of a referee as well. In the dim streetlamp light, he squints to read a drooping newspaper, and I'm sure that if forced face to face with him—if I have to see him squint like that to see who I am—I will blush instantly and say something so irredeemable as to render all future interaction too mortifying to be borne with any dignity. We may as well have already *had* our sex in the turret. And it may as well have been limply, dryly, awkwardly, shamefully terrible.

It's not *that* far to the subway… I can make it through a little summer rain. I pivot before he can look up and notice me. I could probably use a cold shower anyway.

The downtown train is a meat freezer on tracks. Sodden passengers board, and their glasses fog instantly. My blouse isn't drying so much as stiffening with cold. The safety pin I've got in place of the popped placket-button becomes an icicle between my breasts. I take a corner seat. There's a discarded *New York Post* on the floor and I fight the urge to blanket myself in its pages. It's a long ride down to the Biggerstaffs.

Kirk's folks have generously been putting me up since we closed on the sale of my parents' apartment, and though I'm appreciative, I can't say I relish the thought of an evening with Stan and Muffy. Or, as some of us prefer, Man and Stuffy. Four months from Saturday I am to wed their son, John Kirkland Biggerstaff, who I still cannot —after nearly a year of engagement—call "my fiancé." "*The* fiancé" is about as close as I get. Man and Stuffy are "the future in-laws." Kirk will inevitably be "the husband," if I can, in four months' time, train my tongue around that word. It's certainly less odious than the thought of myself as "wife," but "husband" evokes for me odd images of 4-H fairs; the warm, silty flank of a quarter horse; that fertile, loamy stink that rises from a pile of steaming, grassy horseshit. A photograph of me and Kirk will undoubtedly appear in the back pages of the *New York Times*' Sunday Styles section the weekend of our wedding. I'll be one of those brides who will "continue to use her own name," like another neo-Luddite resisting the latest update of Microsoft Word.

The subway peals into a station. I hear the doors shuttle open; my eyelids are too heavy to lift. My lashes may well be frozen together. A pounding racket of footfall sounds fast down the platform, and then I feel someone jump into the car before the doors clamber shut. There can't be a shortage of empty seats, but the new passenger doesn't seem to be taking one; I can feel the unmoving presence over me. My adrenaline rallies to potential danger, but I can barely muster the caution necessary to raise one reluctant eyelid.

And of all people in the world, who is it but Gabriel Weiselberg, wearing a ridiculous orange poncho, beaming down at me, his mouth shaped into the most pleased and private of smiles, brown eyes giddy, eyelashes dewy with rain. (And don't imagine I'm not *well* aware of the restraint required of the daughters of romance novelists with regard to the use of words such as *dewy*. My utmost discretion is always in effect with regard, as well, to *throb, thrust, moist, member, mound, manhood*.) Gabe gives his poncho-ed body a shake, like a dog coming out of the surf, then slides silently in beside me. The warmth of him is miraculous, and before either of us speaks a word I've gotten my arms wriggled up under the poncho and around his middle, where his abs, as always, are exoskeleton-hard. A survival instinct propels me toward his core heat, though this is actually where my hands always go on Gabe. His body is a body that needs to be touched. Or rather, a body that I, in his presence, cannot keep my hands off.

Gabe kisses the crown of my freezing-wet head. "When'd you get to town, pretty lady?"

My voice says, "May…"

He pulls back.

"My father died. I just put my mother into a nursing home in Riverdale…"

And his lovely weathered face opens entirely in sympathy, and then his arm is around me, pulling me back in. "Oh, Milly," he says. "You should have called. I could've helped… Why didn't you call?"

I shake my head a little, lift my shoulders as if to shrug. "You're busy," I say, "your thesis…" The truth: *You have a girlfriend, Gabe; I have a fiancé.* Gabe finished his doctoral coursework seven years ago. He may never *not* be "finishing his thesis." ABD, he jokes, means "Anything But Dissertation." I tell him that ABD is his ERA: a worthy lifelong cause. Success, per se, might remain elusive, but what peace of mind to know you've spent your life fighting the good, right fight. *Right, right*, he says, *right, peace of mind.* Gabe is, at any given moment, an alcoholic, insomniac, exercise junkie, Ritalin-popping transcendental meditator/videogame addict. He says: "I could write a fucking dissertation on peace of mind."

Now what he says is: "Aviva and I broke up."

I lift my head. He's inscrutable as always. "I'm…sorry?"

He's nodding soberly. "It was a matter of time."

"You're in the platitude stage then."

"Yeah," he says, like he hasn't quite heard, and hugs me closer. "Hey." He perks up. "Means I have an apartment to myself though…"

"I'm staying with Man and Stuffy."

"Well I wasn't suggesting you bring me *there*!"

"It might look a little funny if I didn't come home…"

"You're really going to get married, aren't you?"

Again, all I can muster is the helpless suggestion of a shrug. My wedding at this point feels inevitable as aging, as determined as the end of a book.

Gabe pouts. "And you're really going to go monogamous on me, even before that?"

"Look," I say, "it's entirely possible that I just fucked my mother's rest-home orderly in a hospital gable in the middle of a lightning storm, so I don't honestly have any *idea* what I'm doing…"

"Are you serious? You're not serious. You *are* still getting married?"

"Apparently."

"I almost feel *bad* for poor old Biggerstaff."

"Kirk's a big boy."

"So the name implies. You just want to be Millicent *Biggerstaff.*"

"I'm *not* changing my name."

"I've got it! You marry him, and take his name. Then get divorced, marry me, and I'll take *your* name!"

"All that to be Gabriel Biggerstaff?"

"All that to compensate for my tiny, tiny, ashen penis," he corrects.

I laugh.

"Now, now," he chides, "easy on the schadenfreude."

In his high-school yearbook Gabe was voted "Most Likely To Have Trouble Fitting In." The man has—and not un-seriously—contemplated abandoning his doctorate entirely to pursue a career in pornography. It may well be his true calling.

"Anyway," he says, "I think I have V.D."

Something hollows behind my ribcage. My ears and jaw go tingling numb. "*What*? *V.D*? Who says *V.D.* anymore?"

"*E.D., E.D.*," he's saying. Apparently I have misheard. "*E.D.*," he says one last time.

"*E.D.*?"

"Erectile dysfunction."

"Okay, no," I say, flat out. "Okay: the last time I saw you we had sex seven times in twelve hours. You do *not* have erectile dysfunction."

"That was *months* ago… What do you care, anyway? You're getting married…"

And all I can do is burrow closer in to him and hang on.

The train doors open. Forty-second Street. They close again.

"Where are you going anyhow?" I ask.

"Barbecue."

"Nice weather for it."

"Hey, actually—you remember Marco, from college? He was part of that whole Eighth Street scene…? Big communist…?"

"Vaguely."

"The guy we bought the pot from that time…?"

"*He's* a communist?"

"Totally. I ran into him last week. Works for them now. His fucking business cards are like: Marco Hausman, Communist Party. Come on, Mill, come with me! They might even have a washer-dryer. You could dry your clothes. There'll probably be other folks from school, maybe. Otherwise, what? You're just going home to Man and Stuffy?"

"Twist my arm."

"You know I don't like that rough stuff you're into." Gabe lifts an orange wing, points a finger to the center of my chest. "That's dangerous," he says of the safety pin over my heart.

"So's riding the subway with your breasts hanging out."

"Touché."

I mock-kick him, and miss.

"Milly, Milly, Mill, Mill, Mill," Gabe coos, and I close my eyes again until we reach Union Square.

Fourteenth Street is streaky with neon glare. We turn into a bodega and I wait up front while Gabe chooses beer from the back coolers. A wiry little leather-tan man in an undershirt is checking out at the register with a pack of Parliaments and as many pieces of Bazooka gum as he can buy with his leftover change. On the counter beside the Bazooka bin is a cardboard stand, a flyer stapled to it: *Missing* with a Xeroxed photo of Brenda "Bebe" Cleveland. DOB 3/18/60; hair: blond; eyes: hazel; height: 5' 1"; weight: 160; ID marks: tattoo of a green dancing bear on left ankle, Steal-Your-Face skull on right hip. Last seen: 5/16/05, Penn Station.

The outside door swings open then and I have to squeeze aside for a bunch of high-school boys who pour in, posturing like upper-middleclass hoods. The Bazooka-buyer looks up at the *bing-bong* of the door chime and takes me in with the sweep of his glance before he resumes counting change. I watch the candy racks, delirious, like I'm stoned, the candy packages bright and fake as props, cartoon renditions of junk food: blue-razz-fizz, all Juicy, Spree, Zing, mmmm…

"You know, that could be you," says a man's voice. I look up. It's the Bazooka buyer, unwrapping a dusty-pink chunk and feeding it into his mouth while the cashier corrals the rest of the pile into a baggie and rings up the sale.

"Excuse me?" I say. "Were you talking to…?"

He turns to Brenda Cleveland's flyer, then back to me. He wags a finger between us, me and Brenda. "Could be you, you know," he says again.

"O-kay," I say, wary, speaking like he's a child, a slow one. "I suppose it could be any of us, missing, sure…"

"No, no," he says, "look at that. Cut the hair, change the clothes, could be you, no question, for sure." He's going back and forth now, me, the photo, me, Brenda "Bebe" Cleveland.

Now the cashier's doing it too. "That for *sure* could be a picture of you."

I peer a little closer. It's hard to see much of anything on a black-and-white Xerox of a photograph. "Well, I *guess*," I say finally. "It's *not*, but..." And then this seems as dumb a thing as any to say, since it's obviously exactly what I'd say if it *were* me and I was about to get found and didn't want to be. So I'm standing there trying to figure out how to convince these men that I'm not a missing person, and of course anything I do makes me look guiltier.

When Gabe swings into the counter with a six-pack of Anchor Steam and another of PBR—"We'll go high and low brow at the same time," he's saying—the men both look like they're ready to jump and wrestle him to the ground if he tries anything funny, this guy in the orange poncho, clearly my captor. When he pays with cash—to cover his tracks, of course, leave no trace—I imagine the cashier noting the surfaces on which Gabe may have left his fingerprints. And those on which I, Bebe Cleveland, may have left mine. When we exit through the chiming door I'm ready for the SWAT team surround and ambush.

On the street I tell Gabe I've been mistaken for a short, plump, forty-five-year-old, dancing-bear-tattooed, missing Deadhead.

"Now, Milly, what have we said about flashing the tattoos to bodega clerks?"

"I do not look forty-five!"

Gabe lops one beer-laden hand over my shoulder and, half-tripping us both, pulls me to him. "Not a day over forty-four, gorgeous."

"Ow, ow, ow, ow ow ow!" There's a sharp tearing pain at my chest like I'm being stung by a swarm of bees. I try to duck away from the pain, stumbling under Gabe's arm, sending him reeling to keep his balance and save the beer. I'm swatting at my chest until I realize that's worse, like the bee is trapped there, and then I realize: the safety pin! I stop flailing, and freeze. Of course it's the pin, open, tearing my shirt, which I pinch away from my body to inspect the damage: a cluster of red-hot pricks and jagged trails like seismographic markings in my cleavage. I re-clasp the pin, fan my shirt against my skin to cool the spot.

"Oh," Gabe says, "good, right, just leave it there. I'm sure it won't open again."

"Do you have a better suggestion?"

Gabe just stares me down.

"This," I say, "is the reason why you and I cannot have a relationship."

His face spreads in a signature magnanimous grin, arm rising to take me in again. "Honey," he says, "come to Papa."

"And that," I say, snuggling in, "would be another."

Marco Hausman and his communist bride share the rooftop apart-ment of an un-renovated brownstone on 12th Street. I'm nearly grateful to mount six flights of stairs if only for the blood circulation and attendant body heat the climb stimulates. Gabe rang the bell from the street below and announced us as "Gabriel Weiselberg and long-lost surprise guest," and I wonder who Marco imagines might be climbing these steps toward his home. As we reach the final landing, a door flies open at the end of the hall and a thinner, less imposing, no-longer-dreadlocked version of Pothead Marco throws open his arms and cries, "Millicent Russakoff! My god! That's incredible—you two are *still* together!" If our lives were a novel by my mother, this is the moment when Gabe and I would look at each other and realize—At last! And before it's too late!—that we've actually been in love all these years without ever really knowing it.

Gabe laughs. "As *if!*"

"I can't believe you remember my *name*," I tell Marco.

He wraps me in an enormous hug, and doesn't answer, just pulls back as he lets go and looks at me like I'm his grandchild, and possibly also a little bit insane on top of it. He says: "Let's go find you some dry clothes." It's unclear to me if he understands that Gabe and I are not a couple.

We are pulled into the apartment, a shop-worn IKEA display room, communists sold separately. An interior door opens and a wooly-poncho-clad woman with long gray hair steps out, closing the door behind her. "Mr. Zimmerman took a shit in the middle of the floor," she announces, her skinny, bare arms flying up from beneath the poncho in a grand gesture of throwing in the towel.

"Baby," Marco coos, and then he's raising an arm that seems to span the small room and draws her to him. "Gabriel, Millicent—my bride, Letitia."

She is ten years his senior, at least, both of them beaming in-love-ness like they've been irradiated with it. Letitia takes one look at me, says, "Come," and pulls me through a throng of short, dark, spectacled Jews in threadbare suit slacks and sneakers, and into a bedroom where I am outfitted in someone's old Levi's cords cinched at the waist with a strip of Guatemalan macramé. Letitia waits while I unclasp the safety pin at my chest, then trades me my blouse for a green T-shirt from some kayaking outfit in Oahu. I tug the shirt on.

"My boyfriend-fiancé-person-type-person is a kayaker," I tell her.

"Really?" she says, with more interest than I'd expect. "Marco didn't tell me."

"Oh," I say, "there's not, I mean, I don't even know if he knows I'm… Oh! Not *Gabe*. Gabe and I aren't… He's not the—I mean, we dated in college, but we're just friends, essentially, mostly, anyway—my… the… the person I'm getting married to is someone else. In California."

"Oh, oh, oh," Letitia is saying, "I'm sorry, I just assumed, I guess…" I let her lead me back into the party. From there she points me toward a propped-open door leading onto a wooden rooftop patio. There's a free-standing tent, beneath which a man who may very well *be* Fidel Castro is flipping burgers on an enormous gas grill. A table of pot-lucky foodstuffs is suddenly the most inviting spread I've ever seen, and I start piling a plate with beet salad and couscous and something that looks like Chex Mix with peas.

"Turkey burger?" offers Fidel, and I open a bun to accept.

I have to say that I find great comfort in knowing that whatever else is going on in this horrendous war-riddled world tonight, at least one rooftop in New York City is populated with communists eating turkey burgers. Across the table I hear one person ask another, "So what have you been up to?" and the second answers, "Oh, you know, waiting for the revolution…," and I remind myself, again, to be grateful for small gifts, for little things that—even if for the briefest flash—make the world seem less irredeemably horrific.

My father is dead, my mother's sex-crazed with dementia, I'm about to marry a semi-professional kayaking dilettante for personal reasons I don't entirely understand myself, in a country being run by a war-mongering, election-stealing brat with Jesus up his ass, in a world bent on self-annihilation, and there are very few things these days that offer much solace or hope, but drinking PBR on a wet Manhattan rooftop with my sweet ex-boyfriend and a bunch of raving pinkos is one of them. Gabe and I huddle together, sharing a beer, and then another, as Marco tells us the love story of Marco and Letitia, which involves a city-council election, two feral cats, a potentially toxic waste-disposal plant, someone's irresponsible roommate named Bob, an ostensible case of mistaken identity, and Bob Dylan playing "Simple Twist of Fate" on a makeshift stage at a Triple-A ballpark somewhere in the middle of nowhere.

"Gabe says you're getting married too?" Marco asks, leadingly.

I nod, make a face I imagine to be a sort of slapstick version of terror.

"You're getting married, but you're *not* marrying Gabriel here?" Marco guesses, like we're playing charades now and I'm not allowed to speak.

I nod, miming guilt, miming shame. I have lost count of the beers; we seem to be through what we brought, drinking whatever we find in the cooler.

Gabe says, "I'm no kayaker…"

Marco is confused. He points at me—*you*—and mimes a paddle—*dip right, dip left, dip right, dip left*—*kayaker?*

I point at myself, shake my head, no. *Not me. Kirk*, I want to say, but I'm at a loss as to how to indicate him without words. I tap my heart.

"You *love* kayakers…?" Marco tries.

I shake my head again, wave away my last gesture. *Start again.* How to mime *fiancé*? I hold out my left hand where a ring would be if I were a person who'd wear such a thing. I indicate this invisible ring, the band around my fourth finger. I put an imaginary diamond on it, a rock the size of a golf ball. I try to make it shine. I admire it, hold it to my heart, smile, bat my lashes. Then I reenact Marco's paddle-mime.

"You're marrying a kayak!" Marco cries.

Hurrah! I lift my arms, hands clasped in victory.

"Um," says Marco, "and, um, why, exactly?"

"Because I love it," I declare. "And it loves me."

"And what about children?" he asks.

"None yet," I say. "But we hope to have a whole fleet someday. An armada of a family."

And then Letitia is calling Marco inside, the telephone receiver clasped in her hand: *For you,* she's mouthing.

"If you'll excuse me," says Marco, hopping to his feet in one motion like a Russian dancer. He scuttles inside.

I lean my head against Gabe's shoulder. "Why *am* I getting married, Gabe? Do you remember? I feel like I had a good reason once… I can't remember what it is. Did I ever have a good reason?"

Gabe looks at me sternly—the paternal Gabe-mode I've always had a weakness for. "Because you love him," he says. "And he loves you."

"But is that any reason to *marry*?!"

Gabe's shrug is kindly, but it's a shrug nonetheless.

"Why *do* people get married?" I ask. "I mean, *real* people. People like us. People like Marco and Letitia. People who do it for good reasons, not bad reasons."

"Do we know they did it for good reasons?"

"We're giving them the benefit of the doubt. We're *assuming* they had a good reason. Or she needed a green card. Or they did it for health insurance."

"Those are good reasons?"

"They're *understandable* reasons."

"And so what are bad reasons?"

"Okay," I say, "bad reasons to get married… One: fear of loneliness. Two: fear of future loneliness. Three: fear of dying alone."

"Four," Gabe says, "fear of fear."

"Four," I say, "to quote-unquote insure stability. Five: to please your parents. Six: to displease your parents. Seven: to have children. Eight:

to ensure that splitting up would cause an enormous legal, logistical, emotional hassle."

"That's a bad reason?" Gabe asks.

I have no response to this.

"I mean," he clarifies, "what if getting married is like getting a tattoo? You have a realization, some understanding of who you are or how the world works, or what means something, or something like that. And so you get some symbol of that emblazoned on your body so that you can't ever forget that once you knew something. Or with the idea that if a time ever comes when you regret that tattoo, you'll know that you've betrayed the person you once wanted to be…"

"What if you just realize that you were young and stupid? That the Grateful Dead weren't the answer? Or Winnie the Pooh didn't know The Way?"

"Exactly." Gabe's nodding vigorously. "Which is why there's tattoo removal. And why it's painful, and expensive, and a huge pain in the ass. Or ankle, or arm, stomach, that lower-back thing everyone's got now…"

I give him a pun-appreciating snort. "Do you know why Marco and Letitia got married?"

"Because they love each other…?"

We sit sipping our beers a minute. Then I say: "Why can't we be in love, Gabe?"

"With each other?"

I'm nodding. "It could be nice…"

"I know," he says, "I don't know." And that's enough to remind me a little bit of why I'm not in love with Gabe: the only thing he ever seems to *know* is that he doesn't know.

"We *should* be," I say. Now I feel guilty for not being in love with him.

"We could try…," he suggests, though I'm not hearing the commitment in his voice.

"I don't think it's something you can *try* at."

"I know," he admits.

"It *should* be," I say.

"It should."

When Marco returns to us, he's got fresh beers, and somehow that seems like a perfect invitation to say: "Marco, why did you and Letitia decide to get *married*, I mean, you know, like not *why each other*, but why *married*, per se?"

He's nodding at me thoughtfully, like he's heard this question before and is going to wait politely while I finish garbling out the question before he makes it all clear to me at last. "I think," he begins. "I think a few reasons. I think partly out of a crazy, intense, emotional desire to just get up there in front of everyone you know and say, *Oh my god I love this person so much I can't stand it!*, you know?"

Gabe and I nod, as if we do know, and I'm surprised we don't burst out laughing at each other right then, but it seems we're both too eager to hear what Marco has to say next.

"I think also, that it had something to do with having both been people who never did the—" he mimes air-quotes "—right thing. And this idea that there could be something radical in the act of getting married if it was people like us doing it, you know?"

Our nods are growing less nod-like by the second, but Marco seems oblivious. "Why?" he asks me. "You having jitters?" And the lack of irony in that word alone makes me feel certain that whatever Marco and Letitia's reasons were, they're not likely reasons I'd consider "good." He's lost me, and my brain switches half-off, into hibernate, as he launches into some kind of manifesto about the power of reclaiming tradition, and all I can think is: *If the* communists *are this full of shit, what hope* is *there?* And then I can imagine Kirk, looking up from one of his environmental philosophy tomes and peering at me over his glasses, saying: *And where exactly did you get the idea that it's the* communists *who are supposed to be* less *full of shit than everyone else?*

Then, on the rainy rooftop, Gabe's voice takes on that obsequious tone I can't stand, and he's asking a question like Marco's some great, all-knowing sage, and Marco—perfectly happy to play guru—is saying something about making peace with the past. Gabe would defend himself later if I were to accuse him of sycophancy. He'd say that's how you get someone like Marco to really talk: treat him like the Buddha. *He didn't seem to be having any trouble talking*, I'd reply.

"You know, I've had a lot of lovers," Marco says, and what he sounds like is one of the bodice-ripping louts from the seamy depths of my mother's oeuvre, "but then someone comes along who makes you forget the rest of them, or not forget, but just not care anymore. Someone who makes going back to the others not seem important anymore, or not even cross your mind anymore."

Gabe shoots me a look of astonishing smugness, as though every point he's ever made has just been scientifically proven right.

"Oh, so that's supposed to be the ultimate test, then? If I were *really* supposed to marry Kirk—"

Gabe's hands go up in surrender. "I'm just saying…"

"Or maybe, you're kind of working your way through these…," Marco's searching for a word, "…these *others*, so that you can make peace with the past and go on and marry your… what's his name? Kurt?"

"Kirk," Gabe and I say in unison.

"Maybe you need to make peace with, say, the Gabe part of your past before you marry Kirk?"

I think I liked Marco a lot more as an insufferable pothead. "Apparently Gabriel and I have quite a lot of peace to make." I lift my beer bottle to Gabe for a toast, and, though he clinks me, his heart's not in it. "Hey," I say, "maybe I could look up CJ Hultman and make some peace with him too before I get married…"

Gabe snorts, then sighs, exasperated. "I can't believe you're still talking about CJ Hultman."

"CJ Hultman from school?" Marco says.

"Mill spent one night with the guy in like 1980 and *still* hasn't gotten over it."

"It was 1992, thank you very much, and if what you mean by *hasn't gotten over it* is *has incredibly fond memories of what remains one of the most extraordinary sexual experiences of my short life*, then fine, yes, you're right, I haven't gotten over it."

"We'll look him up," Marco says. "We'll call him. He's back living in the Village again. I run into him all the time. We'll invite him over."

"No," I say.

"Why not?" Gabe and Marco sing back at me.

"Because."

"Come on, Mill, it'll be good for you," Gabe says. "You're exorcizing us."

"Shall I make the pun, or would you like to do the honors?" I reply.

Gabe just shakes his head.

"I think," I say, standing shakily. "I think this would be an appropriate and wise juncture for me to take a bathroom break." I plant a kiss on the top of Gabe's head, and make my way as steadily as I can manage toward the apartment door.

The bathroom, of course, is occupied. I'm second in line behind a woman who looks very, very angry. She acknowledges my existence and then allows the brooding to subsume her once again. I lean against a wall. Beside me is a little built-in telephone shelf, and below it another built-in bookshelf, on which, among other things, is a 2003 Manhattan phone book. I pick it up. Casually—which is difficult when it comes to the somewhat drunken handling a New York telephone directory—I flip through to *H*. No listing for Hultman, CJ. The bathroom door opens; it's the angry girl's turn. Christopher? Charles? No, definitely Christopher. But Christopher what? Christopher James? Christopher John? And there it is: Christopher John, Barrow Street. Before I think about it much more than that I've picked up the phone. I tell myself I'm just checking, out of curiosity, to see if it's really him. I'm expecting the machine. He won't be *home*. That possibility doesn't really cross my mind somehow, until someone's saying, "Hello?" and there's no question that it's him: that little twang of Southern drawl that once weakened my knees threatens to melt me once again.

"CJ?"

"Yep."

"Wow," I say, "hi, I, I don't think I expected you to be home."

"Who's this?" he's saying.

"Oh, I… I don't know if you'll remember me. It's been a long time. My name's Millicent Russakoff…?"

"Millicent! Hey, wow. I didn't know you were still friends with Marco."

"Marco?"

"Oh, the caller ID," he says.

"Oh, right," I say. "Yeah, wow, yeah, I just, we were just here and your name came up, I was talking to Marco, and, I don't know if you knew him, Gabriel Weiselberg? We were just talking and somehow… your name came up and Marco said, *CJ Hultman, he lives right down here. We should call him up and invite him over,* and then I came inside and there was a phone book sitting here and there was your name and I don't know why I didn't think you'd be home but…"

"Wow," says CJ. "Millicent Russakoff. It's been a *long* time…"

"Yeah," I say, and it seems pretty clear at that moment that we're both having a very acute memory of what exactly it was that transpired between us that long time ago. It involved an almost exhaustive transpiring of bodily fluids. And though it was only one night, in my memory what transpired just kept transpiring and transpiring and transpiring. There's a marked pause on the line before either of us speaks again, and when we try to it's at the same time. We laugh, try again. Finally I stay quiet—"You go," I say—and he says, "So you're at Marco's?"

My head's gone slow; it takes a second for me to remember who Marco is. "Yes! Right, yeah. Marco's…Big communist…? He used to deal, at school…? He got married, I mean, he's different than he used to be…I don't think he deals anymore. Well, I don't know…I guess maybe he might…I guess…"

"I *know* Marco," says CJ.

"Oh! Oh…"

"And Letitia."

"Yeah! Letitia!" I am a moron. "So, you should—I mean, if you're not doing anything—you should—if you wanted—you could, I mean, you *should,* come over…There're people you'd know I bet…"

"Right," CJ says, "and I do already know you and Letitia and Marco…"

"Right! Letitia and Marco," I cry, like we've just figured out we have mutual friends. I'm a disaster, absolutely flailing, but understanding that I'm tripping doesn't seem to have any relation to figuring out how to balance.

"Right…," CJ says again.

"No," I say, determined: "You should come over. It'd be great to see you. They're at—oh, wait, you probably know where they live…?"

"I know where they live," he echoes, and I must be sounding saner, because the sound of his relief is audible.

"Well, so you should come over, if you want…" I'm going for flirty, unclear as to my success.

"Well maybe I just will," says CJ Hultman.

When I hang up the phone, it's a minute before I realize the bathroom's vacant, and I remember what I was standing here for in the first place.

Marco and Gabe have regressed to lying down on the roof, looking up at the stormy sky, debating whether or not more rain's in store tonight.

"I called him," I announce.

"Who?" they say.

"CJ Hultman."

"No way!" Gabe sits up, then regrets it immediately and lies back down, and his vulnerability in that moment reawakens all my love for him. I slide down to sitting and lift his boozy head gently into my lap. "I think you're right," I say, stroking the damp hair back off his face. "It's time to deal with my unresolved issues."

"Great," Gabe mutters, and I'm sure if he could he'd get up and get away from me, but his own inebriation is holding him down with not much choice but to submit to my mothering. Gabe, lovely as he can be, has a definite tendency toward childish petulance, and he's not above a hearty pout. This is probably, in part, why we get along so well: selfish only-children galled at the other's sense of entitlement and simultaneously enthralled and reviled by the mirrors we inadvertently hold up to one another.

We stay there on the roof for a time, quiet, watching the sky. Marco extracts a pack of cigarettes from the pocket of his cargo shorts and offers them up. I take one and get it lighted for Gabe, then hold it to his lips so he can inhale. We could not, I don't think, if we tried, add up the number of cigarettes I've held for him to smoke in the last seventeen years. This is the order of my thoughts right now: 1) When my mother dies, Gabe will be the closest thing I have to family. And 2) What about Kirk?

When the raindrops start falling again—huge and heavy, like someone's taking aim and firing them down from the sky—we scurry back under the party tent, and I sneak a look in toward the apartment, and catch sight of someone, standing near the door, who might very well be CJ Hultman.

"Okay, kids," I say to Gabe and Marco. "I think my past awaits me…"

They both peer in, squinting, then give up, and stagger back to supine.

I head inside with what I hope looks like boldness, at least to the drunk or unattuned.

CJ Hultman seems somehow diminished, in the way of great homes you've known in childhood that turn out, upon re-visitation as an adult, to be relatively modest and unassuming. He looks much as I remember him looking, and yet all of these attributes strike me as shockingly un-awe-inspiring. It's very disconcerting. He's a good-looking guy, thick brown hair tramped down by the rain he got caught in on the walk over, pleasant face, average height, a little slumpy of posture, burrowing as if to hide a bit of himself in the depths of his jeans' pockets. CJ Hultman is extraordinarily *regular* looking. I'm finding myself at a loss for words. "CJ Hultman," is what I manage. I have this odd sense that our phone conversation half an hour ago never took place and he just happens to have shown up at this party by chance.

"Millicent Russakoff," he says, but the smile cracking on his face is not the smile of the man who's populated my sexual fantasy life for the last decade and a half. It's more the smile of someone who's saying to himself, *I definitely remember the name, but if I saw her on the street I'd've walked right by.*

172

"Wow," I say, "it's been a while…"

"Yeah." He smiles. Sincerely, not creepily. "Maybe since that night…?"

"You know," I say, beer-fortified, and ready to wrangle my demons. "It may not have been even the slightest bit of a big deal or of any deal at all to you, but that night blew my nineteen-year-old mind. That night was…"

It's only a momentary pause, but CJ jumps in: "I remember that night," he says, like he's defending himself against an accusation of Alzheimer's. "I think about that night sometimes, in the times when I let myself lie back and think about things like that…"

And though I'm pretty sure what that means is, *Totally, that night was hot, and I think of it sometimes when I jack off*, what I come out with in response is: "So have you been here in New York since then? Since college?"

"I got married, and we lived in North Carolina awhile," he says, "but otherwise I've been here."

"Oh," I say, so nonchalantly it's patently absurd, "you're married."

"No, not anymore. I moved back to the city when we split up." He's smiling at me in a way I can't quite read. Nervousness? Predation? Insanity?

I don't even know what it is I'm about to say in response when there's some commotion outside; the rain has started to pour down at a velocity greater than the tent can handle. I catch a glimpse of Gabe lurching toward the apartment door. "Hey," I say to CJ, "do you need a drink?" and before he can answer I've grabbed his arm and am herding him though a closed door off the main room that, by process of deduction, has to be the kitchen. I close it behind us.

Though CJ looks mildly alarmed, he almost doesn't look quite alarmed enough for someone who's arrived at a party only to be secreted away by some chick he hasn't seen in fifteen years who may as well have just admitted to harboring an obsession with him that would outlive all dogs and most cats. "Wow, it smells in here," CJ observes.

"It's cat pee," I say, defensive by proxy. "They put their cats here— Marco and Letitia—I mean, not that they're the cats, I mean Marco and Letitia must've closed their cats in here for the party. To keep them from getting out on the roof."

"Yeah?" says CJ, though it almost sounds like he hasn't heard me.

To inhale in this kitchen is like putting your nose to a jug of ammonia, or turpentine, or nail-polish remover, and drawing in deep. My eyes water. In the dim light—only the stove-hood lamp is on—CJ looks a little frightened, like he'd like to be led out of this room as passively as he was pushed into it. I open the fridge, and the brightness inside is comforting, like a safety light flashing on in the dark late at night in a part of town you don't know so well: jarring, and then a relief. There's a lot of food in the fridge—Fresh Direct boxes, and lots of bottled water—but no drinks. "I think maybe all the beer's outside in the cooler," I say, then immediately regret that I've offered him an escape hatch.

"I'd take one of those waters there," he says, and as I pull two out I feel another wave of relief. Almost enough to make up for the loss of the fridge light when I shut the door. I hand CJ a water bottle, and struggle more dramatically than necessary with the plastic safety seal on my own. The rain is pelting the roof over our heads with such force it sounds like hail.

"So," I say, "so, you were married. Wow."

"I guess..." He smiles. Toasts me a plastic, sport-capped-bottle toast.

"Can I ask you a question?" I say. "We were actually just having this whole conversation earlier tonight, about getting married. And I was asking Marco why he and Letitia got married. I don't know, I guess I'm just curious, you know? Like, why *married*? I mean, I get love, and all that, and everything, but, still, you know, why *married*?"

"Is that a question?" CJ says. "Are you asking why I got married?"

"Oh, yeah. But only if you... I mean, only if you want to answer it. I'm sorry, I'm... that's... I've had a bunch of beer... I'm being kind of censor-less, I'm sorry."

"No, no," he says, "no, that's cool." And by this he does not mean *that's hip*, but *that's okay*, and the surfer-dorkiness of it serves to temper my unease. I wait, suddenly mellow, eternally patient, for CJ's explanation as to, *drum roll, please*: Why marry?

"You know," he says, "it feels like a pretty modest reason, really." And I go jittery again, at his use of *modest*, which casts light, I feel, on his intelligence, his worth, his—*god help me!*—his viability as a mate. "I think it was really because, like, there we were, in this relationship, and we loved each other, and there wasn't any reason to break up, and it's not that getting married was the next step in some scheme of expectations, it's more like in order to get at the other things we had to do together…like there was work we had to do together, and in order to do that work we had to have gone through that stage, and taken that step, and said, *I do*, and dealt with the real, imminent possibilities of everything that culturally and historically, and, honestly, emotionally goes along with that. You know? It was like: we had to get married in order to get on with our relationship and figure out that we shouldn't be married."

I am standing with the cool water bottle pressed against the side of my face, and it's not until CJ finishes that I realize I'm giving myself an ice-cream-type headache. He stops and takes a swig from his own bottle.

"That," I say, "was honestly very possibly the single most understandable, sensical case for marriage I think I've ever heard. Hands down."

CJ lets out a *Ha!* of laughter.

"I'm serious," I say. "That actually makes sense."

"Well," he says, shrugging, waffling, looking like he wants to climb back into his own pockets, "we *are* divorced now, so I don't know how *good* a case it makes, but…"

"But you had to get married in order to get divorced in order to know what you know now, right?" I remind him.

"Well, sure, I guess if you can make yourself think that way, sure… It kind of goes assuming what I know now is worth something…"

"It's more than you knew before," I say.

"Touché," he says.

"Why are men always saying *touché* to me? Am I a confrontational person?"

CJ's eyeing me uncomfortably. "You know," he says, "could we…? Do we need to stay here?" And I wish I could claim that for even a moment I thought he might be asking me to leave with him. But this is no proposition; he's just begging for release from the cat-piss room, the desperation flooded through his face like love. It's this beseeching look that I remember, viscerally, when I see it now, again, after fifteen years—the look he gave me that night, all night long, like he couldn't believe where he was, what he was doing, and with whom, and how astounding I was, how astounding we were together. And here it is again, right there on his face as he's asking me, please, to take him away from the kitty-pee stench, and my beery head's trying to wrestle the reconciliation that this is all, absolutely all, he's asking of me, and nothing more, when there's an explosion. Lightning strikes the roof over our heads, plunges through the kitchen ceiling to rend it open like a cavernous illuminated hole through which that jagged bolt—the thunder loud enough that it appears to be shaking the lighting jagged, the idea that lightning might be a sleek-edged light-saber beam if not for the jarring of the thunder around it—shoots as though aimed to separate CJ Hultman from me once again, and this time for good, and it's another second before I understand that the room is still whole, there's just a skylight above us that the lightning's flashing through, but the blast seems to have had force enough to hurl us into each other, me and CJ Hultman, like another horrible scene in my mother's pseudo-literary imagination, because *of course* his hands are, defensively, at his chest, but as we're thrown together his hands are suddenly, *of course*, at *my* chest, brushing my nipples against the soft cotton kayak tee, and for the second time tonight it's like my pelvis drops out from under me in a little rush of wet and warm. And the crash is over then, the dim-dark back as it was, CJ Hultman's body up against mine like we've been struck and charged by that lightning, and now we're fused to each other in an embrace so forced and absurd I'd laugh if it weren't also so fucking arousing at the same time. The confusion of the moment lasts long enough for me to notice the smallness of CJ's body, how delicate it seems beside me, and I wonder if he has actually changed, if he really did used to be bigger. And because it's this night—this surreal, pinball ricochet of a night!—and I seem to have no filters or borders or boundaries left, I don't even think before I say:

"You're smaller than I remember," and CJ, without pulling himself away from me, says into my hair, "Great. Thanks," and then I'm back-pedaling, "No I don't mean…I just mean I remembered you as bigger somehow," which does nothing to ameliorate anything, only it doesn't seem to matter, because what CJ Hultman appears to be doing now is moving his hands around my back like he's going to slide them up under my shirt or down into my borrowed pants, or over the worn corduroy of the ass, pulling me into him like my body remembers him pulling me to him, him into me, and his hand is coming across the small of my back, and I'm desperate with the physical *need* for him to reach his hand down the back seam of the butt of these Levi's, to fit the back of his hand into the cleave of me, and draw me up onto him like fifteen years may have gone by but the body remembers everything, when suddenly he's letting out a cry of alarm, a shriek of fear, jumping backwards, leaping away from me like he's been stabbed by my safety pin, but I've taken it off, there is no safety pin! "What's going on?" I cry, and I'm practically trembling with fear and want and confusion, and the look on CJ Hultman's face is utter revulsion and what he's saying, I realize only gradually—he has to repeat it four or five times before I have any idea what it means—what he's saying is, "I'm terrified of corduroy."

"You're *what*?"

He's scrambling in embarrassment. "It's weird," he's saying, "I know it's weird. I always have been. It just really creeps me out. Just the whole… Agh, I can't, I really, I just can't even talk about it, or think about it, it's the texture, something, it just makes me go all…it's like nails on a chalkboard. Like that. I just can't even stand to think…"

There is, very distinctly, a man in front of me, physically reeling in repulsion, but I cannot put this together with what he's saying: corduroy. "Are you kidding?" I say. "You're kidding."

He says: "I'm not. I'm sorry, I'm really… Can we just get out of here? Could we please just…the smell's awful. I have sinus problems, I really can't breathe here. Do you mind if we…?" And then he's pushing open the door, out into the light, like Dorothy stepping into Oz, and I just stand there in the cat pee, feeling strangely reconciled, and let him go.

• • •

When Gabe has seemingly vomited everything he could possibly have to vomit into Marco and Letitia's toilet bowl, I corral him downstairs and put him in a cab home, then hail one for myself. The rain has stopped again, and the air feels warmer somehow, not muggy warm, just summery. My clothes—my own clothes—have not only been tumble-dried, but someone has replaced the button on my blouse! Sewn a new button right into place! Letitia? The communist elves? It feels like a little miracle.

It's close to midnight when I land back at Man and Stuffy's, unlocking the door bolts with the infinitesimally slow motions of a novice thief, but my caution's for naught, it turns out. As I gingerly ease open the door I hear music. There's low light coming from the archway to the living room, and I follow the muted call of operatic voices. Pausing in the arch, I'm privy to a sudden tableau of Man and Stuffy on their plush velvet sofa, Stuffy leaning into her husband, stocking feet tucked up under her skinny behind. They're both clutching fistfuls of tissues, and each other's hands as well, as if demonstrating a seated square-dance promenade, with improvised bouquet. The music is coming from the stereo speakers, at which they gaze, enraptured. Stuffy looks up as I appear, then turns away, as though ashamed. Man takes up the charge, looks to me over his wife's head, and stage-whispers in a craggy voice thick with tears, "*La Bohème*. On the radio," waving me away impatiently, imperatively, with a puff of tissues, as if to say, *I'm sorry you had to see us like this…Go, run, save yourself!* I back away, practically bowing my apologies, and retreat to Kirk's childhood bedroom-cum-guestroom.

Though I may have been sober compared to Gabe, I'm not actually sober at all; I'm keyed up and exhausted at the same time. I turn out the light, pull off my clothes, and huddle down into Kirk's teenage twin bed with its striped boy-toned sheets: navy, mustard, hunter green. If I could stop my feet from making time with the opera in the living room I feel like I might be able to fall asleep, but then the music stops and I hear Man and Stuffy shutting things down, heading off to bed, and still my feet won't stop conducting Puccini under the sheets. There's a phone on the bedside table, and I pick up the receiver and think to call Kirk, but he doesn't pick up, and I get my own voice on the outgoing recording sounding lispy and cloying, and instead of leaving a message I press seven to see if there are any voicemails. The first is from Sharon, my mother's college roommate, and I don't make it any further than that.

"Millie. Millie, it's Sharon. I'm so excited for your wedding, darling. So happy for you. That there might be a joyous event after such hardship you've been through. Since your mother won't be able to, I want to make a toast to you at your wedding, Millie. And, because it's me, you know how I express myself, in music, always, and I want to make you a toast in song." Sharon is a folksinger from before there were folksingers. The woman anticipated being a Joni Mitchell knockoff twenty years before there was such a person as Joni Mitchell *to* knock off. She married a tycoon. Never worked. Never had kids. I'm the closest thing she has to a daughter, and we're not particularly close. Except, it seems, when my life occasions a folk song… "I'm writing a song for you, for your wedding," Sharon's voicemail goes on, "and I've just finished a draft of it. I want to play it for you. I want to know if you like it, if you'll *approve* of my song to be performed, by me, at your wedding. So I'm going to sing it for you, honey, and you call me and you tell me what you think, okay? I call it 'The Song of Millie's Life, So Far.'" And then there's the knock of phone against table, and the hollow thunk of a guitar body, and a few chords, shaky and vibrato as an old lady's handwriting, and then Sharon's trembling soprano coming twinkly with static through the telephone wire, verses, choruses, and all:

I'm a girl from the city, like my mother before me
But I've left to see the world. Now I'm a California girl

My childhood was happy, I was free and on the loose
Running, jumping, laughing, playing Duck Duck Goose

As a teen I dated lots of handsome boys
But none made me happy. Not one brought me true joy

Oh the pain of youth
And the comfort of age

Thisbe Nissen

I look for answers as I grow up wise and sage

One sad day my father had a stroke and left this world
Now it's just me and Mama, Daddy's own two girls

But Mom's health's not good herself, she's declining rapidly
She's not long for this world. She cannot remember me

Oh the pain of illness
And the comfort of death
I look for answers even when I am bereft

But I've met myself a good, strong man who kayaks the oceans blue
I love him, and—what luck!—he loves me too!

So now I've found a special friend with whom I'll share my life
We'll live happily ever after. He's Kirk, and I'm his wife

Oh the pain of loneliness
And the comfort of love
I have found the answers in the arms of my true love

Oh we'll live happily ever after and have children by the score
I have Kirk and he has me—how could we ask for more?

I hang up and dial Kirk's cell phone. It takes him a while to pick up,
and when he does, he's clearly in a bar.
   "Where are you?" I say.
   "Saturn. Where are you?" It's a lounge. The Saturn Lounge.
   "Your folks'."
   "How *are* Man and Stuffy?"
   "They're awake!" I marvel. "It's midnight, and they're in the living
room, weeping over *La Bohème* on the radio."
   "Sweet Jesus," says Kirk. Then he says, "Did you—?" but at the same
time I know exactly what he's asking so I'm answering already.
   "I just did."
   "We can't have a wedding," he says.
   "I know," I say. Then I say: "Why were we having a wedding in the
first place?"

Kirk says: "I don't know. A party seemed like a nice idea … But seriously, Mill: now? What's the point? Your father's gone. Your mother won't know the difference between being at our wedding or being on the QE2. I'd honestly do just about anything to avoid sharing a meal with my parents, let alone standing at the feet of some justice with them hovering over my shoulder telling me not to slouch…"

"Why are we getting married?" I say.

"Mill," he says, "if you don't want to get married we don't have to get married." And, god, his patience is astounding. He says: "I've said this before and I'll say it again if you need to hear it again. The way I feel about you is, I think, the way people who get married feel, but whether we actually get married or not doesn't really make that much of a difference to me…"

"I know," I say, "I know."

"Okay," Kirk says, "but easy as I am, I'm putting my foot down somewhere, and I am not, never, ever, going to get married in any kind of ceremony or reception or anything where Sharon sings that song. Or any song. Baby, I love you. But I am not marrying you in any anything where that woman sings, *He's Kirk and I'm his wife*, okay? I mean, I draw the line somewhere, okay? That's where I draw the line."

I don't even realize I'm crying until I try to say something and all that comes out is a heave.

"Mill?"

I gulp some air. "We could go to Vegas…?"

There's a second, and I know he's thinking, plotting. Then he says: "Does that mean call in the morning and start trying to cancel things?"

"Will you still marry me anyway?" I say.

There's another long pause, and I'm not sure if I breathe during it or not, but finally Kirk answers, and the magnitude of my relief is, I'm sure, testament to something.

I don't claim to understand a thing more about it than I ever did, but for what it's worth: Reader, I married him. What happens next remains to be seen.

When I get down, I have to take a cue from this girl.

Anasuya Krishnaswamy was born and raised in the San Francisco Bay Area and considers herself a Northern Californian. Her interests include the granola-like activities that you would expect from a Northern California girl: hiking, yoga, and left-wing politics, among other things. Her favorite comfort foods growing up were macaroni and cheese and masala dosa. They still are.

NOTRE BIEN AIMEE

Anasuya Krishnaswamy

Three days before Safa leaves for Senegal, they are shopping. Devi reads the sign outside the door; it advertises "cage-free chickens, live lambs, muttons, sheeps, live cattle, beef hamburgers, fruit jams, and meat and bone meal," among other things. When they step through the door, Devi smells spices, not the sweet-and-sour smell of raw meat that she expects. First she gets a whiff of cumin, then, as the door closes behind them, the odor becomes a blend, and she can make out turmeric and thyme. The workers wear long white coats, with Nehru collars and gray skullcaps. She wanders around reading the signs and staring at the different cuts of meat. The cow's feet, with fur still intact, make her stare in fascination and revulsion at the same time.

Devi has never been to a butcher shop in her life, let alone a Halal market. She ate her first meat when she secretly tasted a piece of beef jerky from a friend in her Portland high school. Eventually she tried all sorts of meat, but she still doesn't admit this to her Brahmin parents. What you will be noshing between your teeth is more transparent at the Halal shop than at the supermarket. There aren't any pseudonyms for the anatomy of the animals. You can just point to a chart. The sight of any carnage or organs or innards disgusts Devi. That is why she studies the small stuff distilled into pipettes and test tubes and beakers.

Devi watches Safa stride up to the counter. Her long, Western, pink sweater covers a full, Western, beige skirt that hides her substantial and curvy figure. She greets the butcher in French and Arabic. "*Ça va?*

Assalaam aleikom." She looks over the selection of chicken thighs and breasts, pointing out to the butcher the ones she wants. There will be another stop at the fish market where Safa will be just as selective when she picks out the fresh sockeye salmon. In July, the king have already had their run and the coho won't yet have begun.

The week before Devi had taken Safa to the hospital because of the pain.

Devi pulled up directly to the entrance of the beige three-story medical clinic. She didn't see anyone who could help her, so she pulled Safa out of the car. Devi walked with her arm around Safa's midsection, while Safa draped her arm over Devi's shoulder, until they reached a bench right inside the entrance where Safa could sit. Then she jumped back into the car, pulled into a spot in the first row of parking, and jogged back to the clinic doors where Safa was lying motionless on the bench.

"I'm dizzy," Safa reached out for her. "Dizzy and nauseous."

Devi held her hand and rubbed her arm. Still no one around, and Safa seemed to want her close by, which meant she couldn't go searching for help. In that moment, she wished she could bench three hundred pounds, so she could pick her friend up and carry her inside.

"I just need a minute to rest," Safa said. Devi considered this option with skepticism, and then a nurse appeared in the entrance area.

"How are we doing? Do we need a wheelchair?"

While they examined Safa, Devi surveyed the assortment of used and outdated magazines. She picked up a fashion magazine and flipped through the perfumed pages, looking at the models. Aside from their skinny bodies, there was something alike about all of the faces. She wondered, if you drew lines between the centers of their foreheads to their cheekbones, noses, and chins, would the shapes be identical? She looked at the couple in front of her. Old, dark skinned, perhaps farm workers. Both tired. She had just brought him some coffee. Which one was sick? Then Devi saw purple oval patches on the woman's arms where an unskilled nurse had not been able to find a vein.

This was always the problem they had with Safa, until they fixed a more permanent attachment into her arm, so they could conveniently hook up an I.V., a chemo line. Devi had gone once with her to the treatment. She tried not to stare at the other patients while Safa asked about their families, and made them laugh. Devi's stomach became queasy even before the nurse started describing her responsibilities, which included helping Safa to vomit into the "receptacle." It turned out that day that Safa didn't need to throw up. But when another patient did, Devi found *herself* bending over the receptacle.

To her right in the waiting room, Devi glanced at an old man with his daughter. Clearly he was the one. He read an article in a magazine and muttered to his daughter every few seconds. When he turned to mutter, Devi saw his sunken cheeks. The daughter's expression—no smile, no frown, vacant eyes—never changed. Two more older couples sat to her left. Safa was too young for this. Then behind her she heard a child's voice, a conversation between a mother and son who came out from the exam rooms. "Now ice cream in the park." The boy had been bribed before his lab tests. The ice cream, the park, the present were his focus, and he didn't seem afraid. Devi envied him.

She remembered other times she'd been afraid. The time she broke her collarbone, and she couldn't move her body without it hurting. The time her father went on his first business trip and flew away without her. The time she and Mark got lost in the wilderness in a late snowstorm. In all those situations she found the action needed or the patience to wait it out.

When she turned back around, Mandy was wheeling Safa out from the back.

"She's ready to go home and rest after you stop at the pharmacy."

For weeks, the doctors had seemed to bumble through, unable to pinpoint the problem. Devi asked them both, "Do you know what's wrong?"

"They're not certain," Safa said. "They have another medicine for the pain and something for the nausea. Last time they found my white-blood-cell count very increased, so they think I maybe have an infection. How do you call it?"

"Pleurisy?"

"Yes."

"What exactly is that?" Devi asked.

The nurse said, "The pleura is infected. It's near the lung."

"I cannot have an infection and receive the treatments," Safa said.

H & K Meats (Halal and Kosher Meats) is the place where Safa can get meats from animals that are raised and slaughtered in the permitted way—raised cleanly and humanely, prayer said before slaughter, neck sliced with a sharp knife, carcasses bled out quickly to drain out disease and impurities. Some say it takes less than a minute for the animal to die. Devi remembers that Safa was not so particular when she first came to Oregon from Senegal four years before. Now she wears the head covering all the time. Three and a half years ago, after the first round of chemo, she covered her bare head with a variety of things from solid colored cotton pieces tied like an American hippie would wear a bandana, to some of her fancy head wraps from home. Then her woolly hair grew back and she wove it into long braids. Now she prays five times a day. She has purchased a special prayer rug. Devi went with her on two day-trips to Portland to find it. Now she will not buy chicken even from the local co-op that advertises organic free range, because the rest of the permitted way has been neglected.

They are planning for a Fourth of July party and Safa has decided they will make yassa poulet. In the car on the way back from the shopping she calls out a list of things left to get and menu items.

"Lemons for the chicken. Spicy fish and rice. Special couscous…"

These aren't questions and require no responses. To play, Devi can add a list item if she wants, or ask a question about the dish or the French or Wolof words that Safa uses.

"That's the one with the dark millet?" Devi asks.

"Yes. Bissap juice. Ginger juice for Massamba. Salad…"

"Will you make your to-die-for mustard dressing?"

"Yes." Safa laughs. "Americans like to die for strange things."

They cruise down I-5 in Mark's Jeep passing Mt. Jefferson off to the east. Looking at the steep faces, curling ridges, and wide base usually makes the organs in Devi's core vibrate. But today there is a pressure keeping them jailed in stillness.

"Have you and Mark climbed this one?" Safa asks from the passenger seat.

"Not yet," Devi says. All plans have been on hold. "We're fighting."

"*De que?*"

"Yesterday it was whether or not the fan needs to be on in the bathroom."

"Eh?" Safa turns to look at Devi, seeming to study the side of her face for a minute. "Why?"

"At the end, I wonder what it was really about, you know?"

"He is afraid you will leave him."

"I've never said anything like that."

"But you might leave," Safa says.

"Maybe I'm afraid he'll leave me."

"You are not afraid of that." Safa undoes her headscarf, which has slid forward too far, and re-wraps it. "Why don't you want to get married, Devi?"

Devi has to slow for a logging truck laden with Doug firs, then she changes lanes and speeds up to pass. The vents are open and she can smell the woodsy pepper and vanilla coming off the fresh bark. She thinks of the summer she first started her lab internship, before she met Mark and said hello to his dimple and his green eyes. If only it had happened sooner, before she met a married staff researcher in the lab who befriended her. Their breaks turned into long walks and lunches and eventually sex. It wasn't something she ever imagined herself doing. The fact that Devi's parents have been married so long, she feels, is more the result of a cultural pressure, from a culture 13,000 miles away.

"You and Massamba seem to make it work," Devi says.

"Yes. But there has been forgiveness."

"For what?"

"He was gone, in the states, so long," Safa says.

"He picked up a girlfriend?"

"As much as I didn't like it, I was not so surprised." Safa shifts to face Devi, and leans her shoulder against the back of the car seat. "It's what *I* did. I, how do you say? I shook him."

"You shook him?"

"He asked his good friend to take care of me." Safa twists back and sinks into her seat. "And I came to rely on him, and we were living everyday like *we* were married. He stayed in my parent's house, we would go for the shopping together; when Massamba wasn't there for some ceremony or duty, he would fill in." Safa pauses and looks east again at Mt. Jefferson. "You have not climbed that one?"

"What else happened?" Devi asks.

"After I had the diagnosis." Safa turns her head away from the window and picks lint from her skirt. She puts the pieces into the palm of her hand and stares at them. "He came into my room one night. And I didn't turn him... *comment dites-vous?*"

"Away. You didn't turn him away. And, '*It* shook Massamba.'"

"Yes. It shook Massamba."

The road narrows to one lane and winds through some construction barriers, and Devi slows to a pace that Mark's Jeep can handle through the curves. Safa rests her head back against the seat and stares straight ahead.

"You needed someone," Devi says. "Sometimes we just need a physical someone."

Safa is quiet for a while before she says, "Tell me how you do it. How you climb that mountain." She tilts her head in the direction of Mt. Jefferson.

"You mean the route?"

"The whole, how do you say, expedition?"

"It's not like the Himalayas." Devi laughs. "It's more like a two- or three-day trip."

Safa shouts, "Two days! For something that looks so frightening?" Safa pulls the edges of her sweater together. "I never knew why you would want to get so cold."

Devi imagines a foray into the wilderness: scrambling up scree slopes, bouldering over a rocky outcropping, taking in vistas of dormant volcanoes with their rugged couloirs, cliffs, and crevasses, smelling the pungent sulfur vents and tasting the crisp, clean, air. Her range is the Southern Cascades; the magnificent slumbering presence belies the violent history, until a Mt. St. Helens reveals her hidden secrets. Devi has read about the volcanoes of the Pacific Rim, and climbed many of them. When she puts her hands and feet on the volcano, she can sense the power that nature has to tear down and re-create over time, or in some cases in a few minutes, and this is what brings her back out into the wilderness again and again.

"The views, the sounds, the smells. And a feeling. You can't get those exact ones anywhere else."

"Tell me how you do it, what it is like."

"The route along the south ridge is easiest," Devi says. "You have to pack in all your gear and food. The first camp is five miles in, which in the snow with a full backpack can be quite a slog."

"Slog?"

"Long, hard hike."

Safa nods. Her scarf has slid to the side, and she removes it. Devi notes the features of Safa's face—the curve of her forehead sloping into the bridge of her nose, the roundness of her nostrils, the broadness of her lips. These things have persisted through the rounds of treatment, but Devi sees them sliding, like a lost ice axe, down a hard frozen slope.

"Tell me what you are wearing," Safa says.

"Fleece underwear. A second thicker layer of fleece. Rainproof pants or a bib."

"Bib?"

"Like overalls."

"Ah, *qui*."

"A down jacket."

"Down?"

"Feather."

"What else?" Safa's eyes are closed and she touches the parts of her body where the clothing would be.

"Thick wool socks inside thick plastic boots with an insulated lining. Some people wear leather boots."

"You must wear the crampon, no?"

"Yes. Or if there is a lot of snow, you can wear snowshoes, or even ski."

"Ski? It is beautiful."

"But we don't ski."

Eyes still closed, she pats the car seat. "The snow is soft?"

"In places, yes. On the glaciers it is icy."

"You have the pick, to help you?"

"Yes, an ice axe."

"What does the snow taste like?" Safa leans her head back and swallows.

"It's like ice, but a very fresh taste on the mountain. Sometimes it tastes like pine, if it's fallen or blown off a tree."

"You smell the trees, the other plants?"

"Mostly fir and pine below tree line. Then it's mostly rock and ice."

"What does the rock taste like?" Safa giggles. "I know you tasted it."

"Chalky."

"The rock is solid." Safa pats her legs. Her legs are still substantial. Her body, beaten up over time, in constant pain, has not withered away.

"Sometimes the rocks move, or there is a slope of loose gravel that washes down—a little more each year."

"Your body. After the first day, how does it feel?"

"A good relaxed tired. Unless you get blisters. Then you have a constant burn in places on your feet."

"Oooh! But the next day. Your body is stiff?"

"Maybe a little in the morning. But then you start moving and everything warms up. Everything becomes loose. You feel very free."

Safa bends her head slightly to one side. "And at night. What do you hear?"

Devi tries to remember the sounds without closing her eyes. "Sometimes some birds. But mostly wind—whirling the snow around, beating against the rock, whapping the tent."

"You can sleep?"

"I need earplugs."

Safa sits upright and crosses her arms. "So you go up and up, and then you come near the top and you reach and you feel very, very happy?"

"Yes, happy. Exhilarated. Excitement and joy."

As they head farther south, Safa looks west across grass fields and grazing sheep toward the coastal range.

"Your body on the way down. It is stiff?"

"Not yet. You are still loose, maybe running on adrenaline." Devi notices the thing she does after a while, when talking to Safa—she stops making contractions.

"Ah, *qui*. The next day, after you sleep in your bed at home, and wake up. Then you are stiff."

"Exactly."

"That is when you complain to me. 'Safietou, my legs are so sore, I can not go for a walk around the neighborhood!' And I am always thinking, Eh? What happened?" Safa shakes her head and chuckles.

The week before, they had gone to the hospital instead of their usual walk. The pain had been in Safa's side for months: it waxed and waned but never left, it migrated from one place to another through another round of treatment, a pain that started while she was pregnant with Amina more than two years ago. They had hoped the pain in her back was due to the separation of the bones that occurs during pregnancy, but it wasn't. Instead, while Amina was growing, so was the cancer, and Safa's health was drooping like the mint plant on her balcony she always forgot to water.

Right before their exit they pass the last grass fields, raised for the seeds that grow the perfect lawns. Now Safa's chuckle has turned into a laugh, rising from a deeper place, the same infectious laugh that she arrived with four years before—the thing Devi understood before they shared a common language. After she catches a few sideways peeks at Safa, Devi realizes that her own mouth is stretched into a smile and the pressure in her chest has eased up.

"Mint," Safa says. "Massamba will brew the tea. Raphael will barbecue."

When they get back to the apartment, Devi sends Safa in and unloads the car by herself. In the kitchen Devi re-examines the pictures Safa has stuck to the refrigerator—Amina in the hospital held in the crook of Massamba's arm, Amina at the crawling stage opening the drawer of pots and pans in the kitchen, Fatima's most recent school picture—Devi remembers that mother and daughter fought over whether Fatima should wear a Senegalese outfit—Fatima at her first rollerblade lesson, decked out in helmet and pads. One picture is of whole seashells lacing a sandy beach on an island near St. Louis in northern Senegal. Devi would like to visit that place, see the land and water that cradled Safa's childhood. She sets the bags in a row next to the toaster oven that a friend from the mosque gave her, the blender that Raphael and Laura gave her, and the Cuisinart that Massamba bought her for a birthday. As Devi is setting the last bag down in the kitchen, she wonders where Safa has gone, and crooks her head around the corner to the bedroom. She sees Safa in the dark in all-out supplication on her prayer rug. Devi knows she has been attending the mosque more often. She recalls a four-year-old late-night discussion over coffee at the local beanery. Polygamy was the topic, allowed in Senegal for the man. Safa said, "It should be for both the woman and the man. I may be from a patriarchy, but *je suis une femme moderne.*"

Devi thinks the patriarchy of Western medicine has had its run with this modern woman. Devi knows all the ways they find new drugs, all the ways they test them in the lab. Her dissertation is full of examples, organized and well written, sitting in a black binding on her bookshelf.

When Safa comes back into the kitchen, she tells Devi, "I prayed for you and Mark, so you can relax."

"It's gonna take more than a prayer," Devi says, and then realizes she has just condemned Safa by extension. "I mean for Mark and me. It's gonna take more than a prayer for Mark and me."

"You, how do you say, *tu minores?*"

"Minimize?"

"Yes, something like that, or *sous-estimons?*"

"Estimate?"

"When it is bigger than you think it will be."

"Oh, underestimate?"

"Yes. Underestimate. You underestimate, Devi."

Two days before Safa leaves for Senegal, they are dancing. Devi and Mark arrive early to find Massamba sleeping on the couch with Fatima curled up next to him. Massamba's seriousness, usually held in the furrows along his forehead or the set of his jaw, are absent as he sleeps. Father and daughter are undisturbed by the eighty-decibel background noise of a CNN World Report. Devi smells the lemon juice, already squeezed for the marinade, and ginger, already shredded for the juice. Safa has covered the dining table with a white cloth and the clutter has been gathered and stored somewhere else. A large quilt is draped across the chairs. It is the one she has been making for Fatima. The dark-red, green, and white floral patterns radiate from the center, and one corner is left to complete—some pieces pinned in place and others still missing. Safa and Colette, a friend from Benin, stand in the kitchen. Colette's bright yellow head wrap replicates the crown of the moon goddess of the Fon people of Benin. She says something soothing to Safa—half French, half Wolof. They are putting the fish and chicken into big bowls to marinate.

Colette tells them that Fatima is grounded because she misbehaved in school—too much talking again. Safa says, "I don't understand that child." She minces up the garlic by holding one end of the clove, punching a crisscross pattern on the top, and then slicing through it with a knife so all the little pieces fall neatly into the bowl. "Fatima keeps talking and talking. Do you remember when we asked her why and she said that she must have swallowed a boom box?"

Their laughter is interrupted by the arrival of Raphael, Laura, and their daughter, Isabel. Isabel is small for her age, and quiet, with ruby cheeks that hint at her spunkiness. Raphael and Laura are the same height, and fit from all their dancing. At the moment her hair is cropped shorter than his, and as she tells him where to put the supplies, he teases her about who wears the pants in the family. They have brought all the fixings to barbecue Argentinian style, and all the CDs needed to complement Massamba's stash and lend endurance to the party. Raphael shuffles through the CDs, and slides salsa music into the CD player, and Massamba, Laura, and Isabel start dancing. Devi helps Colette and Safa in the kitchen, and they all move to the salsa music as they chop and stir and mix.

When Fatima offers to help her mother mix up the ginger juice, Safa eyes her daughter, tosses the grated ginger shreds into a pitcher, hands it to Fatima, asks her to fill it with water, and "make sure to put the lid on" before carrying it to the table. Fatima is in a hurry to finish, so she can join the dancing that has begun. She forgets the lid. The white beads in her braids click together as she rushes over to the table, and right before she reaches it, her elbow bangs into one of the chairs, tilting the pitcher to one side and sending most of the ginger and water onto the carpet and patio door.

"Fati*mata!*"

Safa's falsetto bounces off the walls, suspending the dancing. Fatima's entire body holds still; frozen like a Rodin in the exact position she occupied just before the Ginger Juice Disaster. The only motion comes from two tears, one leading the other down her face.

Mark puts a hand on Safa's shoulder and says, "Who wants to go to the store with me to get more ginger?"

"Me!" Isabel and Fatima volunteer in unison. Safa does not bring up the grounding, and Mark grabs them around the waist and lumbers out to the car, one giggly, screaming girl in each arm.

Raphael turns up the music and goes out to set up his barbecue, and the women gather back in the kitchen. Safa sighs, "She doesn't slow down. She's wild. I don't know what's going to happen to her." Colette clucks something, in French only. Safa responds, "If she were in Senegal, one slip to an elder and she would get a good whacking."

Devi likes how free-spirited Fatima is. Her willfulness, Devi hopes, is the sign of a strong, independent woman to be. Respect for elders is one thing, but being a servant to their every whim is another. She thinks Fatima is more American now than Senegalese. Devi is more worried about who will buy Fatima her first bra or hand her the first maxi pad. Who will tell her stories of her grandmother and who will braid her hair without making her cry out in pain?

When Mark returns with the children, the meal is cooking, everyone has a drink of some kind, Raphael replaces the salsa with a merengue, and Amina, the most natural dancer of them all, bebops vigorously on her two-year-old legs. By nine o'clock the other guests arrive, dinner is ready, and Safa spreads out a tablecloth on the floor. She chooses the one that Mark and Devi have given her, a Moroccan design elaborately embroidered in silky maroon and orange threads.

She puts the large serving dishes in the middle with an ample supply of spoons, and they eat Senegalese style, everyone gathering around the serving dishes and eating directly out of them, keeping their portions of food carefully separate from the others. Devi remembers the first time she ate this way and how cramped she felt. Now she is used to the close quarters. Now she has become a little bit Senegalese, and it has happily worn into her.

After the food settles, Massamba changes the music to Baaba Maal, and a combination of West African, funk, and reggae rhythms punctuate the air. The voices of the singers, the talking drums, and the hair strings of the *hoddus* combine with the keyboards, horns, and electric guitars of Baaba Maal's generation, coaxing people onto their feet. The dancing begins again. Hops and stomps and bumps. Hips swinging in twirls and spins. Mark whirls Fatima and Amina around. Devi comes out of a solo pirouette and Raphael grabs her hand and swings her into a merengue step. Even though he's from Argentina, he prefers a merengue to a tango. The tune doesn't matter, as long as the drums beat the right rhythm.

As he leads Devi around the living room, she catches a glimpse of Safa curled up on the couch, her usual perch. Safa isn't the most fervent dancer of the group, and she often sits watching or clapping, sometimes playing Raphael's hand drum. Devi wonders if she danced more in Senegal before she got sick and came to the states for treatment. She is smiling, and Devi follows her eyes to Massamba dancing with both his daughters. Devi breaks away from Raphael and heads to the couch. She holds out her hand to Safa, who refuses it with a tilt of her head. "Too tired?" Devi says.

"A little. I like watching."

Raphael merengues solo over to Safa. "You can't let me go on by myself, Safa. I'll look crazy."

She laughs, "You *are* crazy, Raphael," but declines with a wave of her hand.

Devi says, "Please, Safa." And then, "If you're well enough to cook, you're well enough to dance a little."

It comes out all wrong, as if she is scolding a six year old who doesn't want to go to school. Safa's face clouds, and she turns her head to the side, so Devi can't see her eyes. Devi feels her stomach sink back into her kidneys. Massamba sidles over toward the mini-congregation; Safa begins to giggle. He has his hands carefully set on his hips and stomps and lifts his feet in perfect time with the complex rhythms, twisting suggestively as he approaches Safa. Now her face turns serious. She unfolds her legs, rises from the couch in a graceful sweep, and joins Massamba in the dance.

Devi feels weak from relief, but Raphael's hands clasp hers and steady her, and by the end of the set she is exhausted and flops onto the couch. Soon Massamba will start the tea brewing and the dancing will go on until early the next morning. She hears the first notes of the next song, sees Safa motion to her from across the room, and her heart drags her protesting body back into the middle of the revelers.

The day before Safa leaves for Senegal, they are buying gifts for Safa's friends and family in Senegal. Everyone says that the family will visit and return before Fatima must start school, and Safa will start her next round of treatments. Everyone repeats this, in these words or their own, adding a dollop of hope, repeating the mantra, trying to churn a lie into the truth.

Safa looks over the lip glosses and eye shadows, telling Devi which colors might look good on one friend but not on another. Devi reads the names of the colors: burgundy, cabernet, cocoa, cayenne, mango, golden brown. The eye shadow: banana, blond, bone, camel, desert, nude.

Safa holds a lipstick up to Devi's lips. "My cousin, she is lighter, slightly lighter than you."

Every time Devi looks at Safa now she can't believe how dull and ashen her West African skin has become, how her eyes have receded and dimmed, how her cheeks take on a prominence that is unexpected, and uncomplimentary.

Safa's arrival, on a cold and rainy October weekend four years before, lit up the gray Oregon day. Her dark caramel skin was shiny and supple. She walked upright, with a slow, serene step, wearing her West African boubou and head wrap, a brilliant purple with complex gold weaves and textures. No sign that she was ill. She spoke little English, but melodic French. "Better French than the French," is what she would say later on, when she learned English.

"What do you think for the eyes?" Safa asks Devi. She motions to her to sit in the tall chair by the vanity mirror and opens a sample.

Tomorrow she will fly to Senegal, and Devi imagines that she will stop speaking English when, or perhaps before, she lands. At first she will "make parties" with her friends. The heat—how had Safa described it? Take the hottest day in the summer in Oregon, soak a blanket in water at the same temperature, and keep it wrapped around you all day. A constant sauna dress. She will wear her sauna dress and go visiting the people and places she has missed over the last four years, that made up her life before, and that made up her.

Then she will deteriorate, because her immune system will be too weak to fight off disease, and she will die in Senegal, in the hospital, with her family, the blood relatives, around her.

Safa whisks the brush back and forth and says, "Close." Devi closes her eyelids and Safa brushes and dabs over one eye. "Camel," she says.

Her mother, sister, and women friends will bathe and wrap her for the burial.

Her father, husband, and brothers will dig the grave and lay the casket into it.

Her body will finish disintegrating underneath a headstone that says, *Notre Bien Aimee*. Our Well-Loved One.

Devi opens her eyes and Safa says, "No. Keep closed."

For three days, according to custom, the mourning will continue.

Safa brushes and dabs over the other eye. "Desert," she says. "Now open. What do you think?"

Devi thinks of the mountains: slogging through an approach, riding their exteriors, sensing their interiors, sitting on their summits. She has negotiated long, soft ridges, open bowls, and narrow gaps. Icy flows and powdery piles. Some part of every mountain stays with her—implants a sound, a smell, a color, a line, an arc, a form, a spirit. When Devi encounters a mountain, she knows how to greet her, take what she gives, and go on.

*Even at an early age I had this hunger to document. Almost
everything that mattered was already at hand: a bowl of browning
bananas, my sister's refusal to eat one, the winter sky beyond the
window just starting to offer up snow. Lamentably, it would take me
another fifteen years to realize that my lens was actually a keg cup.*

Garth Risk Hallberg holds an MFA from New York University. His stories have appeared or are forthcoming in *Canteen, h2so4, Evergreen Review, Em,* and *Best New American Voices 2008.* Mark Batty Publisher brought out his illustrated novella, *A Field Guide to the North American Family,* earlier this year. Please visit www.afieldguide .com.

JUBILEE

Garth Risk Hallberg

Nothing stayed new for long there. Take, for example, the pizza franchise that opened in Jerusalem when I was twelve. My father and I had flown over that summer to bury my grandfather's second wife—the only grandmother I'd known—and I remember passing it on the way from the airport to the southern suburb where my grandfather lived. Plastic pennants beckoned from the far side of the taxicab window. The red, white, and green awning promised a slice tolerably like the ones back home. My father told me he'd bring me back later in the week if I managed to behave myself during the shiva. I'm not sure if he forgot about it, or if, more likely, I somehow failed to live up to my end of the deal, but we didn't end up going to the pizzeria. Eight years later, when we passed the site again en route to my grandfather's seventy-fifth birthday party, rubble was all that remained.

I might not even have noticed it if my father hadn't pointed it out. "Animals," he said. I knew my liberal brother, David, would bristle at this. I monitored his profile for his secret anger signs—the slight tightening of his lips, the red flush in his ears. In his lap, his right hand wrestled with his left, where, the next time I saw him, his wedding band would be. We'd both learned, however, that you can't win an argument with my father, who was always on edge before seeing his own brothers, and David remained quiet in the seat behind my mom as the sun-bleached streets rolled by.

In the late-model rental car, that silence felt, in its own way, ancient.

Even the shopping malls we passed looked somehow medieval, their high walls windowless, their access roads snaking like moats. Over there, fortifications and checkpoints and soldiers were as ubiquitous as dust and heat. It all wore away at everything, so that whatever landmarks, people, and conflicts were hardy enough to last seemed like monuments—though to what, I couldn't quite figure out.

For fifty years my grandfather, prematurely weathered by the war that took his parents, had been clinging to the land of our ancestors like a tree. In family photographs taken just after his arrival, at age twenty-five, he looks like my brother: thin, nearly unto invisibility. But surrounded by sun and wind and sand, and the Arabs, he had laid away a hundred pounds of gut and haunch. He had laid the foundations for three houses, two marriages, six sons, and a daughter, now deceased.

I remember marveling, as a kid, at his appetite, watching in wonder as he grunted his way through five meals a day. He combined the customs of his native Poland with those of London, where he'd ridden out the war: he took a cooked breakfast, brunch, dinner, tea, and supper. I remember seeing him eat a dozen hard-boiled eggs during the *seudat havra'ah* after my grandmother died. At first, watching those white orbs disappear one by one into his silent mouth, I thought it was a sign of grief, like the way the Irish in movies drank too much at wakes. But later, around midnight, I heard him tromping barefoot past the room where I was sleeping and into the kitchen, to eat again. Just in case there was no food the next day, I guess. Maybe the hunger that overtakes you during wartime never really goes away. We could never afford airfare to Israel for the high holidays, so I don't know how he survived Passover.

He was holding court in his wheelchair when we got to the house. Aunts and uncles and cousins had formed a kind of receiving line at that end of the yard. In the space between them and us, a half-dozen tables gleamed, wedding-dress white. I'd left my glasses in the car, and only when I approached the makeshift bar to fetch drinks for my mother and father could I see the fine shroud of dust that had settled into the linens. I poured two glasses of sweet red wine and then waited dutifully for my parents to pay their respects before I greeted my grandfather. David was somewhere behind me. A cousin had waylaid him. I could hear her congratulating him loudly on his engagement.

"Hello, young man," my grandfather said, looking me over.

"Hello, Grandfather. It's Josh."

"Joshua. I know." Although I knew he hadn't remembered my name, his eyes, deep in their sockets, weren't misty or confused like Sasta's had been, toward the end, but hard and coal-black, impervious to time or loss. Like my father's.

Our embrace was awkward; I could barely get my arms around him. He was still, seventy-five and wheelchair-bound, a giant. And though I know now that his solidity was illusory, in my arms he seemed hewn from rock.

I kissed his cheek. "It's good to see you," I said.

"Your father tells me you study the law."

"That's David. My brother David." I felt small next to him. Up to that point, I hadn't done much of anything that anyone could be proud of.

But he seemed not to hear me. "You're a good boy, David. And you're to be married, I hear. Mazel tov."

I considered the range of responses. Directly behind me, my divorced uncle Ephraim bobbed on his toes, anxious, supplicant. "Thank you, Grandfather," I said, and moved off to the round table where my parents were seated. I generally tried to take it as a compliment when people confused me with my brother. It was better, at least, than being measured against him. David had cleared all the hoops with apparent effortlessness. He had been salutatorian of his high-school class, and, a semester into his free ride at NYU, had declared pre-law. My father had been quietly pleased when David turned down a scholarship from Cardozo to pay his own way through the University of Chicago law school.

Then, on the Thanksgiving break of his first year in the Midwest, David had brought home a protestant from the North Shore. She managed to charm my mother, which was about the best we could hope for under the circumstances.

But Annemarie aside, David had been winning for so long that, by the time of the birthday party, I'd given up trying to compete. Despite his slender build and impassive exterior, he never lost a single one of the wrestling matches we used to get into. And although I was faster and had a better handle, he still whipped me nine times out of ten in basketball. His jumpshot was like something out of a geometry text-book, a parabola burnished clean of human error. It had lost none of its purity since varsity. His fiancée and I were probably the only people who knew he spent a half-hour every weekday morning at the gym, shooting from beyond the three-point line and chasing down his own rebounds. Even with a shot like that, there had to be rebounds.

My grandfather's extra girth had survived his colon resection, and now, riddled with tumors, he managed to eat an entire fish and some unleavened bread, and to drink the two toasts proposed by my uncle Ron—one to the family and one to Israel.

My father had ostensibly spent four thousand dollars on plane tick-ets so that we could all be present for this birthday extravaganza, but I didn't see any crepe streamers or party hats. Though no one talked about it, we all knew that we had really converged here so that my grandfather could settle his estate before he died. While my mother and father ate their dinners, they kept glancing toward him, as if to make sure he was still breathing. During dessert, my father and David distracted us all from the question of my grandfather's health by get-ting into a protracted debate about whether or not a shortstop should be earning twenty million dollars—"More for an inning than I bring home in a year," my father said. "Of course I can't anymore expect you to have an appreciation for that. You've moved beyond us, I'm sure." Before my mother could intervene, David dropped his napkin on his plate and excused himself.

Following the post-meal thanksgiving, the forty-odd guests began to rise from the tables. Arabs in starched shirts, previously invisible, emerged from the kitchen and fanned out between the tables, col-lecting what we'd left behind—crumpled napkins, stained silver, plates heaped with tangerine skin and the fine bones of fish.

My father and his brothers gathered around my grandfather to discuss what he'd summoned them to discuss. Ron was the oldest, followed by my father, and then Daniel, Eli, Ari, and Ephraim. They were like casts from a single mold: the later the issue, the more evident the imperfections. Uncle Ron, despite being seven years older than his baby brother, had a full head of black hair and the same boxer's build as my father, while Uncle Eph was balding and squat. Their sister, my aunt Rachel, had died with my real grandmother when I was very young, in a car crash that only the driver, Uncle Eph, had walked away from. I vaguely remember a month from my early childhood when my father, the only American citizen among the siblings, was absent from our apartment for the burials. I never got to meet my aunt. I can't remember my real grandmother, either; my grandfather's second wife was always Sasta to me.

The aunts took over another table to catch up and compare notes. When I was younger, my mom, with her Bensonhurst brogue, had seemed out of place among her sisters-in-law, women who wore tasteful pantsuits and designer sunglasses, spoke politely in barely accented English, knew from a salad fork. Eventually, though, she had learned what to talk about—illness, children, the reliability of maids—and what to avoid—fathers-in-law, sex, current events—and, now that we were going to inherit a little money, could give the appearance of fitting in.

My older cousins hovered close to the bar, drinking, joking, rehashing the plots of American movies. Uncle Eph's twins, Benji and Nathan, who lived with their mom in Tel Aviv, kept trying to kindle interest in the only subject that interested them—politics—but the knot of cousins, well trained by their mothers, gradually isolated them on its perimeter, like a cell expelling a foreign body. The twins seemed not to notice. They simply turned to one another and were soon going back and forth about a separating wall with the kind of ardent jargon that guys in my neighborhood reserved for the Knicks or Jay-Z. My brother was nowhere to be seen.

Some of the younger kids played a version of whiffleball in the open space beyond the tables, where the long shadows of the trees did not reach. After delivering another glass of wine to my mother, I leaned against the low clay wall that bordered the yard to the south and watched them play, feeling jealous of their carelessness. I tried to let this distract me from my post-meal nicotine craving.

The late afternoon sunlight gave their game the air of a thing remembered. There was something Edenic about kids in a yard playing ball. I had always preferred basketball and football to the endless stoopball games of South Brooklyn or the uniformed courtliness of the summer leagues. But as I watched the cousins it occurred to me that baseball was the one sport that wasn't a metaphor for war. There was no struggle for turf, no real contact. The point, if there was one, was to get home safe. The rest of the time you just tried to keep things from happening. This I could appreciate (though I couldn't have said what it was I personally was trying to forestall), and maybe it was what my father had always found so appealing. I don't know; he never bothered to articulate why he thought David and I should care about the Yankees games he dragged us to, or about the players he'd decided were running the game into the ground. Anyway, I could have stood there forever in the gold light of my grandfather's yard, watching over my prepubescent cousins with their exaggerated wind-ups, their tenuous grasp of the rules, the wild, free way they swung for the fences.

In high school, my brother had developed the ability to become almost invisible when it was convenient. I was just entering the age of scuffles in the subway, of missing curfew and coming in after midnight smelling like liquor. Our apartment suddenly seemed like an extension of my father's body; he could sense the minute I stepped in the door that I'd done something wrong. I'd find him still awake after a night beat, watching TV with the sound turned down and the closed captions on. "You've got a black eye," he'd tell me, or, "The trash didn't get taken," or, "You smell like a distillery," or, "Your report card came today." Then he'd tell me I was grounded. Or later, after grounding had failed to cool me down, he would simply stand between me and the hallway that led to my bedroom, radiating silent disapproval until I muttered an apology. The absolute worst was when my father, who as a young boxer had compiled a record of 27-2, smacked me on the forehead with the stiffened tips of his fingers. "Stupid," he'd say. It didn't hurt, really, but I would have done almost anything to avoid standing there taking it, staring into the burning black eyes that I guess must have mirrored my own.

This forehead smack was a private ritual between the two of us; as far as I knew, my father had never laid a hand on David. My brother never got in fights with the Italians on our block, never "dressed like a rapper," never got caught sneaking in late in a cloud of beer. Instead, he brought home enough trophies and certificates to fill the top shelf of his closet. And if he ever doubted the stuff about G-d, he knew better than to let on. He had figured out how to fold himself into himself until all that you could see was a crisp leading edge.

I didn't quite register that he was standing beside me until he grabbed the back of my neck and shook me gently.

"You snuck up on me," I said, recovering.

"I was spying." He had this way of letting his voice hang halfway between sarcasm and whatever is the opposite of sarcasm, so that I couldn't quite tell if he was saying something or saying nothing. I figured it would serve him well in the legal profession.

"Me too," I said, gesturing with my head to the whiffleball game. "They don't seem to care much about winning, over here."

He leaned against the fence, bracing his back against the stone, and looked out over the yard. "You look like you're dying for a smoke."

"I wouldn't say dying."

"I can tell," he said. "Smokers put out this smell." It was David who had taught me to smoke cigarettes up on top of our building, one afternoon in summer, after I'd threatened to tell on him if he didn't show me. We'd hunkered down on the tar paper, eye level with the little parapet that edged the roof, paranoid that other parents from the neighborhood might see. He'd taught me how to blow smoke rings and how to French inhale, and how to cover the smell with aftershave. But ever since he left for school, he'd been lobbying me to quit.

"I didn't remember Grandfather being so old," I said to change the subject. "I think he thought I was you."

"I bet he outlives both of us," David said.

We both looked up to watch a helicopter roar by overhead. The kids playing ball didn't seem to notice, nor did any of the wives, except for my mother. Over there, you could identify Americans by the way we looked up nervously at noises in the sky.

"Do you remember how we used to go see the Yankees with Dad?" I said.

"Back in the day."

"Way back in the day. I was just realizing, I was always a little bored. It wasn't action-oriented enough for me. No contested territory. No shot clock."

"Now?"

"I think I'm finally grown up enough to appreciate a game that's about, like, civilization."

"Sounds like premature nostalgia to me."

"What's that supposed to mean?"

"Meaning *Field of Dreams* aside, baseball's not poetry. There's still a struggle for dominance; it's just more strategic. More underneath the surface."

"I'm saying, it's the surface that interests me now. That steadiness. I can't believe I was so hungry for drama. He would buy us those peanuts, remember?"

My brother corrected me. "He would buy *you* peanuts."

"I think sitting in the bleachers was the longest Dad and I went without fighting until maybe last year, and I never thought to enjoy it."

"What happened last year?"

"We both kind of gave up."

"Come on, Josh." His mouth was suddenly thin. "Do you not re-member how it got in the bleachers after the Yankees lost?" he asked. "When they'd throw trash and shit down onto the field, trying to hit the players on the other team? That Quiet Riot song would be playing on the P.A. What's that song?"

"'We're Not Gonna Take It.' Twisted Sister."

"Dee Snyder knew. Everything that's not war is war by proxy."

"I guess."

"It's true, and don't forget it. Peanuts are the opiate of the masses."
Another helicopter cruised by overhead, ripping the air in two. "Damn,
I can't get used to that."

"What, they don't have helicopters in Chicago?" I said snidely.

He sighed. "I guess I can see where you're coming from, though.
There's a pastoral element that's appealing." Once he'd triumphed,
David liked to wax philosophical, to try to see all sides. Maybe I would
have, too, if he'd ever given me a chance to win.

The light began to fade, entropy prevailed, and my little cousins
got bored and drifted away from their game. The cluster around my
grandfather's table was dispersing, too. I was mildly surprised to see
the fireplug figure of our uncle Ephraim, blurred at the edges by my
nearsightedness, detach from the others and lurch toward us. He avoided
without appearing to notice the white-clad bodies of the catering staff.
My father and my uncle Ron remained behind with my grandfather,
nodding as he talked.

"David," my uncle said with a smile when he reached us. He pro-
nounced it the Hebrew way. He thrust his free hand out, a little wine
sloshing over the rim of his cup and splashing on the dirt.

David extended a hand without lifting his weight off the fence.
"Uncle Eph."

"Your father has told me about your nuptials. Congratulations!"

"Thanks," David said, looking down toward his dust-powdered
shoes.

"If you keep these things confidential from your uncles, you will not
get as many gifts." His laugh was like small-arms fire, semiautomatic.
Almost twenty years had passed since his divorce, and we saw him
so infrequently that I couldn't tell whether his intense manner was a
symptom or a cause of his loneliness; at any rate, it tended to create
friction in an already fractious family. There had been some talk, after
the divorce, of him coming to the U.S. to stay with us for a while, but
I think my father and my uncle realized at roughly the same time that
it was better that he remain in Israel. This was around the time of the

car crash. Uncle Eph had been drinking. They'd never been able to stand each other, anyway.

"I keep meaning to send out announcements," David said.

"Leave the invitations to your wife-to-be. You're busy at university. Tell me again which one."

"Chicago." He was in the habit of calling it Chicago, as if the school was the same thing as the city.

"The often-heard-of University of Chicago. You finish when?"

"A month ago."

"A month ago? Why go back to the States? I can always make a place for young talent in my bureau," Uncle Ephraim said. He worked in the civil service, in some sort of legal position the details of which I could never remember.

"Your own personal bureau?" David cocked an eyebrow. "I'll have to take it under advisement. I'm planning for two now."

"There will not be a better time to be young here. Things will only get worse. Your grandfather will not always be here, you know."

"We know."

"So spend your conjugal years in Israel. Give your children the gift of dual citizenship. Of course it's a commitment—"

"We'll think about it, Ephraim."

"Your father has told you our father has the cancer?" This was the way it always went in my family, the pressure that got passed from older to younger in an obscure ritual designed maybe to shape you. Or to see if you would break.

"He has," David said. "As much as cancer sweetens the offer, I can't see us living here with things the way they are. Bombs and occupations and such."

My uncle seemed briefly at a loss. A shadow passed over his face for a moment. Then he brightened. "My little nephew the lawyer. I hope you will not be so flippant when you come before the judge." He patted David's shoulder. "You remind me of someone. Anyway, this engagement deserves a toast, I think."

"What do you think, Josh?"

"Yes, Joshua. Come have a drink," my uncle said.

"He's drunk too many toasts already, I think," David murmured in my ear as we followed our uncle toward the bar.

"What is your focus in school, Joshua?" Uncle Ephraim had filled three glasses to the very lip. The wine seemed to slow the sunlight, like liquid amber.

"I don't know. I'm thinking accounting, maybe."

David shot me a weird look as our uncle handed us the glasses.

"To the prosperity of my little nephews."

I tried to drink surreptitiously, so that my mom wouldn't catch me. Though I was almost a junior in college, she was in the habit of reminding me that I was underage. "Just think, in three months you can have wine with dinner!" Maybe it was because I used to get in so much trouble for it, or because my father was a cop. I hadn't yet figured out whether I was expected to observe New York state law in Israel. But after too many forehead smacks I'd decided that it was better to live within the limits than to test them.

"Who is this lucky young woman, anyway?" Ephraim asked, though he must have heard the rumors.

"You probably don't know her, Uncle Eph."

"Help me, then. What's her name?"

"Annemarie," David said.

Already I could feel the wine warming my face. I really was craving a cigarette.

"Your brother is a subtle character," my uncle said to me, sotto voce, listing forward like a dog on a scent. "Interesting name. What is she like?"

David took a breath. "She's studying architecture. She's well read. Turn-ons include Chopin and walks on the Lake. We share a sense of humor. And she's not converting." He drained his glass. "Anything else you want to know?"

Uncle Ephraim paused for a moment in mid-gulp, whether for effect or not it was impossible to say. "Anne," he said, after finishing off his wine. "Marie. What does your father think?"

Now I was interested. While I knew my father was less than pleased with the prospect of David marrying a shiksa, I had no idea what he'd actually said about it to my brother.

"What do you think he thinks?" David said.

My uncle clucked and refilled his drink. I shook my head no when he moved to top me off. "I remember your father saying to me once, We will end up doing to ourselves what Germany couldn't."

Although David didn't flinch, there was scarlet at the tips of his ears. "And what do *you* think, Uncle. Don't hold back now, I wouldn't want you to spare my feelings."

"I think another toast," my uncle said, raising his glass. "To the lucky Anne Marie!" He gulped down the wine, the color of which his face was fast approaching. David didn't drink, and neither did I. "He can be stubborn, I know—try talking to him about money. But I say, Why let fifty generations of tradition stand in the way of true love? Who does this father of yours think he is?"

"The whole family is stubborn. You should have seen Josh here when he was younger. Even grandfather."

"If your grandfather is less stubborn, none of us exist."

"I suppose so," David said. His tone was impossible to read.

"Your grandfather earned his right to be stubborn. Your father merely thinks he inherited it."

"Maybe he's got a point, though, in this case," David said. "Maybe actually sustaining a marriage gives you some kind of authority on the subject. Otherwise maybe we're just running our mouths."

Uncle Ephraim cocked his head funnily and froze. "You've turned out just like him, do you know that? Though even he would never marry an Annemarie."

David grabbed the shoulders of my uncle's shirt. "Stop," he said quietly. "Whatever you're trying to do, stop it,"

My uncle reached for David's collar. I thought I heard fabric ripping. "But you both confuse conversation with battle." He nearly spat the words out. "People get hurt that way." His face blazed like a wall at sunset, filled with bloody light. I put a hand on each, preparing to pull them apart. I caught the scent of spoiled wine on my uncle's breath and the gleam of perspiration on his bald skull just before he shoved me away. And that's when David punched him, the way our father taught us, rotating the fist a quarter turn before it hit the cheekbone. He pulled his arm back smoothly, without showing the pain I knew came with a blow like that. We learned that from our father, too.

David stood there, tensed, in his fighting stance. I couldn't remember ever seeing him like that, full of whatever it was that filled my father up, and had filled me up too, once. My uncle backed away, then reached up to touch the side of his shocked face. "Son of a bitch." He lunged at David.

Suddenly, my father was with us, looming like a mountain over the two of them, pulling at my brother's biceps with his enormous hands. "David," he barked, his accent returning as it always did under duress. "David. Stop this." David released my uncle and my father spun him around. My brother's face was set in the blank mask he'd cultivated years ago, the military face with which he'd taken the punishment meted out to him, on those rare occasions when he got caught. My father's eyes were black fires. He jammed his face into the space six inches away from my brother's, and I realized for the first time that he was actually shorter than David, that the illusion of power was just that. "You need to relax, son!" he said, and even though he was yelling and his nostrils were flaring, I had time, before my brother swung at him, to wonder in some subverbal part of my consciousness if this wasn't the closest he'd come with either of us to a spontaneous demonstration of love.

David got in only one good shot, connecting with my father's cheek. It took my father, the onetime middleweight champion of the state of Israel, less than two seconds to put the insurrection down.

This is how the evening ended: with my brother storming off on foot down the drive, not saying goodbye. With my mother in tears. With my father calling my uncle "a plague that never ends." With me in the backseat of a silent rental car several hours later, moving through suburbs as silent as a distant planet, staring up and out the dust-covered window at the stars of my ancestors. Something was happening, but I couldn't figure out what, or how to stop it.

. . .

After a month back in Brooklyn, I still hadn't found a summer job. My mother kept telling me, "Call back and ask about your applications." I couldn't bring myself to tell her that all the applications I'd filled out were still sitting in the top drawer of the desk my brother and I used to share.

None of us had heard from him since he walked away that night. Despite my assurances that he must have flown back to Chicago, my mother worried aloud. "He could return his messages, at least," she said. "He's got to know I'm going crazy here." For his part, my father maintained a three-week silence on the topic of David. Then a call came from my Uncle Ron, summoning him back to Israel to await the inevitable.

On one of those July afternoons that blur into evenings, I was up on the roof of our building, smoking and studying the clouds and the far-off skyline, trying not to think about any of this. The light was still strong at seven o' clock, and down below in the street three kids were staging a home-run derby with a broomstick and a tennis ball. My cell phone trembled in my pocket.

I was somehow unsurprised to hear David's characteristically formal *Hello*. It was as if he had felt me reaching out to him over the buildings and water. These things happen sometimes, between brothers.

"Where are you calling from?" I said. "Mom's been worried."

"How about you?"

I took a puff, then let the smoke spill lazily out of my mouth, obscuring the Williamsburgh Bank tower in the distance. "I'm not such a worrier these days."

"Right. Well, I'm in Chicago."

"What's in Chicago?" I asked.

"My wife, for one thing."

"Your wife."

"We're married," he said matter-of-factly, as if *married* was just another adjective, like *thirsty*, or *tired*.

"Everything okay?"

"I'm okay. I'm doing okay. We went the JOP route, or I would have sent you an invitation. You can pass all this along to Mom, by the way."

"If that's what you're calling for, you should just dial her directly."

"Actually, I'm calling to apologize, Josh. To you, specifically."

I asked him what for.

"I don't know," he said. "For having to grow up with me. I've been thinking."

The shadows of buildings had begun to fill my street, though it was still light up on the roof. The kids were heading indoors for dinner. I could see the flickering of TV sets in the windows of apartments across the way. I remembered spying on the neighbors like this with David, back when my vision had been clearer. We knew who watched *Cosby*, who watched the news, who watched soft porn on Skinemax. Without my glasses, I couldn't make out the programs.

"Forget about it," I told him.

"I want to atone. I want you to come out here this summer. Take a vacation from everything."

"I don't think I can," I said.

"This is the voice of experience, Josh. You need to get free of that pressure."

"I've got to get a job, man."

"What are you going to do in Brooklyn you can't do in Chicago?"

"Get an internship. I don't know."

"You've obviously given this thought."

"You're turning into Dad again," I said. It just came out. I braced myself.

"No, wait. This is the opposite of why I called. I called to tell you not to let us break you down. You should do whatever you want. That was always your best thing. I'd hate to see you waste your life worrying about what everybody else wants you to be."

"I don't know what you're talking about right now."

"You can do anything, Josh, and it turns out amazing. It used to drive me crazy, you'd been given this freedom, but now I realize how much I envy it. You want to ride a Harley cross-country, do it. Write the great American novel. Start a jug band."

"I'm too digressive to be a writer. I don't see things."

"The point is, don't just give in. Or however you said it. Give up. Turn into an accountant or whatever. Don't be like us. Be free."

I had assumed this conversation would be about him, as our conversations tended to be. I wasn't sure what to say. I settled on, "Okay." An awkward silence followed, like the ones in class after the professor opens the floor up for questions.

"How's Grandfather?" he asked, finally.

"He's close to the end, I think. Dad's over there right now."

There was a long pause. "You know you were always the favorite."

"Are you high? He can't even remember my name."

"I mean Dad."

One possible definition of déjà vu is hearing put into words a thing you've been thinking about for your whole life, without really knowing it.

"You know exactly what I'm talking about. Who got to go over when Sasta died?"

"You had a job then, David."

"Who got the peanuts?"

I had an image of the two of us, on our way to a game. I was around four. David would have been eight. Wearing our mitts, in case a foul ball found us, we had followed our father down into the subway. On the way, as we racketed through the tunnel, we sat while he stood in the aisle, a giant, his head nearly touching the bar. We were under standing orders not to get separated. The car grew more and more packed as we moved through the city, until, forty-five minutes later, we emerged in the Bronx. Then the doors swept back and the surging tide of fans washed us across the platform, up the stairs, and onto the shores of light, David still holding my hand in his. I couldn't imagine then loving a game whose charms lay in the gaps between the action, in the nods, the crouches, the unhurried chatter, so this was my favorite part: standing on the curb beneath the jutting blue ribs of the stadium, holding my brother's hand, waiting for my dad to appear from a hole in the earth.

"You never asked," I said. "All you ever have to do is ask him, and he'll give you anything."

The streetlights chose this instant to flicker on. The sidewalks had been blown free of trash that morning, and from where I was standing, the apparent absence of debris and dirt made the neighborhood feel like a soundstage, hollow and uncompromised by actors. I knew, though, that as soon as dinner was over, the kids would return. Maybe I'd go down and offer to pitch.

Or maybe David was on to something, in his own problematic way. Maybe this would be my last summer in Brooklyn.

"David, say the word and you know he'll forgive you. Or whatever it is we do. Give his blessing. Move on."

"I hope you'll never know how hard it is to have to ask, little brother."

There wasn't a lot to say beyond that, so we said our goodbyes and hung up, having agreed to talk again before the fall.

INTERVIEW WITH STEVE ALMOND

by Aaron Gilbreath

Steve Almond, a writer whose work deals with deep, raw emotions—vulnerability, loneliness, desperation, heartbreak, and, as he's put it, "the suffering of desire"—is a major publishing force in the small press. Raised in Palo Alto, California, he worked as a journalist for seven years in both El Paso and Miami before earning an MFA at the University of North Carolina at Greensboro. His books include the cult classic My Life in Heavy Metal; *the story collection* The Evil B.B. Chow; *his personal, chocolate-centered exorcism* Candyfreak; *and now, a novel-in-letters coauthored with Juliana Baggott,* Which Brings Me to You. *His nonfiction has appeared nearly as widely as his short fiction, with regular contributions to such places as* Poets & Writers, Boston Phoenix, Boston Magazine, Virginia Quarterly Review, *and* NPR, *some of which will soon appear in a book of essays by Random House. His interactive and eclectic website, www.stevenalmond.com, features reprinted short stories, sex advice for lonely Jews, even a forum for fans to contribute their stories, as well as his enthusiastic music e-zine,* The Tip. *Steve used to teach creative writing at Boston College, though he recently resigned, in protest over the school's decision to invite Condoleeza Rice as commencement speaker. He spoke to me during the tour for his new book.*

Photo credit: Stephen Sette Ducati

Steve Almond

Your stories have appeared in over thirty literary journals, including countless upper-tier magazines like the Georgia Review, Tin House, MAR, Other Voices, *and* Zoetrope, *yet you still publish in new and relatively obscure outlets like* Faultline, Tatlin's Tower, *and* Night Train. *Is that a way of throwing a bone to the upstarts, or just an expression of your creative output?*

Some writers just starting out, and I'm just generalizing, are ready to write a novel. I certainly wasn't, so I was writing short stories, and that was my entire world. When you're a short-story writer at the beginning of your career, those literary magazines are the laboratory for the writers who hopefully, at some point, will write great short stories, novels, nonfiction, whatever it is. But they have to have a laboratory, a place where they feel like their work can get into the world. And it's not going to go into the *New Yorker*. That's not how it's going to happen. I mean, unless you're extraordinarily talented or you're extraordinarily lucky, you need the small magazines.

I edited the *Greensboro Review* [in college], and I sent to *a million* of these places, and *Red Cedar Review* finally took one of my stories. You know, *Georgia Review* took a story fourteen months after I sent it to them, and I had no idea even that that was a big deal. People said, "Oh my god," but I just thought, "Hey, they're all kinda little magazines, they're run by mostly volunteer staffs at universities." Well, now I've gotten to a point in my "career" where smaller magazines will send me a note and some editor or sub-editor, somebody, will say, "Hey, I like your work, will you consider sending us something?" Now who, especially in the world of short stories, would not say yes to that? No, I'm sorry, I'm too *big* now, I'm a *short-story* writer. I mean, God, forget it. Also, I don't have a big sponsor, like a big publishing house that's gonna say, "Almond: buy his shit!" or the *New Yorker* saying, "He's one of the hot new guys!" So I feel like I have to use all the different possible avenues for people to find their way to my work. That's another rationale.

So part of it is soliciting. But a problem for fledgling writers is that many of these magazines don't pay anything but contributor copies, and when you're just starting out, you send out to everyone because you're desperate for publishing credits as much as, if not more than, money.

If you want some advice, as someone who's writing for the small press, what I do now is, if I think I have a good longer story, I send it to the best places first. I wait for it to get rejected by all of them, and then I send it to the next tier down. What I try not to do is to put shitty work into the world.

Basically what you're doing then is taking the space of a young writer whose story could have appeared there instead. You're using your name in a really cynical way. So what I tend to do now is send short-shorts to these smaller magazines because I figure, Hey, it's one page, and I figure the shorts are pretty good.

Short-short stories work especially well in online venues. Do you think this is because peoples' concentration wanes when reading on a screen, like how e-books didn't really fly?

The book is the perfect artifact, as is a literary magazine for that matter. It's a lot of consciousness in a very small space. People, when they are in front of the computer, are basically watching TV, you know. They might be slightly more active, but they're still in that "I'm watching a screen" mode. So I still publish online in places like *Nerve* where some of my dirty stuff can find a home, but if I had the opportunity, I'd rather publish a story in a magazine that's a physical artifact.

That brings me to another question: because you've published in Nerve, *One-Story,* failbetter, SmokeLong Quarterly, *do you still think, because we're a staring-at-a-screen type of culture, that there is a permanent place for online journals alongside print journals? Or do you think that online publishing will peak and crest?*

What I think these online magazines represent are little communities. The people that read *SmokeLong*, there's a community there, and it's part of the great American mission to find community when everything's become so atomized. So that's partly what those online journals are about, and that's never going to go away, because people are always looking for a chance to find other people. Also, it's much more convenient, frankly, than getting a magazine in the mail every six months. I tend to think that publishing a long story online is a losing proposition, because it's very hard for people to sit there and read five thousand words on a screen. You know, it's not like turning pages where the physical artifact is there, they can change the light if they want to, they don't have pop-up messages or the temptation to check their email right there. Computer screens and the internet were not set up for long periods of concentration, and that's what reading requires.

Another problem within the slew of new online magazines is that they don't bring new readers into the world. An article in the May/June 2006 issue of Poets & Writers *described the increasing amount of literary writers and the diminishing readers of literature. That author's solution was to have every writer who submits work simultaneously recommend books to other readers in order to increase readership. However unlikely, it at least makes sense mathematically, but are our technological means for escape too deeply embedded in the cultural matrix for this trend to reverse?*

Diminishing readers is the major issue. This generation I'm seeing is screen-addicted. Technology has changed so much and the world has become so chaotic; at the same time the avenues for escape, for basically tuning out of the real world and tuning into some set of screen narratives—instant messages, cell phones, Blackberries, internet, videos, video games, TV in myriad forms, DVDs—have multiplied, and present ways of not being in the present moment, of not being *with* somebody in a room, of not being conscious of your surroundings and the fact that you are a human being on the earth with other human beings. But it's also true that as people feel more and more lonely and isolated from each other, they look to these screens as a way of feeling less alone, comforted. I think it's a false fix, but it's very compelling to people, and it also makes it more and more difficult for people to do the lonely, dogged work of reading.

Reading is not easy. It engages your full imagination and your concentration, and as people are raised from the time they're little kids, every two seconds there's a new image on TV; I think it is changing the way their brains function. I mean, if you took the average human being now and transported them back a hundred years, they would *all* be clinically ADD. They would *all* be bored out of their skulls if they just had to fuckin' sit in the parlor and listen to their uncle tell stories. Or play jacks, or whatever the fuck they did before all this crap came around. I mean, look, a hundred and fifty years ago, people didn't fuckin' fight over the TV remote. They fought over the latest installment of Dickens. And it's not as if our brains have fundamentally changed in a hundred and fifty years. We're still capable of that greater concentration and that greater sense of empathy, and having our imaginations fully engaged and activated by literary art. So it is *possible*. It's just that I feel like writers now have to be absolute, ass-kicking zealots about it. My suspicion is that reading will only rise again if the pace of life slows, and we start to turn away from the false gods of convenience. The end of peak oil offers this possibility. It may also offer widespread famine and bloodshed. The question is whether our culture can grow up and face our moral duties to one another. That's where writers—artists of all genres—have to step up and lead the way.

The proliferation of upper-tier online journals like failbetter, Drunken Boat, Tatlin's Tower, *and* storySouth *provides more outlets for writers' work, but there are countless more online sites that do not hold submissions to the same literary standard as the print journals. Even though having work published does boost your confidence as a fledgling writer, is this a source for false confidence, or just a great way to practice?*

Good question. I guess the answer would be different for different writers. It's really a matter of how stubborn you are after excellence—authentic danger and love in your work. I mean by this that it's gotten easier to publish work that is competent, but not new or special.

There are a number of changes in print mags where they've recently switched over to online submissions, such as Fence *and* Meridian, *who've added the online submission option. And certain other ones—*Land-Grant College Review *and* A Public Space—*only accept online submissions rather than snail mail. Do you think that's something that will potentially change in the future?*

Well, I just know as a submitter that that's the way it goes now. I think it's great in the sense that it doesn't waste paper, but I also think it's a bummer because, as I've said, it's a different experience to read something on the page than it is to read it on the screen. I just think you value something more when it's on the page. That said, as long as I feel like the editors are paying careful attention to the submissions, the format doesn't matter.

When I was just starting to send stories out I would get very angry if they didn't get taken. I'd get these rejections with nothing on them, just a mimeographed sheet. But having worked at the *Greensboro Review*, I know the fact of the matter is every submission does get pretty careful attention, and the ones that almost make it get *really* careful attention. What I tried to do with the *Greensboro Review* is make sure that if a story was in the top one hundred, they got ink, and the top fifty, they got a letter saying, "Here's what we thought," because I think it sucks that people can form all sorts of opinions about a particular story, and maybe even have useful advice for the writer, but unless it gets in the magazine the writers don't hear any of it. And editors worry that by sending personal responses they're going to encourage people to send more stuff—well, if you liked a story enough to debate it, and it was one of the top fifty considered for your issue, then you should let that writer know. "Hey, we really gave this careful attention, and we're going to share a little bit of it with you."

What other things did working from 1996 to '97 at the Greensboro Review *as fiction editor teach you about the world of publishing?*

That was the boot camp for me as a story writer. When you read twelve hundred stories in the space of a year, you see all the bad moves, all the evasions, all the extra words, all the bogus, you know, "Let's give this character a dead mother or a crippled sister, or make them sexually abused when they were a kid," all the ways inexperienced writers try to lend their characters weight, meaning, as defined by tragedy. The editorial experience was just incredible. I learned more doing that than I did in any other aspect of my MFA program. The classes, the workshops, those were all helpful, but there was nothing like seeing the same mistakes over and over and over again. Writers who don't give the reader enough basic facts to figure out what's happening 'cause they think that's making the story "mysterious" and it's gonna make people read on when it's really just confusing the fuck out of them. I mean, all those common mistakes, all the totally obvious similes and metaphors that get in the way of actually being in the world of the characters—I was just pounded by them day after day, and I think it made my prose, through that sheer process, at least less stupid, if not suddenly elegant and poetic.

What about cover letters?

I didn't even pay attention to them. All the editors wanna see is what you got. Can you bring them into your fictional world and make them care about your characters? Can you tell a story about something that matters to you deeply?

While submitting, it's easy to get wrapped up in the minutia of presentation and make OCD-type associations between how clearly you wrote the address on the envelope and the likelihood that editors will read past the first line. Neurosis can creep in to every aspect of the submission: attaching the stamps in an aesthetically appealing way; writing the journal's address in all caps, like a bow to the journal's supremacy and your humility before it. Did you suffer from any submission or other creative neurosis?

All that matters is the work. That's it. The rest is just filigree. Trust me.

In your piece "Pretty Authors Make Graves," you dish the honest dirt about the love-hate, need-'em-hate-'em nature of writers' relationships with literary publishing outlets and its effect on your ego.

...you'll start to send your work out to the bad parents of the world and they'll find it (and you) ugly and send you little slips of paper with passive-aggressive inscriptions printed by machines, and you'll start to see yourself, finally, as they do: an ugly little wannabe freak with no business card and a car that makes guys stop you in the parking lot of your supermarket and offer body work for cheap. This is called progress. If you're truly unlucky, some of the bad parents out there will start to accept your crap and you'll move on to the next set of bad parents until finally you're dealing with the world of New York Publishing, which is inhabited by bright, ambitious people who hate your guts for still trying. They will make you feel worse and worse and uglier and uglier and in the end you'll need to thank them, because they, too, are helping you find that inner ugly schmuck kid I keep mentioning. It is perfectly reasonable to fantasize about punching these asswipes for years and years, because that is precisely what they deserve. They deserve to be punched. But they are only emissaries from the world of commerce, bit players, pimps and petty tyrants, and they have only the numbers to defend them; which is to say, they have no defense, whereas all of us, the artists, we have our ugliness and the resultant beauty pinned to our lapels.

Are there any alternatives? Or are writers, for now, stuck?

I don't really see any way to strip humiliation and self-loathing from the artistic equation. If there is one, I haven't found it.

The fact that you have a website speaks to your faith in the web's ability to get good work out there and reach readers. But posting your previously published stories also shows how limited the readership of literary journals is. Besides the Oxford American, Playboy, *and* Heeb, *do you want to one day publish in the big slicks like the* New Yorker *and* Harper's?

Of course. Everyone does. I spent a lot of years reading the stories in those magazines, being inspired by them, and fantasizing about landing a story there. But I've gotten less slavish over the years. I guess I've just sort of decided that I'm going to have to find my audience in a more incremental way.

You have a blurb on the Heat City Literary Review's *website: "It's great to see a lit journal that isn't afraid to take chances, to get reckless in the matter of the human heart and its perverse proclivities.* Heat City *is that kind of joint. Plenty of heat, plenty of light." What do you mean by heat? Is that sort of an emotional connection to the characters? The dramatic element?*

I guess it's my own dorky way of saying, "I'm interested in work that's dangerous." I'm not interested in the kind of work that's emotionally restrained to the point of tepidity. That's just what I wanna read. Barry Hannah, Denis Johnson, Lorrie Moore when she's cookin', Carver, François Camoin—the kind of writers where I know their characters are in a crisis. Frank O'Connor, "Guests of the Nation." A short story—a novel also, but the short story in a much more compressed way—should capture *a* moment in a person's life when everything fuckin' changes, and if it's not approaching that kind of danger then what are you doing? You're at the penny-ante table. You know, it's a short story, man, it's not an anecdote, it's not a slice of life, it's *the day* that everything *isn't* just average.

It's sort of sad, because that's the kind of writing editors should be finding and publishing in their journals, and a ton of new journals have debuted in the last few years: the Cincinnati Review *in 2003,* Swink *in 2003,* Ninth Letter *in 2004,* Backwards City Review *in 2004, the* Los Angeles Review *in 2003,* Loraine and James *in 2005. What besides great writing do you* think is important for a magazine to have to stay afloat. Because the average lifespan of a new journal, sadly, is around eight years.

Right. Well, I don't know exactly, but, in the world of literary magazines, they've got to find some way to get subsidized. But I think for the most part, places like the *Cincinnati Review* or *Swink* are usually a few people in a university setting, or even more rarely outside of it, who just work their ass off, basically, who spend hours and hours and hours, because they believe in the idea of putting forward their version of what literature, short fiction, essays, and interviews should be.

I like the kind of journal where they're doing a variety of different things at the same time, so in other words, I got some fiction, hopefully an interesting, kickass interview, maybe some criticism, some essays that are funny and irreverent. My feeling is, and I hope this is true of my work, there aren't enough readers in this culture, and you cannot expect to just write beautiful, quiet, tragic stories about suburban anomie and expect to reach a generation that is being bombarded with these frantic buy-messages, where every two seconds there's some other place for their attention to be. I think you have to find a way to write about contemporary culture and the kind of chaotic, consumerist, fuckin' crazy cauldron we're in, in a way that gets beneath the surface—to how lonely and frightened people are. So that's what I mean by "dangerous work." *That's* what I'm interested in.

To give you a good example, *Tin House* had this essay that Bret Anthony Johnston wrote about being a pro skateboarder. It was this funny, irreverent, sad, quirky personal history full of personality, and I just thought, Yeah, I want to be able to look at a table of contents, and if I wanna read quiet, serious, beautiful, great, but I also want a choice to read some fuckin' crazy-ass essay about being a skateboard pro, a lonely kid, in the seventies and eighties.

Beyond what editors hope is their journal's "unique editorial voice," many journals include unique features that help distinguish them from others: Swink *has its Damaged Darlings section (where one author with an unfinished or abandoned story hands the work-in-progress to another author, who reworks and finishes it),* Backwards City *includes comics, the* Cincinnati Review *publishes multiple reviews of the same book in every issue, and* New Letters

224

has its "on air" feature. But how important is creating a demand among writers to keeping a mag afloat? Making a journal a place where writers want to submit their work?

I love all these kinds of features, but I'm not sure that they can keep a mag afloat. You need a core of committed folks, and some dough.

All booksellers know the sad fact that covers help attract shoppers. Be it funky French candies or new novels, many people shop with their eyes and their consumptive lust. Last summer Fence *magazine used a ploy more prevalent in glossies like* GQ *to attract attention: their cover featured a young, topless, tattooed woman clutching her breasts. Many fans and subscribers were outraged at what they thought was a sophisticated literary journal stooping to cheap marketing tricks. In the issue's editorial notes, titled "Summer Fiction Tits," Rebecca Wolff describes how she saw the previous issue's poor sales as a partial reflection of the charcoal drawing on the cover, and how she decided that tits would sell more issues than artsy, subdued charcoal drawings:*

> Metaphorically speaking, it's tits that make us want to buy something, whether it be a journal or a car or a handbag or a sweater for a baby. So why not, I thought, give the people what they can also be understood to want. It is a more than slightly ironic comment on my own initial promise to make *Fence* "visually appealing and desirable as a consumer product."

Is this the future of lit mags?

I hope not. I mean, putting some great art on the cover of a magazine is terrific. But I don't think aping the tropes of pornography for the sake of attracting attention is going to get people excited about poems. It gets them excited about tits.

Let's switch gears a bit. Your work is incredibly emotionally raw. People get totally sidetracked by the sex, which clearly is just surface-level B.S. What was it during your seven years of journalism that led you to fiction? Was it the people and horrible situations that journalism brought you in contact with that made you want to write about their inner worlds?

Yeah, I think so. What journalism is interested in is how and why and when, and, "Get me that guy's balls and nail 'em to the wall."

And I kept finding myself going, Okay, I get that I'm supposed to write about the lawyer who stole all that money and embezzled it and fucked up his life and now his wife committed suicide, blah blah blah, I get that that's my job as a reporter, but I don't ever get to answer *why*. The human question of why someone would behave so self-destructively—it just nagged at me. I felt like I wasn't allowed to write about the inside of people, you know, why they make these calamitous decisions, how unbearable pleasure is for them, how they manage to screw their lives up. That's what most forms of journalism don't do.

I was exposed to a lot of people in dire circumstances, but in a very vultury way. Reporters parachute in, and you gather all the tragic data, and you leave and write it up in a thousand or two thousand words, but you don't ever really try to understand or empathize with who these people are and what's gonna happen after you leave, so I think in some sense in my fiction I'm always trying to find characters that I can love enough to see them through their trouble.

How did you get into journalism in the first place? Were you a writerly kid? A scribbling teen?

I wasn't writerly, exactly, but I was mouthy. I talked a lot. It was clear that language was my thing. Journalism seemed like the surest—really, the only known route to making a career out of words.

Your first published piece of fiction, "Alteration," appeared in the summer of 1996 in the Rio Grande Review. *At the time you'd spent seven years as a working journalist, so was this one of the first nods that your fiction could be as viable as your nonfiction?*

Oh yeah, I remember getting the acceptance for that story. I just went berserk. It was one of the great moments of my life.

What was that moment like? Paint me a picture.

I was in grad school, sending out lots of wretched stories, and checking the mailbox every five minutes. I got the envelope from the *Rio Grande Review* and it was a little slip of paper, so I thought it was a rejection. But there was a note on one corner, sort of chickenscratched there, saying, "We enjoyed this story and want to run it in our next volume." It took me a minute to process. Then I just let out a big whoop. And I had this euphoric surge, this sense that I could do this thing, it was going to happen.

This feeling lasted approximately three minutes.

How long had you been writing fiction before that first publication?

Off and on for three years, consistently for a year and change.

Besides candy, how did you deal with the loneliness of writing in your earliest days of fiction? And how about now?

Music mostly. The company of friends. Poker. Squash. The occasional pot binge. Sex. Not necessarily in that order.

Author Larry Brown died November 24, 2004. He's one of the greatest examples of someone with dedication and passion who taught themselves to write well enough to get published—novels, short stories, nonfiction. He spent eight years writing, while working day jobs, before his first book came out, and chalked up three failed novels and eighty to ninety trashed stories to the necessity of practice. What do you think about such anomalies?

Well, I mean, Larry Brown was a badass. I remember reading one of his stories to this friend of mine, Frankie Tomasino. Frankie was one of my Miami homeboys. Not a literary dude. But he fucking loved Larry Brown. My sense is that most writers have a pretty big pile of failures before they start producing stronger work. I know I have a shitload of trashed stories and novels.

What kind of writer would you say is the best fit for an MFA program?

I say this all the time—MFAs are like any educational opportunity: you get out what you put in. Period. If you want a couple of years to study the craft of writing, and be taken seriously, do an MFA. You don't want to, don't. In the end, dedication talks and bullshit walks.

You still get rejected as you mentioned earlier. What's your ratio right now, your miss-to-hit?

Probably five-to-one, something like that.

That's pretty damn good.

It's pretty damn good. It used to be like thirty-to-one. It used to be forty-to-one. I mean, I'm thinking of a story that I sent out for seven or eight years called "The Darkness Together." I knew it was a good story, and I sent it to forty places, and finally, finally, finally, I think the second time I sent it to, I think it was the *Southern Review*, they finally took it.

And it won a Pushcart, and I thought, "I have a list of forty magazines that had said no to it," some of them very small magazines. And it's not like I rewrote the thing. I knew it was a solid story. So what do you do with that? You just have to develop calluses. You just have to go, "Okay, fine, I'm going to ignore that rejection," because those are the odds. There's a zillion people—the MFA programs crank them out every year—who wanna write, and all you can do is control how deeply you can be with your characters, how much trouble you can get 'em into, how long you can bear to stick with them in those moments where it's really coming apart inside. And the rest of it, all the jealousy and shock and the long odds and the bitter punching of the mailbox, all of which I've done in spades, that's your life, you know, that's where we are. Not enough people read in the culture, not enough people want to experience their internal lives, and that's the reason that you have to be stubborn.

And that's probably one of the things you tell your students when they come in with the sort of universal, naïve dreams.

Mmmm. I don't have the burden of dealing with graduate students who really feel like they wanna get published, so all I tell my undergrads is, "You know what, dude, you want to impress me, you want me to like you and respect you and think you're a badass? Just fuckin' tell me the truth about something that matters to you. You know, show me how naked you can get, and then I'll respect you." Because so much of a young writers' life is, basically, wanting to tell the truth, but also being terribly frightened to let it out of the bag.

I've become very comfortable with my own humiliation. It's like my subject, my own humiliation. It's incessant. But it actually makes my life a lot easier to lead because every time a bad, fucked-up thing happens to me, I can say, "Oh, that's just material. I'm being fucked with? Fine, just material." And that actually is more useful than trying to weave some narrative about the planet Galactica or whatever.

That openness and willingness to deal with your warts seems to be crucial to what makes someone both a better person and a better writer—that emotional honesty.

Yeah, the better person's tricky. I hope so. But I've learned the lesson that just because someone's a great writer doesn't mean they're a great person. Like Saul Bellow: to me, he is *it* in terms of the sentence, but it doesn't mean that Saul Bellow has to be a nice guy to me. Or a nice guy to anybody. Because he gave me *Herzog*, and that should be enough. He gave us a lot of books. But I do think that if you're truly empathetic to your characters, it makes an implicit promise that you should be nice to people in the world around you. To be extra empathetic is kind of your job. I don't think that's true always, but someone like George Saunders, having met him a couple times, his work is incredibly compassionate, and it makes sense to me that he's a good egg. He's not just preaching it on the page and then he goes home and says, "Get me a beer, honey!" and smacks his wife around.

You've said you wanted to publish a book in every major genre: novel, short stories, nonfiction, poetry. Three down, one to go: tell me about your poetry.

It sucks. I wrote an entire manuscript five or six years ago. Some nice lines here or there, but overall I was a prose writer trying to hammer poems out of ideas. Once I've written an actual novel on my own, I'll give myself the reward of writing a book of poems. That doesn't suck.

Will your novel-in-letters with Julianna Baggott, Which Brings Me to You, *help you finally craft a novel of your own that you're satisfied with?*

That's the hope. It's that, or back to peyote.

An author who read from her first story collection at Powell's Books once said that her biggest regret from the early part of her career was not keeping in touch with the editors of the journals she first published in. Do you have any career regrets?

I have a ton: that I didn't start reading sooner, that I haven't read more, that I haven't shown enough patience as a writer, that I gave away too much of my power to agents and editors, that I focused too much on my disappointments and downplayed the good news. Shall I go on? Regret just means you're paying attention.

Aaron Gilbreath was raised in central Arizona's cactus country, but six years as a retail bookseller in Portland, Oregon has turned his once sturdy hide to veal. He's written for places like *Poets & Writers*, *HARP*, *Sacramento News & Review*, *42opus*, and *High Country News*.

The Last Pages

Susan, in front of the hickory tree, 1960.

I promised Cousin David that I'd put him in a story. I'm pretty sure he'd like this one—be tickled, in fact, though he would find fault. Not in his characterization—I think he would love that—but in my grammar, perhaps, or in my lack of *je ne sais quoi* (God knows how he'd spell it), my awful literalness, my lack of intuition, *something* I didn't get right, or just didn't get. He was Jungian. I am Freudian. What could you expect?

The story is fiction. I hope David is largely David, but the narrator is only a little bit me. The facts of her life are different from mine. I have three children, not two. My husband is not a workaholic stiff. And, as it happens, my family came over from Europe a generation before his family did, and from farther west. I've been a professional writer since my undergraduate days at Syracuse University.

—*Rolaine Hochstein*

The rebirth of the sweater-vest was noble but short lived. As was (on a slightly different chronometric scale) the Renaissance that built the Vatican. What endures is wonder.

I'm imagining some Roman five centuries ago looking up from the piazza San Pietro to have his heart blown open by saints. And some tourist five centuries from now finding himself arrested by angels in the form of stone; by the way the light hits the shoulders of the girl taking his hologram—the way it all passes away from us, continually.

One of my many failings is that I never write anything down at these moments when a sense of possession takes hold. For example, I remember hearing an anecdote about a family reunion over the phone from my friend Walker, but don't remember how it became "Jubilee." Presumably, I began typing. Then one day it was done. All that stayed with me was that guiding sense of wonderment, like a voice in my ear, saying, *Shh... slow down...listen...*

—Garth Risk Hallberg

My friend Peter Baldassari has devoted his life to the saints. Next time you visit Boston's North End, you should go see his alley full of shrines, called All Saints Way. I visited him mostly during the winter, and we'd sit in his basement workshop and drink Michelob Ultras while I asked a lot of questions. The workshop itself is covered with hundreds of statues of all sizes. One day Peter told me about a plaster saint that kept disappearing and reappearing in different people's homes. It was as if the saint acted on its own and chose to bless those homes for a certain time and then move on. "Saints Alive" grew from there. Mamma Idelfa just happened to receive that blessing.

This is a picture of Saint Anthony. I never saw a procession for Saint Jude.

—Scott Alan Anderson

Here's a picture of me with some of my favorite women in Tuskegee, Alabama at Booker T. Washington High School. My friend, Viviane La Pread, is a teacher there and invited me to talk to her English class of tenth and eleventh graders. I also spent happy afternoons talking with Shana and Chasity and Brittany and their mothers. To whet Mrs. LaPread's appetite about the winter attributes of Iowa City, I sent her a glorious picture of snow. She replied:

Dear Patricia,

...got your "snail mail" and the pictures; however, we would never be lucky enough to get snow! You see, in Tuskegee, snow means *no* school...*no* shopping...*no* snow plows...*no* snow tires...in other words, everything *stops* and we are all as happy as hell...It's only happened three times since 1945.

And so I wish them a one-day snowstorm this winter: Happy hours with nothing to do.

—*Patricia Foster*

I wrote "The Shelter" very quickly, a few weeks after finishing my first novel, and a few days after realizing no one was going to publish it any time soon. It was the first story I had written in nearly three years, and I think of it now as a gift from my subconscious, a consolation for three years of frustration.

It was August and I'd been spending a lot of time moping and watching CNN. There was a segment about a dog that had been abandoned in a war zone. They showed it pushing its snout through a crack in a window, recorded its horrible whimpering. I cried until my sinuses clogged, and when I collapsed on my bed to collect myself, André's voice was narrating the story to me and all I had to do was sit down and write it. I was enchanted by this character—his bravery and his pain and his imperfect devotion. His voice and story consoled me during a difficult time, similar to the way he and Yalla are able to console each other, offer each other a glimmer of something untainted in a place of desolation.

—Kim Brooks

My mother says that when I was several months old I climbed out of my crib. When I was little I climbed trees, and then later houses, to get on the roof so that I could look around and follow through on dares to jump off. When I was a teenager I climbed large rock formations in Navajo country. And when I met someone who wanted to take me hiking and mountain climbing, I joyfully went along.

—*Anasuya Krishnaswamy*

My dad, Tony Nissen, died soon after this story was accepted for publication. He'd been sick a long time, technically with Parkinson's disease, but it was more like Alzheimer's. Back in 1999, I was visiting my folks in New York when I got word that my first book was going to be published. I'd just spent our family vacation scribbling fiction—on yellow legal pads propped on my old camp-counselor clipboard—which I'd later transcribe into my ancient Mac Classic. My dad was still somewhat mobile and cognizant then, and he and my mom greeted the publication news with tears of joy, and some measure of relief. Later, Mom herded Dad into my room and, still weeping, he said, "We want to establish the Nissen Award and buy you a laptop computer, so you can write faster!" My dad was an economist, and infinitely supportive of his weird-hippie-writer daughter; still I think it was the first time he imagined I might someday support myself writing. If I could only crank it out faster! This photo of the two of us is how I like to remember him, in all his handlebar-mustachioed glory. I miss you, Papa.

—*Thisbe Nissen*

"The Man Who Fell from the Sky" came from many sources—a desire to write a short story after working on a long novel for several years, my love of football, and my fascination with the way prophecies (even two-dollar fortunes or the little slips of paper in fortune cookies) can define and shape a life. My father was obsessed with fortune tellers and believed their predictions that he was destined for greatness. The first draft of this story came in an exuberant rush, and it was my first new piece after writing *The Girl from Charnelle*. After revising the story and sending it out, I discovered that I wasn't ready to leave Neil and Ben and the world of this story. I wanted to see where the brothers would wind up, and how they would respond, over the course of their lives, to Madame Tsontakis's prophecies. I kept asking myself, "What happens next?" And the story has now blossomed into a novel.

—*K. L. Cook*

With my wife, Charissa Menefee, and my kids—shamelessly hocking my wares.

This is a painting I made shortly after I was diagnosed with breast cancer in 2002. I made a full recovery, as did all my "chemo buddies."

—*Jennifer Moses*

Uncle Hermann, Travemunde, circa 1950.

COMING SOON

As you can imagine, we have these things that we care about passionately, but if you die too quickly, if you die too soon, you've got all these unfinished projects.

from an interview with Ruth Ozeki by Kyoko Amano

Enough sunlight filtered in for Rico to see what he was doing, so he left the lights in the big room turned off. The weather was unusually cool, so the swamp cooler was off too, and the windows all stood open.

from "Soledad" by Al Sim

Back when we were having trouble, Inge planted three hundred bulbs in the backyard. She tucked them into the rock-studded earth one bleary afternoon just before the ground froze. Later she said, "I didn't know if I'd be here when they came up, but I figured seeing those flowers might be nice for you, might make you happy.

from "The Pretty Lady Brand" by Andrea Cohen